KU-507-050

KILLING CUPID

Louise Voss and
Mark Edwards

WINDSOR
PARAGON

First published in book form
by Harper
This Large Print edition published 2012
by AudioGO Ltd
by arrangement with
HarperCollins*Publishers*

Hardcover   ISBN: 978 1 445 84792 4
Softcover   ISBN: 978 1 445 84793 1

Copyright © Mark Edwards and Louise Voss 2011

Mark Edwards and Louise Voss assert the moral
right to be identified as the authors of this work

This novel is entirely a work of fiction. The names,
characters and incidents portrayed in it are the
work of the author's imagination. Any resemblance
to actual persons, living or dead, events or localities
is entirely coincidental.

All rights reserved.

ROTHERHAM LIBRARY &
INFORMATION SERVICES

BS200071720
R00054679

British Library Cataloguing in Publication Data available

Printed and bound in Great Britain by
MPG Books Group Limited

For Sara

ACKNOWLEDGEMENTS

Killing Cupid had a long journey to publication and lots of people helped us along the way. Mark and Louise would like to thank:

Pier Wilkie for believing in this book from the start and giving us the incentive to finish it.

Jennifer Vince for the original cover design.

Julie Baugh for being our very first reader.

Everyone at studentbeans.com and Kingston University for their support.

Sam Copeland and Kate Bradley for their fantastic work so far.

The amazing 'indie' writing community for endless encouragement and openness, including, but not limited to, Mark Williams, Lexi Revellian, J Carson Black, Sibel Hodge, HP Mallory, Saffina Desforges, David Gaughran, Scott Nicholson, Victorine Lieske, Cheryl Shireman, Stephen Leather and Dan Holloway.

And, of course, to our families and especially our partners, Sara and Nick, for their belief and patience and for never giving in to the temptation to throw our Kindles out the window.

Prologue

Alex

It was the sound of Kathy's body hitting the concrete that kept me awake at night afterwards. It was like a hard-boiled egg dropped from a great height onto a wooden floor. A muffled thud, something splintering, a crack. And then the great silence that followed.

From my position up on the fire escape, I couldn't see her. The moon had slipped behind a cloud. I peered down at the black shapes, thought I saw something dart over the back wall—a cat, a small fox?—and that fleeing creature woke me from my stunned state and made me move. There was only one thing to do.

Panic.

The metal steps were slippery from the rain that had fallen that afternoon, and as I walked backwards down the fire escape I slipped and banged my knee, scraping skin, hissing a curse that seemed to echo around me. With tears in my eyes I stood upright and looked out across London, at the jumble of shapes silhouetted on the horizon. The city looked different now. More dangerous. Another secret—mine, my latest—crawled through the city and joined the millions that hid in London's nooks and basements and hearts.

Back inside Kathy's flat, I tried to gather my thoughts and work out what needed to be done. Had I left fingerprints? What had I touched? I'd

1

come in from the pub, stood by the window, taken the beer that my temporary friend had handed me, chilled and cracked open, a wisp rising from its neck.

There was the bottle, standing on the table by the window. I picked it up and took it with me, tucking it into my jacket pocket. Had I touched anything else? Had I? My thoughts were drowned out by the rush of fear. I had to get out. Using my sleeve to cover my fingers, I opened the door of the flat and peered up and down the stairwell, leaving the light off. Surely the neighbours would hear my heart? I heard a noise through the wall and froze. Then, trying and failing to make myself weightless, I completed my journey down the stairs, out into the night.

I stopped by the gate. Her body was just around the corner. If I took a few steps to the right, I might see it. I . . . shit, how did I know it was actually 'a body'? She might have survived the fall. It was possible. She could be merely paralysed. Merely. I had to check. Looking around again to make sure no one was coming, I dragged my heavy legs—I felt like I was wearing antique diving boots—to the corner of the house and peered around the corner. I could see her on the floor—a dark shape, motionless, about twelve feet away. There were no sounds, no whimpering, no laboured breathing, sounds that would have told me she was still alive. Though she could be unconscious. I mean, Jesus, if she was still alive, of course she'd be unconscious.

I crept closer, and as I did, the security lights came on, lighting up the whole world, pointing a blazing finger at me. Here's Alex, everyone. Over here.

I jumped backwards, banging into the wall, stumbling and almost falling. But as I spun away I

2

saw all I needed to see: her head cast at an unnatural angle, neck broken—it was unmistakeable—and her eyes, open, staring. Right at me. My stomach lurched, and I fought it. That would be the worst thing I could do—splattering my dinner and DNA all over the yard. I turned and walked, head down, eyes half-closed, thinking if I can't see anyone else they won't see me, and made my way out onto the pavement and along the street. I forced myself not to run, though I was desperate to, wanting more than anything else to flee, to sprint, to put as much distance as possible between me and that dead woman. But I could imagine some curtain-twitcher glimpsing this man running from the scene; a man that police wanted to help them with their enquiries. So I made myself walk, calmly; just a bloke on his way home from the pub. I walked all the way home.

When I got there, I shut my bedroom door behind me and tried to work out if I'd made any mistakes. And most importantly, I thought about how Siobhan would feel when she found out. Because that was what mattered to me most.

Siobhan. My love. The woman I'd die for.

The woman I'd kill for.

PART ONE

PART ONE

1

Siobhan

Wednesday 10.30 pm

I've got to take out my contact lenses, they're sticking. I hate those moments between taking out my lenses and finding my glasses—I feel so myopic and helpless. I gave myself a real fright last night: I'd removed my lenses in the bathroom then realised my specs were beside the laptop in the living room. When I went out into the hall to get them, a figure loomed up at me. I jumped out of my skin and nearly screamed—before I realised I'd been scared by my own blurry reflection in the hall mirror.

'Come on, Siobhan,' I said under my breath. 'Sort yourself out.'

Talking to myself again . . . But I guess I'm still not used to living alone. I get jittery at night, when the walls make strange sounds, or voices float in from outside. Or when Biggles suddenly thumps down on the duvet, mewing, as if he's somehow fallen off the ceiling. It's pathetic, I know, to be so afraid of nothing. The product of an overly fertile imagination and too many TV crime reconstructions, I fear. And that's no excuse for my astounding ability to mislay my possessions, which is the other thing currently bugging me.

It was bad enough when I left my keys in the front door for hours the other week—Mum's speciality: ringing me up nearly in tears, wailing that she's torn

7

the house apart and can't find them anywhere, until I ask her if she's checked the door. So for me to then go and do it too—oh help, I'm turning into my mother.

Found my glasses. They were in my coat pocket.

Anyway, the writing class . . . I didn't think it would be so scary. I mean, I've done readings and things before, but somehow having responsibility for your own students is much more terrifying, even if it is just an evening class at the local college. I wonder what they thought of me? I tried to project an air of authority and confidence, even though my fingernails were carving curves into my palms.

'OK, I think it would be a good idea if we all introduced ourselves,' I said, feeling sorry for them already. I know it's necessary, but it's always so excruciating. Somebody once described it as the Creeping Death. You sit there and wait, trying to mentally rehearse what to say, as your turn creeps closer . . . At least as the teacher, I could go first.

I was about to begin, but I caught the eye of one of the two guys present. He was slouching right at the back, like a schoolboy, two rows behind everyone else. It made me want to laugh, the way he was half-grinning at me, sort of smug and 'Hey, look at me, aren't I a rebel?'

What a prat, I thought, and made him come forward to join the group. He skulked a bit nearer, giving me what he obviously thought was a smouldering look, but which actually just looked as if he was swallowing a belch. Although when I studied him more closely, I saw he wasn't bad looking.

I gave them my carefully prepared spiel, trying to make it sound spontaneous:

8

'Hi, I'm Siobhan, this is the first creative writing class I've taught, so please be gentle.' They all laughed softly, which helped me relax into it a bit more. 'I live locally; I'm thirty-five . . .'

'Any children?' asked an elderly woman at the front.

'No kids, no husband, just a cat,' I said, too willing to offer information. As if they cared about the cat! I'm amazed I didn't volunteer to tell them about my chosen method of contraception and that I hate anchovies . . .

I couldn't resist telling them that I'm a writer—although that is relevant, so I didn't feel bad about it. Told them I'd had a novel published a few years ago. I suppose I was hoping at least one of them might have heard of me, but they all looked blank, so I ploughed on:

'. . . and now I do bits and pieces of freelance journalism, mostly for women's magazines. I play tennis and have a weakness for eighties music . . .

'Oh, this is hard!' I simpered out loud, willing myself to shut up. 'Someone else go now?' Before I start telling you about that nasty yeast infection I had last month, or the flying ants nesting behind my kitchen units . . .

The others took their turns. There was Barbara, a retired dentist's assistant; Jane, a city worker in an expensive suit; Mary, a middle-aged woman with two grown-up sons; Kathy, who told us straight away that she was a lesbian, mainly—I guessed—because she thought it would shock the more mainstream women who went before her. She had a glint in her eye that appealed to me—in a non-lesbian way, I hasten to add.

Then came Brian. He kept scratching his head,

9

and colossal flakes of dandruff were frosting the shoulders of his leather jacket. The poor guy also had a slight stammer and the charming habit of rubbing his nose then wiping his hands on his trousers. He was really giving me the eye, too. Ugh. And he told us he writes fantasy novels. Uugh.

Then it was the Rebel's turn. His name was Alex, and he wasn't exactly forthcoming.

'I work for Bookjungle.com,' he said, 'selling other people's books and wishing I was writing my own. That's it.'

So, only six of them. But it might be fine. Jane was great, really sparky—I bet her writing's good. And the gay one, Kathy, seemed quite interesting. Alex acts like he's allergic to all of the other students, sitting as far away from the rest of them as possible and wrinkling his nose whenever they speak.

No decent men, though. I must say I did have a small fantasy about some gorgeous late-thirties guy with devastatingly sharp prose and a wicked smile, whilst also being sensitive and modest . . . Alas, I fear that both my male students will be purveyors of the 'aren't I wonderful' school of writing. The blokes so often are. Throw in some tepid one-liners—or in Brian's case, six thousand headless Snark warriors—and they think they've got a best-seller on their hands.

Poor scrofulous Brian—he was probably christened 'Poor Brian', bless him. I'm sure he's a sweetheart really, for all the ogling and acne. Not that Alex was much better. Thinks he's the dog's bollocks. He was ogling me too, but in that way men sometimes do when they don't remotely fancy you, they just want you to fancy them.

Anyway, I told them they had to keep journals,

and that I wanted them to start by writing up a recent, important conversation. Alex asked if I would look at what they'd written, so I said, 'No, it's private. You can write anything you like. You can even write about me, if you want.'

It was a joke, but Alex jotted something in his notepad, eyebrows raised. He'd better not, the little bastard.

By the time I'd talked them all through the wretched paperwork that the college requires—register, assessment forms, syllabus, etc.—it was nearly time to go. The class ended on a bit of a downer for me, with the question I'd been dreading ever since mentioning I was a writer: Mary asked me when the next book was coming out.

Like some kind of production line. I couldn't bear to explain that I only got a one-book deal, and they never renewed my contract. I know I'm going to have to admit it at some point, when we get to talking about submissions to agents and so on; but for now I just told her it was coming along slowly. 'That difficult second novel . . .' Clichéd, but true.

Thursday

I feel so low this morning. I never realised it before, but the thing I hate most about being on my own is waking up alone. I miss Phil's body in the bed with me. I miss him when I get up in the night for a drink of water, then go back to bed and he's not there to wrap my cold legs around. I loved the solidity of his chest, heavy with sleep, almost burning hot. His skin always felt somehow softer when he was asleep, and his breathing was steady and comforting, in a way

11

that Biggles's fluttery little cat breaths never are.

Later. Went for a soya milk decaf at the High Street Starbucks—I just had the urge for one—and who do I bloody well bump into? Phil, of course. He was just passing the door as I came out.

'I thought you were boycotting Starbucks,' he said.

'I am,' I said, and we both stared at the coffee in my hand. He can still make me feel so inferior. 'I am, on principle. And The Gap. It's my own little anti-capitalist stand. It's just that since I'm detoxing, I'm off dairy, and they don't do soya cappuccinos at the Italian coffee shop.'

Phil just smiled in that rather patronising way of his, and I thought, no wonder I only miss him when he's asleep. He's far too smug when he's awake. Asleep, snug; awake, smug.

To change the subject, I asked him how Lynn was. I guess I must have been desperate to change the subject.

'Fine,' he said. 'We're going away to Portugal next week.'

I had an instant flash of them on a beach with pale sand, Phil rubbing suntan lotion into Lynn's back. Hopefully they'll get so sunburned they won't be able to have sex. Still, sunburn fades, doesn't it? Unlike . . . oh, bugger it, Siobhan, stop. Be strong. Bring back that image of Phil with sunburn. That's it. Now picture yourself slapping it.

2

Alex

My day off. Simon and Natalie were at work, and being in the house on my own with nothing to do made me feel like a polar bear at the zoo. I roamed from room to room, unable to rest or concentrate on anything; spent hours flicking through photos of people I barely know on Facebook, stopping every now and then if an attractive friend of a friend caught my eye. I was so bored that I decided to do a bit of housework, put some washing on.

Checking my jeans pockets before shoving them in the machine, I found a folded-up tenner. A sign from God for me to get off my bored skinny arse and go and do something. Anything. I decided to get on a tube and see where I ended up.

On the way to the station, my thoughts returned to the writing class. I've been thinking about it a lot over the last few days. I'm glad I took the plunge and signed up. The hours at work pass quicker now I have something to look forward to. Okay, they don't exactly skip by, but previously they moved like a wounded soldier dragging himself across a battlefield. Writing this journal makes me feel better too. Getting my thoughts onto paper—or, more accurately, onto the computer screen; paper is so old-fashioned—stops them festering in my head.

I wonder what my fellow students will write about in their journals? It's not hard to imagine. Brian will be writing his in the guise of a mythical character from one of his fantasy stories: Brian the Bloody

Awful, roving the land and bewitching lusty maidens with his magic staff. Kathy will detail her lipstick-lesbian affairs in her journal: blow by blow, or lick by lick, accounts of Sapphic escapades. I'd love to read it. Barbara will stick pictures of her grandchildren in hers, confusing it with a scrapbook, and write long poems about Des Lynam. I can barely remember the names of the other students, so nondescript were they.

Unlike the teacher.

Siobhan. She came into the room with a knowing smile on her face, unhooking her bag from her shoulder and studying her new students in turn. Her hair was cut in that short, boyish style that I like, and she had big, bright eyes, though I couldn't quite work out their colour. They seemed to change as I looked at her—or maybe it was just my opinion about them changing: blue—no, grey—no, green—no, hazel. She said she was 35—I've always thought I'd like an experienced older woman. She also said she had no husband, and I wondered if she was divorced. She was too attractive not to have been snapped up at some point. There was something in her eyes that betrayed pain, disappointment. But she looked confident, standing there in front of us, as if whatever trials she'd been through had made her stronger. I like that. I like women to be strong. Intelligent. The kind of woman who can put up a fight when she needs to. I couldn't imagine ending up with a wimpy girl. I would have been shitting myself if you asked me to stand up—or sit on a desk—in front of a group of strangers, but Siobhan clearly took it in her stride.

I'm sure that her eyes lingered on me for an extra beat when she looked around the class. She touched

14

the bridge of her nose, as if she was pushing back a pair of glasses. A part-time contact lens wearer, like me. The gesture made me think she wanted a better look at me, that she was evaluating me. When she spoke and introduced herself, her voice was musical, but quiet. I had to lean forward and concentrate to understand what she was saying. It was night music; a lullaby. I noticed Barbara fiddling with her hearing aid.

When my turn came to speak, my voice trembled with nerves and I only managed to get out one sentence before coming to a halt. I'm sure this didn't make Siobhan think badly of me, though. She's a writer: she's almost certainly into sensitive men. I was sad when the class ended, because it meant I had to say goodbye to her for a week. Still, that week is almost up now. I'll see her again in a few hours.

*   *   *

The tube train got stuck in a tunnel just outside Oxford Circus. The lights flickered and electricity hummed through the carriage. Nobody looked at anyone else; nobody said anything.

There was a crackly, inaudible attempt at an announcement and I could feel myself getting hot, tense. Nobody else seemed to have even noticed that we'd stopped. I had an image of that scene in *The Rats*, passengers traipsing through the tunnels, savaged in the dark by razor-teethed rodents.

The woman opposite gave me a look. She chewed the inside of her cheek for a moment then said, 'You okay?' She was American.

'I'm fine.'

15

'It's just that you made this noise . . .'

I felt my cheeks heat up.

I put my head down, concentrated on the litter. The train lurched into motion and I got off at the next stop. I waited till the next train came along.

I eventually emerged from Leicester Square station. I needed something to read and immediately thought of the second-hand bookshops on Charing Cross Road. I trawled around the shops, scanning the tables, picking up yellowed paperbacks, sniffing them and putting them back again. I like second-hand bookshops for their cheapness, but there's something revolting about them too. The thought of all those greasy fingers handling the pages, all that dead skin gathering in the folds. Examining one book, I found a squashed spider between the pages. Perhaps someone had used it as a bookmark.

I passed a pleasant couple of hours wandering in and out of shops, until I found myself in a pokey bookshop back near the tube. If I don't find anything here, I decided, I will spend my money on alcohol. Which was when something caught my eye.

It was lying on a table. The title was *Tara Lies Awake*. The author, Siobhan McGowan. My teacher. I tingled. It felt like a sacred moment, and I lifted the book with slow reverence, stroking the hardback cover like it was a holy artefact. Siobhan's book. I flipped open the cover and the scrawled pencil mark told me it was only £2. I would have paid a lot more for it. Without any hesitation, I took it up to the counter and practically threw my money at the old bloke behind the till.

'Hey, your change . . .' he called as I pushed the door open.

Out in the street, my change now safely in my

16

pocket, I looked at the cover. There was a naked woman on it—artfully done, of course. And there, on the inner flap of the dust jacket, was Siobhan herself. She was a few years younger, with a broad smile on her face, but . . . well, I've got the book lying open in front of me now. She doesn't look as good in the photo as she does in real life. It looks a bit posed, fake. When she stood up in front of us in the classroom she seemed real. I mean, of course, she was real, but . . . oh, I don't know what I'm trying to say. I suppose what I mean is that although Siobhan looks good in the picture, she could be any woman. But the woman who stood in front of us in the classroom last week seemed special.

I stopped at the off-licence on the way home and bought a bottle of wine, then shut myself in my room with the book and stayed there all evening.

*   *   *

God, the dreams I had after reading *Tara Lies Awake*. It's so erotic. So . . . sensual. Or is it sensuous? I'll have to look it up. Don't want to say the wrong thing when I discuss it with the author, do I? Whatever, it's damn sexy. And beautifully written. Sexy and beautiful—and surely a book is a reflection of its author? I saw a hint of it last week in the classroom, but only a hint. I expect she has to hide it in front of most people. It can be dangerous being that passionate. You have to keep it in check, wear masks. But I feel like I've learned so much about her from reading the book, and I can't wait for her to show more of herself.

Siobhan's novel is about this woman called Tara who is a virgin until she's 21. She's always been

17

scared of men and relationships, and then she meets this guy called Luke. He's married, and older than her. And they fuck. Christ, do they fuck. I've been around the world. I've been to Bangkok where girls are supposed to know every trick in the Kama Sutra. But I bet those Thai girls wouldn't have heard of some of the things Tara and Luke get up to in *Tara Lies Awake*. The book is written from Tara's perspective after the affair ended. She's lying in bed, thinking about all the stuff they did, touching herself. She ended the relationship because of his wife, but she still craves him. And on the last page, there's a knock at the door.

And that's how it ends.

Oh Siobhan, you seem so calm, so placid on the surface. But underneath . . . I know what's inside you.

Oh Siobhan.

I want to be inside you.

*   *   *

Imagine how thrilled she'll be when I turn up with her book tonight. No—wait, though, I won't take her book along with me. That's too unsubtle, and one of the others might ask to borrow it and I won't be able to say no. I don't want to let the book out of my clutches. I have uses for it. So what can I do to make Siobhan happy?

Of course. It's obvious . . .

3

Siobhan

Well. That was quite an evening.

I got to college early—I wanted to be the first one there, rather than drifting in with the other students as I did last week. I want to project more authority. I dressed up a bit more this week, too, I'm not sure why. Maybe because I feel a little more confident now I know that they aren't the world's most intimidating bunch. So I put on my high boots and my fishnet tights. Decided against the denim miniskirt—too slapperish, with the fishnets—but went for my knee length black cord skirt, and a polo neck. It must really be true, what they say about attractiveness being all about confidence. I felt pretty good.

As I walked past the main office area, Betty the receptionist called out to me: 'Ms McGowan? Someone left this for you.'

She reached over the desk and handed me an envelope; wrapped in a pink ribbon, no less. I mean, who puts a ribbon round an envelope? I thanked her, and she gave me a knowing look over the top of her half-moon specs. I didn't want to open it then and there, so I went into the disabled toilet and locked the door, before ripping open the envelope. I'd thought it would be a card, so I was surprised to pull out a single, typed sheet of A4, in one of those fancy fonts meant to look like handwriting.

I was even more surprised at the heading: 'Bookjungle.com:' it said. 'This reader, Aparkinson,

19

has awarded this product * * * * *.' Five stars. It was a review of *TLA*.

'Sublime, erotic masterpiece,' was the sub-heading. I quickly scanned the page, superlatives jumping out all over the place at me. It was a rave review, so glowing it was almost neon. In fact—and I never thought I'd say this—it was almost too glowing. Pleased as I was, it was embarrassing, too. Like that creep at the gym that time, who kept going on about how sexy my calves were. Nice to have the compliment, but a bit much really.

I couldn't even think who Aparkinson was, until I saw the note at the end:

'Dear Siobhan, I read your book. In case you don't look at Bookjungle,' (As if! All authors look at Bookjungle.) 'I thought you might appreciate my posting. I really loved it. All the very best, see you in class. Alex.'

Alex—the boy rebel. How weird! I wouldn't have put him down for a pink-ribbon gushy kind of guy. But I had wondered if he fancied me.

He might not, though. Perhaps he just genuinely loved the book. It's very sweet of him.

I wasn't quite sure how to react. I mean, what was I supposed to say? Thanks?

I re-read the review more slowly. I can't say I wasn't chuffed—it's been years since anyone posted a review of *TLA*, not since that bastard who proclaimed it, 'Unreadable—the worst book I ever read,' and gave it no stars.

It was, admittedly, lovely to see such a nice one, and to know it's on the Internet for all to see. I kind of wish he hadn't put his name, though, so the other students, when they eventually—and inevitably—look it up, don't discount it because they know that he knows me.

Can't resist transcribing a few choice quotes:

'The central character, Tara, is incandescent, shining on the page, the kind of person we all dream of meeting in real life but so seldom do; we cannot help but fall for her.'

Aah—sweet!

'The prose is rich and sweet as marzipan, but never cloying, never too much. Instead, we are happy to gorge ourselves on these delicious words, to get drunk on sugar, to be giddy like E-numbered-up children.'

Hmm, that's a bit OTT.

'Sex scenes are notoriously difficult to get right, but McGowan seduces the reader in the same way the handsome Luke seduces the lovely Tara; a verdant eroticism moistens these pages, as sexy as hell, as blissful as heaven.'

Yeah, baby! Love it.

Anyway, I slid the review back into the envelope and put it, plus ribbon (Biggles will enjoy playing with it) back into my bag, and exited the toilet, glad that there wasn't a queue of cross people in wheelchairs waiting outside.

When I got into the classroom, I expected to see Alex, waiting cockily for my reaction, but the room was empty except for Poor Brian. It was funny, because when he clocked my boots and the tights, his eyes opened so wide you'd have thought I was naked.

'H-h-h-hello,' he said, gulping like a cartoon character who's just swallowed a pikestaff.

We chatted for a bit—I asked him a bit about his fantasy book, but I have to admit that it sounded as if he was talking in a foreign language, with all the

21

place names and weird aliens and so on. I told him that I'd loved *The Blind Assassin*, and that had a sci-fi story within it, but he hadn't even heard of Margaret Atwood!

Then he glanced towards the door, and for a moment I thought he was going to lunge at me; he had this rather worryingly expectant look in his eyes. Or else do a runner. But to my astonishment, he produced a copy of *TLA*! That's doubled my annual sales figures then. I wonder if they've all gone out and bought it? I hope so. But I wasn't sure what he wanted me to do with it—he sort of waved it at me.

'Would you like me to sign it?' I asked, and he blushed gratefully, nodding. I duly inscribed it, and the poor chap looked as if he was about to die with gratitude—but it was a lot more straightforward than Alex's big gesture.

The others all arrived together, just as I was handing back the book to Brian. I smiled briefly at Alex, but didn't make real eye contact with him. I felt a bit . . . flustered, I suppose. Like he somehow had one over on me now—although of course that's silly. I don't know what it was, but as soon as I saw him, I felt uneasy. When I looked at him, skinny and cockier than he seemed last week, the review and the pink ribbon seemed a bit inappropriate. I casually leaned over and pushed it right down to the bottom of my handbag, so it was hidden. I suddenly wanted him to be unsure as to whether or not I'd even received it, and I decided not to mention it at all, unless he asked me outright. Perhaps I'll thank him, next week, without making a big deal out of it.

At the end of the class, I could see Alex beginning to loiter behind the others as they filed out, chatting.

Only Kathy was left, so I wandered over to her desk and told her how much I'd enjoyed the piece she'd read out earlier.

'I'm so glad you liked it!' she said, her face lighting up. She looks really pretty when she smiles, under that harsh jagged haircut. I subtly edged my shoulders round until my back was to Alex, and he wasn't in my line of vision at all—although I was somehow still very aware of him there, lurking.

'Actually,' Kathy said after a minute chatting about the task, 'I was wondering if I could have a word?'

Phew, I thought—a reason to ask Alex to leave. But when I turned back around, he was marching out of the classroom, without a farewell.

I turned back, and Kathy was standing there, beaming—with a copy of *TLA* in her hands! I couldn't believe it, and started to laugh.

'I'll be able to retire on the royalties soon,' I said. 'It's brilliant—you're all buying it! I knew there was a reason I should take up teaching.'

Kathy laughed too, and good-naturedly handed me a biro. 'Loved it,' she said. 'I really couldn't put it down.'

'Thanks,' I said, blushing. Her praise somehow felt more valid than Alex's overblown words and Poor Brian's stammered compliments, and I felt foolish for over-reacting, even in my own head, about Alex's review. At least I hadn't made a fool of myself by mentioning it in any way. And having three of them comment on it definitely diluted the impact.

I wonder if there's any chance that Kathy fancies me too? She certainly seems to glow when she talks to me. But perhaps I'm just being arrogant.

I left the college feeling far more cheerful than of late, all the evening's words of flattery echoing around my head. Perhaps it wasn't too late to get another book deal after all. I must have some talent, to provoke such a reaction. I'd just forgotten, that's all.

Either that, or I've got three new admirers! Can't be bad, however you look at it.

4

Alex

Wednesday

I spent all afternoon working on my online review of *Tara Lies Awake*. I submitted it to the site and printed it out, kissing the paper before sealing it in an envelope. I wrote my home number on the printout (haven't been able to afford to get a new mobile since mine was nicked from my pocket the other week in the pub, and of course it wasn't bloody insured) and wrapped the envelope with ribbon I'd found in Simon's room. Nat's always making cards and doing fancy stuff with parcels, so I expect the ribbon belonged to her. I was sure she wouldn't mind me borrowing a bit.

On the way to class, I kept imagining how impressed Siobhan would be when she read my review. The more I thought about it the more excited I got. I found myself walking really fast, marching in time with my heartbeat.

I wasn't sure exactly how to give my review to Siobhan. Ideally, I'd have liked her to stumble across it on the website, but I couldn't be sure enough that she would see it—authors apparently always check their own Bookjungle rankings, but since the book had been out for so many years, I couldn't be sure that she would still be checking it. I didn't want to leave the printout on her desk in case someone else picked it up. And if I handed it to her in class the others might wonder if there was something going on between us. But it had nothing to do with any of them—this was a private matter between Siobhan and me.

Entering the college, I saw the receptionist and decided she was the best person to leave the envelope with, mainly because I couldn't give a flying one what she thought of me.

'Has Siobhan McGowan come in yet?' I asked.

'I don't think so, love.'

'Could you pass this to her when she does?'

She took it and set it aside.

'You won't forget, will you? It's very important.'

She looked at me, then at the pink ribbon wrapped around the envelope and raised a well-plucked eyebrow. 'No, love, I won't forget.'

'Thank you.'

After that, I needed the loo. I must have been in there longer than I thought because when I reached the classroom, everyone, including Siobhan, was already there.

I opened the door and saw Siobhan look me up and down. I swear she seemed impressed. And kind of hungry. Like I was a Mars Bar and she was Marianne Faithfull. She must have read my review already and—well, it looked like it had had the most positive effect I could have hoped for. Could it be that praise makes her horny? Makes her want the person praising her?

Is she that similar to me?

To my delight, I saw a hint of pink poking out of her bag—the envelope I put the card and review in. So the receptionist didn't let me down. And when I saw what Siobhan was wearing . . . wow! The boots, below what looked like they could be stockings on her long, sexy legs, and more make-up than last time—though not too much, nothing tarty or cheap. She looked sensational.

She asked me to sit down, and I could feel her eyes on me as I walked to my chair. I had this rushing sensation in my stomach and chest, that feeling you get when something very exciting is about to happen. I was trying not to stare at Siobhan too hard, trying to be cool, trying to stay calm. And then she turned all the lights out.

It was a shock at first, suddenly being in pitch darkness with a group of near strangers. But, very quickly, I became accustomed to it. I even forgot the others were there, and it felt like it was just me and Siobhan. Brian wasn't scratching like a mangy hamster, Kathy wasn't sending me hate rays for being a man, Barbara wasn't snoring. It was just me and Siobhan, Siobhan and me, and it was so dark with the blackout blinds down that I couldn't even see my own hands, and nobody else could see how aroused I was as I listened to Siobhan's deliciously husky voice.

She asked us to think of a character, but the only character I could think of was her, and then there were two of us in the story in my head, her and me. I couldn't manage the bit about standing in my childhood bedroom. All I could picture was my bedroom now, rucked-up sheets beneath two entwined bodies.

I felt like she was caressing me with her words, reaching across the room to me and stroking my hair, my face, touching my eyelids and running her hand down the back of my neck, then around to the front and—oh God—into my lap. I could smell her— her skin and perfume and hair—and when the lights came on I nearly fell out of my chair in my desperate attempt to cross my legs.

Have to admit, though, the mood was spoiled a bit by the sight of the drool on Grandma's hairy chin. But when my eyes adjusted to the brightness I couldn't stop myself gazing at Siobhan. She caught my eye then quickly looked away, shy, sweet, coquettish.

When I had to write down what I'd visualised, I had to make something up. I couldn't be honest, could I? This journal is the only place where I can be fully honest.

The class ended and the others started to file out. Brian stuttered something to her as he passed and she smiled at him, sympathetically. I hung back, waiting for all the others to leave. I wanted to talk to Siobhan about her book and my review. I wanted to give her the chance to say how pleased she was. But bloody Kathy wasn't leaving. She stayed in her seat, scribbling something, and Siobhan came over and started talking to her. It didn't seem that Kathy would be leaving too quickly. Realising there was no way I could hang around without seeming like a weirdo, I slunk out.

But I wasn't too worried because I knew Siobhan would love what I'd written—and I was confident that she'd want to call me to talk about it. She . . . shit, there's the phone now.

It wasn't her. Someone for Simon. Of course it wouldn't be her. She'll want to play it cool, won't want to let me know how excited she was to read my words straight away. I expect she'll call tomorrow, Thursday. I wish I still had my mobile—I'd forgotten what it's like to have to literally wait by the phone.

I doubt I'll be able to sleep tonight. Too excited.

Thursday

Had a terrible evening. Sat in the living room watching TV and waiting for the phone to ring. Nothing on except a programme about lions: all they seem to do is sleep and shag. Looked at the cover of Siobhan's novel; the naked woman, Siobhan's picture, the two merging into one. I stared at the phone. It stared back, mocking me. It rang at one point, making me leap off the sofa. It was Si, asking if I wanted to join him and Nat for a drink.

'I can't.'

He sighed. 'You need to get out more, Alex. You couldn't come out the other night because of your writing class. You can't keep turning down our invitations. We'll get offended.' I could hear the clink of glasses in the background, Lady Gaga on the jukebox. I put the phone down, worried about blocking the line.

I smoked six cigarettes and rummaged through Si's bedside cabinet, trying to find his dope stash. Just a few hard crumbs. I ate them. They

28

didn't do anything.

At ten, I checked the phone connection. At this point, I realised how sad I was being. Maybe I should unplug the phone, I thought. Then when she tried to ring she wouldn't be able to get hold of me; it would just ring and ring, and she'd be there getting worried, wondering where I was. I knelt down to pull the cord out of the wall. But I couldn't do it.

I wish I'd had the chance to talk to her after the class. Maybe I was too subtle, simply writing my phone number. Perhaps I should have made some 'call me' sign in class. But that would have made me look like a twat. And I'm sure Siobhan's the kind of person who understands subtlety. Her novel is subtle. So why hasn't she taken the hint and called? Does she think I'm just a loser who doesn't even have a mobile phone?

Or maybe she's just shyer than she seems.

Friday

Maybe she lost my number. That could be it. She might have lost the card I gave her somehow. She might even have lost her bag. Maybe she's been searching her flat or house, getting frantic, wanting to call me, worrying that I'll be upset. Of course, I'll reassure her, I'll tell her it's fine, let's go for a drink, a meal, and who knows what will follow.

Friday night, and I'm in my bedroom. It's eleven thirty and, through the thin walls, Si and Nat are at it again, doing more for Anglo-French relations than Concorde, hypermarkets and Julian Barnes combined. I've put my headphones on, to drown it

29

out, but when I close my eyes all I can see is flesh.

But it's not just sex. It isn't. No, no, I'm not being dirty. Not like when mum caught me in the bathroom, caught me with the magazine. And she made me scrub with the pumice stone: made me scrub my hands and . . . no, that's the past. I don't want to remember it.

Saturday

No call again. I went out for a walk, up towards the college. I wasn't sure if Siobhan teaches there at the weekend; thought I might bump into her. I didn't.

When I got home, I knocked on Simon's door.

'Enter at your own risk.'

I went in. The room stank of dope and sex. No sign of Natalie. Simon was on his iMac, looking at porn on the Web. The girl on the screen looked very young; I had to look away.

'Did anyone call for me?' I asked.

He reached for his cigarettes and lit up.

'Yeah . . . actually, some chick did ring.'

'What? When?'

'Yesterday afternoon when you were at work.'

'What did she say?'

He grinned. 'She asked if I wanted to save money on my gas bill.'

'You git.'

'She was nice, actually. Maybe I could have fixed you up on a blind date.' He laughed and coughed simultaneously.

In my mind, I grabbed hold of his stupid, grinning head and shoved it through the screen of his computer. In reality, I just muttered, 'Arsehole,' and left the room.

'Don't get eggy, Alex,' he called after me. 'It was only a joke.'

I came into my room and slammed the door. Then I turned on my own PC, staring at the flickering screen while it booted up, the hard disk grinding away. I could see my reflection in the monitor screen. My hair was all over the place and my eyes looked puffy. I needed a bath.

But if the phone rang while I was in there . . .

I logged onto Facebook and typed Siobhan's name into the search bar. There were five Siobhan McGowan's in the UK, plus some more in Ireland and a page full in the States. Two of them were listed as living in London on the search results. Of those two, one had a picture of a baby as their profile picture; the other had a picture of a cat.

Siobhan doesn't have a baby—but I remembered her telling us she had a cat when she first introduced herself to the class. I clicked through. Because her privacy settings were preventing me from seeing her full profile, I was only able to see a small amount of information, including the fact that she had 82 friends. Twice as many as me. I scanned the list. None of the others from class were on there.

My mouse cursor hovered over the 'Add as friend' button. Should I do it? Why not. After all, we were friends, weren't we? Certainly better friends than half of the people I have listed as friends, most of whom are colleagues or people I haven't seen or wanted to see since I left school.

I clicked the button then had a tremulous little daydream about how long it would be before I saw the words 'In a relationship with Alex Parkinson' appear on her page.

31

Then I hovered over the 'Poke' button, but thought on reflection that was taking things a bit too far.

For the next two hours I refreshed the page repeatedly. I learned that one of my 'friends' was bored, that another had a cold, and that one of them had just finished watching the second series of *Prison Break* on box set. But Siobhan hadn't yet confirmed me as a friend. I checked Twitter but all I found was an account in the name Siobhan MacGowan with a single tweet that had been made six months ago: 'So this is Twitter, eh? Wonder what all the fuss is about. Am going to tweet every day.' Couldn't be her, unless she'd accidentally added an extra 'a' into her surname—unlikely, I'd say.

Monday

I decided this morning it was time to stop moping around. Stop being pathetic and passive. Do something, Alex. I went into work with a plan, albeit a dangerous one. I was going to commit one of the few sackable offences.

I sat down at my desk and put my headset on. My supervisor, Jackie, looked over at me, making sure I wasn't wasting time before logging on. As we're consistently being told, Bookjungle is the biggest online retailer in the world—not that you'd know it from our wages—and we have to keep our customers happy by letting them talk to us like we're shit and not keeping them waiting when they want to tell us this.

I took a couple of calls from people moaning about delays in receiving their books, then did what I'm not supposed to do.

Checking that nobody was watching, I went into what we call the 'back office'; the part of the computer system that the public can't see. It's the database where we keep all our customers' details. We need to be able to access it in order to answer their queries: we can see their address and all the books and CDs they've ordered. But we're only allowed to look up the details of customers we speak to, and only if we need the information to deal with their enquiry, to prevent you looking up the details of your friends and enemies. To deter us, the system generates random reports, which mean that you have to be able to show the supervisor that you spoke to the customer you were looking up. These reports only capture one in fifty of the customers we look up, but it's not usually worth taking that chance.

Today, it was worth that chance.

I was quietly confident that Siobhan would be a customer of ours. After all, we are the biggest of our kind, and anyone who reads a lot, like Siobhan must, was more than likely to have ordered a book from us.

I typed her name.

There were 13 Siobhan McGowans on the database. Most were in Ireland, but three were in London, one more than on Facebook. Two of them had North London postcodes. I wasn't sure which one it would be so I looked at them both. I felt jumpy and sweaty as I hurried to look up the details. The first Siobhan McGowan had bought a few CDs (Norah Jones, Gareth Gates—Jesus wept) and one Delia Smith cookbook. Surely that wasn't my Siobhan? I'd be very disappointed if it was. I clicked on the second

Siobhan and looked at her list of purchases. It was huge. I quickly scanned the list: Ryan Adams, The Cure, Belle and Sebastian, Sting . . . well, nobody's perfect. And among the many books was one about teaching creative writing—and *Tara Lies Awake* by Siobhan McGowan! In fact, she'd ordered her own book several times. I clicked another icon and there were her personal details. Her home and mobile numbers and email address. I copied them, pasted them into an email, then sent it to myself at home, deleting the message from my sent items folder.

I couldn't concentrate for the rest of the day.

All I could think was, I know where she lives.

* * *

Victoria Gardens was a pleasant little street: nice and quiet, curving off the main road, a small Victorian terrace, aptly enough. Close enough to Camden to be hip, and close enough to Hampstead to be respectable and safe. Siobhan lived at number 54. I walked down the odd-numbered side of the street, trying to act casual, trying not to look like I was reading the numbers on the doors. I was having a job in the dim light anyway, but luckily number 54 had a big brass sign on the front door. Siobhan's house. Just a few feet away.

Close enough to sense her.

After this initial recce, I came home to check there were no phone messages. There weren't. Then I went on to Google Maps and found the location of her house. It was only a thirty minute walk from my place, if I took the short cuts I carefully worked out.

I couldn't phone her because she'd want to know where I'd got her number from. Oh, I was snooping on the computers at work, breaking the Data Protection Act, Siobhan. No. I couldn't do it. I couldn't email her either, for the same reason. But I could walk by her house again, and maybe, just maybe, I'd get lucky. She'd come outside and look surprised and I'd say, 'How strange, I've got a friend who lives down here. I've just been to see him. Yes, I'd love a cup of coffee. You lost the card with my number? No, don't worry, I knew it would be something like that. And I do have a mobile, by the way, it's just been nicked. Ha ha.'

I had a bath and downed a couple of glasses of Absolut. Not enough to get me pissed; just a bit of Dutch courage. Or Swedish courage, I should say.

It was nearly nine by the time I had enough Swedish courage to return to Siobhan's house. It was dark, the sodium orange streetlights illuminating the alleys I cut through. There weren't many people around: a few dog walkers, a bunch of teenage boys and girls hanging out by the Lock, buckling under the weight of their facial jewellery. I walked past them and on towards Hampstead.

When I got to number 54, I didn't stop—just walked straight by, glancing to my right. The lights were off downstairs, but there was a light on in the first floor front room which I assumed was the bedroom: not a bright light, maybe a lamp, or candles. It was just before ten—too early for her to be in bed, surely?

I walked to the end of the road then back, again sticking to the odd-numbered side. I lit a cigarette. I wasn't sure what to do. I couldn't keep walking up and down, could I? I felt sick. Should I go and knock on the door? No, of course not. What excuse would I give? There were none.

35

I thought it would be okay to walk by one more time. I felt like there were hundreds of little butterflies going crazy inside me; a thousand newborn spiders wriggling in my stomach.

I was about five houses down from Siobhan's when her downstairs light came on. Very quickly afterwards, the front door opened.

I ducked behind a car before anyone emerged. My breathing seemed so loud to me I was worried she might be able to hear it from across the road. But when I risked a glimpse around the car's bonnet, I saw that the person who emerged wasn't her. It was a bloke, a big, dark-haired rugger-bugger type. My heart sank.

Then I heard the door shut, and the next thing I knew footsteps were coming straight towards me.

I held my breath, wondering what the hell I should do. But then the footsteps ceased, and a car door opened and closed. The engine revved up and I peered through the window of the car I was crouching behind. I could see him in his car; a huge exhausted-looking man. He gripped the steering wheel and drove off.

I memorised his licence plate number.

And after all the lights had gone off in Siobhan's house, I came home.

5

Siobhan

Monday

As soon as he was through my front door, Phil told me that he and Lynn had split up.

'Why?' I asked, trying not to gloat visibly.

'We want different things,' he said. I nearly laughed out loud. That easy, catch-all, convenience excuse, like bands breaking up because of 'musical differences'. In my opinion, couples *should* want different things. Life would be pretty excruciating if couples wore matching clothes, ordered the same things off menus, went to the same place on holiday every year for the rest of their lives because they both liked it. Of course I knew he really meant 'she wants kids and I don't', but I didn't care. I didn't even feel sorry for her, which surprised me. I suppose I always imagined myself as more empathic than that.

'So the holiday's off?'

He nodded, looking so crestfallen that I forgot he was technically out of bounds now, and touched his shoulder. It made me shiver with possibilities and remembered sensations, the way his solid body felt underneath that stripy shirt. I'd forgotten that he always really turned me on—until we actually got down to it, that is. With Phil, the idea was always better than the reality: anticipation was everything. It's weird how my body used to dupe me into thinking it was going to be great. I must be a sexual optimist,

37

if such a term exists.

'And what are you doing here?' I asked. 'You know I'm not a fan of unannounced visitors—what if the house had been a mess?'

He half laughed, stretching out on the sofa the way he used to, having to bend his knees so his feet didn't stick over the end. He was flattening all my cushions and I wanted to pull them out from under him and bang them together to fluff them up again.

'Your house is never a mess, Shuv. I just wanted to talk to an old friend, that's all. You don't mind, do you?'

An old friend? I'm not a sodding old friend! His socks were worn thin on the soles and I thought, I'd have chucked that pair away long ago. I hadn't noticed him take his shoes off, but when I looked over, there they were in the hall, just like old times. I wondered if the next time I turned around he'd be stark naked and I wouldn't have noticed him undressing either.

'It was nice to see you the other day outside Starbucks. I'm sorry if I was a bit short—Lynn and I were rowing then too, and I—well—seeing you just made me miss you more than ever.'

I must have looked at him with a particularly gormless expression on my face. He reached out and touched my cheek, and I felt a callous on his finger scrape against my skin. 'I really miss you, Siobhan,' he said.

Suddenly I just wanted him so badly that I thought I was going to cry, like craving chocolate when your blood sugar is at rock bottom, or that overwhelming desire for a glass of wine at the end of a long, hard day. I wanted the familiarity of his skin and his soft clumsy kisses, even his hairy chest. I wanted someone

38

to bring me tea in the morning.

I practically dragged him up to the bedroom and ripped off his clothes, and then there was the shock of the cold bedclothes over and under our hot flesh . . .

. . . and nothing had changed. The cat hair still made him sneeze. He squashed me under his weight. He moaned and grunted and thrust, ripping at my hair and using his fingers in all the wrong places. I'd been really turned on for the first two minutes but then I just kept thinking, I want a real man. I wanted to be fucked by a man with a dick like a truncheon, not this skinny little excuse for a penis. I want to come three times in a night.

I'm sorry, but Phil is ridiculous in bed. I'd forgotten quite how ridiculous, but really, all that contrived ass-slapping and cringe-worthy fantasy-whispering. How can he think it's a turn-on? And worse: now he's started using all this yucky babytalk—'Does my 'ikkle Shuvvie want it bad from her big boy Phil?' Ugh!! (And 'big boy?' I mean, hello? Who's he trying to kid?) I was rolling my eyes when he came. The baby talk must be Lynn's influence—he never used to do that.

All in all, the idea of Phil is still way better than the reality of Phil. He's a lovely bloke, and we did care about each other, and he made me laugh and bought me tampons without blanching if I needed him to—but now I remember why I wasn't heartbroken when he finished with me. Now I remember that I'd thought, oh well, might get a decent shag now, if anyone will still have me.

Nice as it was to think about getting tea brought to me in the morning, I suddenly couldn't countenance the idea of Phil staying the night; this night, or any other. I'd get my own tea—no big deal. But before I could say 'yes, well, thanks for that, Phil, but I really must be getting on with my life now', he'd jumped out of bed and headed for the bathroom to wash his willy in the sink, as he always did. (It's such an unpleasant thought—really, the male anatomy is pretty revolting, once you take away the components of arousal. Perhaps I ought to become a lesbian instead, like Kathy.)

I pulled on my bathrobe and followed him to the bathroom, giving him a respectable couple of willy-washing minutes to himself first. When I got there, he'd wrapped a towel round his waist, and was enthusiastically brushing his teeth with the old green toothbrush he used to call his. He must have unearthed it from the back of the bathroom cabinet.

I leaned against the door frame and just said it straight out: 'We're not back on, so don't get too comfortable.' It came out a lot more harshly than I intended.

I wasn't wearing my glasses so I couldn't see the hurt in his eyes, reflected in the mirrored door of the cabinet, but I could hear it in his voice, indistinct through a mouthful of toothpaste: 'But—I thought we . . . I need you, Shuv.'

With my blurry vision and his hairy back, he looked like a large doleful black bear standing by the basin. When he turned to face me, foaming at the mouth, I thought how his chest made me feel as if I'm suffocating, all that thick hair up my nose when we're in bed. I'd forgotten about that, too.

'No, you don't,' I said. 'Don't settle for something that's less than what you want. You finished with me, remember? Don't think that because you've been dumped, that makes things suddenly perfect with us.'

'I haven't been dumped,' he said, turning back to the basin, brushing furiously again and then spitting violently. He always cleaned his teeth like someone trying to scrub barnacles off the bottom of a boat. I'd be surprised if there was any enamel at all left on them.

'Oh. You dumped her, then, did you?'

He didn't answer, although I saw in the mirror that he'd closed his eyes like a small child who thinks that if he can't see you, you can't see him either.

I had a brief pang, thinking of that fortnight in Portugal going to waste. I'm glad I had the writing class to think of, otherwise I might have been tempted to ask if I could take Lynn's place. Perhaps I was being too hasty. There was a lot about Phil that was great, too; sweet and loving and patient. And his hairy body was lovely and warm on a cold night . . .

But no. I really don't think it would work out between us. It was just one of those things—probably as much my fault as his.

'Sorry,' I conceded. 'I'm being pissy. It doesn't matter who dumped who. This is about you and me, not you and Lynn. We shouldn't have slept together just now—it's always a mistake to go back, I think. Let's just call it one for old times' sake, shall we?'

His shoulders slumped, and I felt really sorry for him. I went over and put my arms around him.

'Oh Phil, it's been lovely to see you, honestly, and I'm sorry that things haven't worked out for you and Lynn. But I just don't think it would be a good idea for us to try and pick up where we left off. I think you did the right thing, to break up with me.'

That was about as diplomatic as I could be, without

recourse to the words 'pencil' and 'dick'. It wasn't his fault that he was bad in bed. And maybe he'd meet a girl who liked his little . . . foibles. I had loved him once. I didn't wish him any harm, not really. It was just the sting of rejection that hurt—but now we'd had this liaison, actually, I felt better about it. For the first time I really started to believe that I could do better than Phil.

'So I suppose you want me to leave, then,' he said, drying his mouth on another of my towels.

I nodded, wincing at the rejection. 'Sorry,' I repeated. 'I do care about you, Phil, but . . .'

'I understand,' he said dolefully, and took himself back off to the bedroom to get dressed. I left him to it, and went to fold my washing off the drying rack I'd positioned by the radiator in the living room. Biggles was curled up asleep underneath it—he loved it under there, playing with bra straps in the damp curtained hideyhole.

'See you around, Siobhan.' Phil came into the room, dressed once more, and jingling his car keys. He wouldn't look me in the eye as he gave me a brief, minty kiss goodbye.

'Take care of yourself, OK?' I said, annoyed to feel tears stinging my eyes. I folded a pair of socks and threw them into the laundry basket, so he couldn't see that I was upset.

He nodded brusquely, and let himself out of the house. I pulled back the curtain to watch him lower his bulky frame into his car, and heard the slam of the door echo round the deserted street. As his headlights flooded the stationary vehicles in front of him, I was sure I saw a sudden movement, like someone ducking down behind a car. I stared harder, but nothing else moved, so I thought it must have been a fox, or a cat jumping off the car roof. I hope it wasn't a burglar.

I went to both front and back doors to check they were double-locked, sighing as I walked back upstairs. Alone again—naturally—as the song goes . . . Just as I got back into my bedroom, surveying the rumpled bedclothes, the phone rang. I sighed again, this time with irritation, and picked up. What had he forgotten?

'Phil?'

Nothing. The line was dead.

I sat on the bed for a long time, not moving, wondering if I'd done the right thing.

Sunday

My resolve is much stronger now. By the next morning I was sure that I had done the right thing—better to be on my own than compromise with someone I wasn't entirely convinced about. I spent the weekend at Mum's in case Phil came over again and I let him talk me back into the relationship, but there's been no sign of him since last week . . . I told Mum a little about what had happened, about him splitting up with Lynn—the censored version, of course, although it made it very difficult to explain to her why I don't want to get back with him, without telling her that he's got a willy like a cocktail sausage and has no idea what to do with it. Mum always had a soft spot for Phil. I think she was more upset when we split up than I was.

She's constantly telling me how worried she is about me, regardless of how often I reassure her that there's nothing wrong: I'm just single, that's all.

It's not a disease. Sometimes I feel like telling her I am ill, just so that she's got something concrete to fixate on instead of this nebulous and misguided concern over nothing. Having said that, I suppose I do like knowing somebody cares about me enough to worry so much. And she's my mum; it's her job to worry.

*   *   *

It's nice to be home again, although I'm not getting much work done today. I've been on a huge cleaning jag, running the duster all round the skirting boards, rolling up the rugs and washing the floors, chasing out the tumbleweeds of dust from behind the sofa. These Victorian houses are so hard to keep clean. No matter what I do, I can still feel decades of grime pressing down on me. I'd like to rip up all this woodblock flooring and replace it with laminate, but the original floors do look so much nicer. Plus, the thought of all the dust and crap that would be disturbed in the process makes my skin crawl.

While I was dusting the books, I caught sight of *TLA* on the shelf. It's funny, I haven't looked at it for months and months. I suppose I'm so used to it sitting there that I just don't see it any more—it's as much a fixture of my flat as the velvet cushions and the Paul Klee print above the fireplace. I don't get that shiver of pride at tracing my fingers over the letters on the spine; don't pick it out and flip through the pages, unable to believe that I personally came up with all those words. (Although I do still wonder how on earth I did it. When did I have the time?)

But today I looked at it in a different light. Its

appearance in class last week has made me feel aware of it as somehow an extension of myself, that old vulnerable feeling that I had when it was first published. I feel particularly concerned about Alex, for some reason—probably because of the review he wrote. What if he thinks that Tara is me? Worse— what if he thinks that what Tara does in bed is what I would do? At least there isn't a lot of sex; I'd be mortified to put my name to a bonkbuster. There are only two real sex scenes in *TLA* and I'd say they're both artistically appropriate, and necessary for insight into the characters . . . I wish I *did* have that sort of sex!

10 pm

Well, guess what? Phil's just been round again. I'd thought after what I told him on Monday that he'd have got the message. But it seems that he hasn't.

'I can't stop thinking about you,' he said. 'That sex was so mind-blowing last week.'

I was practically biting my knuckle at this point. But he really did seem upset. If he's that upset, why did he dump me in the first place? It seems churlish to ask him, though.

'Did you call me, by the way, after you left that night?'

He looked surprised. 'No. Did someone call? Bit late, wasn't it?'

'That's what I thought. There was no one there when I picked up.'

'Probably just a wrong number then.'

I nodded, although I couldn't help thinking about the dark shape I saw moving behind the car. 'I'm

45

sorry you're feeling low, Phil,' I said.

He bent down to kiss me but I moved my head away, and his lips connected with my ear. I felt a faint twinge of lust, but told myself to get a grip. I tried to be nice, to say again that I'd moved on—I even trotted out his own excuse and told him that we both wanted different things (a decent shag being top of my list). But he didn't seem to be hearing me. Eventually I had to put it to him straight.

'Phil. You're a lovely guy and a great friend, but I really feel that we aren't sexually compatible.'

His jaw dropped and he blinked at me in amazement.

'You never complained before,' he said suspiciously.

I made some excuse about not realising it until last week—I wouldn't want to hurt his feelings that much—but Phil does have extraordinarily thin skin. He jerked away from me, grabbed his coat, and headed out the door. I followed him into the street.

'Don't go like this, Phil, please,' I said, trying to keep my voice low so as not to give the neighbours a free show. This wasn't *Sex and the* bloody *City*, after all. 'I'm really sorry. I don't want to hurt you. I just don't want to go back to where we were before. Please let's stay friends. I don't want to spoil that.'

He looked at me, and I could see humiliation in his eyes. 'I'll see you around then,' he said, without a trace of his habitual smugness.

Men and their pride! Especially where it concerns their sexual prowess.

Still, I don't suppose I'd be overly happy if some ex announced that I was rubbish in the sack. Poor Phil. But I guess he's really got the message now. And I really do feel OK about it.

Wednesday

Something very weird happened this morning. I've had this card, and it's anonymous. It's—well, it's weird. I don't know what to make of it.

The post came, just as I was leaving to meet Dennis Tennis. I scooped it all up off the mat and stuck it in my tennis bag. I got to the courts on time, but Dennis was late, as usual. I tried to warm up by practicing my serve, but I'd only brought four balls with me, and after a few goes I got tired of having to run down the other end of the court to retrieve the balls and try again.

Nobody else was around except a lone jogger doing circuits of the park, and a man in bright green dungarees digging up a flowerbed about a hundred feet away. He was listening to REM 'Losing My Religion', which was coming out of a flatbed truck parked next to him. I was quite glad Dennis wasn't there—I was enjoying the feeling of being almost alone in a wide open space, the trees around me starting to change colour, squirrels bouncing along branches over my head, fresh air in my lungs.

I went and sat down on the court, leaning against the net post, and pulled out the mail. Two bills, a postcard from Paula in Phuket, and this interesting-looking letter with my name and address typed on the front. A good, thick envelope.

There was a postcard inside it, of a Gustav Klimt painting: *Water Snakes I (Girlfriends)*. It's one of his beautiful golden erotic ones, a woman on her back with that frowny, closed-eyed expression which is more likely to be orgasm than sleep. One naked breast is showing, and her arm is around another woman, who looks as though she's sucking the other breast. The two look like one. It's weird how he so often painted his women with their heads at ninety degree angles to their bodies.

When I turned it over it had a few lines printed on it, by hand. It said:

. . . I don't think I can even write it. I'm not a prude or anything, but it makes me feel embarrassed because of the way it describes what somebody wants to do to me. It wasn't signed. I'll stick it in here when I find my sellotape—it's not something I'd want to leave around for Mum to find.

I didn't recognise the handwriting, but Phil knows I like Klimt. And it figures that he'd be trying to dispel his bad rap in bed—although it's not like him to go in for soft porn. I thought I knew him well enough to know that it's just not his style.

I was really shocked, actually. I didn't realise how shocked until Dennis Tennis turned up, lolloping across the park like a daddy long legs, and when I stood up to meet him I sort of almost lost my balance. Dennis looked really concerned.

'Are you OK?' he asked, in his funny Wiltshire accent. 'You look a bit pale.'

Normally I'd never confide in Dennis Tennis; the 6' 5" religious tennis-playing plumber. He carries his tennis racket and his Bible around with his toilet plunger and his spanners. Ours is a strictly tennis relationship, I have no idea where he even lives—but suddenly I just wanted to talk to someone, so I blurted it out. Not what the card said, of course, just that I was a bit taken aback by its content. And

48

that I'd sort of finished with an old boyfriend, and was worried that he'd taken it badly. Dennis looked utterly mortified, and muttered something that sounded suspiciously like he'd pray for me if I liked. I felt like saying, 'No, that's OK, just let me win at tennis for once.'

Then I suddenly thought; what if the card's from him? The quiet ones are often the worst.

I dismissed this idea instantly. But then I thought, it can't be Phil, either. I know Phil well enough to know that he's not that imaginative—I lived with the man for eight months. Not Phil, not Dennis, then.

What about Poor Brian, gutted that I knocked him back? But no, how would he know where I live? And the same goes for Alex, too, my other potential admirer. It's a picture of two women . . . couldn't be from Kathy, could it? No—a woman wouldn't be anatomically capable of doing some of the things described on the card. I can't think of any other ex-boyfriends who would suddenly come out of the woodwork. Why is it anonymous, if they did? It must be Phil.

*   *   *

Needless to say, tennis was a disaster. I played atrociously, and Dennis thrashed me 6-1, 6-0, which irritated me beyond measure, even though I deserved to lose that badly. I couldn't concentrate at all. My mind was like the ball, flying all over the place, everywhere except where I wanted it to go. I just kept thinking of those words, and seeing the rapture on the face of that Klimt woman with her long hair streaming down over her shoulders and

49

mingling with the other woman's hair.

*   *   *

When I got home, I looked at the envelope again. It's postmarked Kentish Town, so whoever it's from is not far away. My hands were clammy as I took out the card and re-read it, holding it between finger and thumb like it was going to contaminate me.

On second reading, I thought, maybe it's not that obscene. It's quite, well, erotic. It's just the fact that it's not signed that makes it so creepy. If I got that card from someone I was madly in love with, I'd actually be rather flattered. And turned on.

*   *   *

Who fancies me enough to fantasise these things, and to let me know—albeit anonymously—that they do?

6

Alex

Tuesday

It took me almost an hour to choose the Klimt card, but once I'd bought it and got it home, I wrote the message in a feverish rush, letting my feelings spill from my pen and sealing the envelope before I could change my mind.

I printed her address on the envelope then took

it down to the post box. I stood there, gripping it hard, not sure what to do. I wanted her to read it and feel good. I wanted her to know that she could arouse those feelings, even though I'm not sure I want her to know it's me yet. I need to play it cool— don't want to seem too keen. That always frightens them off or leads to misunderstandings.

I may have to fight for Siobhan's affections. Who was that man who left her house the other night? A lover? A friend? Maybe it was just her brother. No need to get violently jealous yet.

Standing beside the postbox, my hand was trembling; my resolve was wavering. And then I heard, 'That for me?'

It was a postman. He must have unlocked the post box and emptied the contents without me even noticing. (Sometimes, strangely, I just seem to black out, lose all sense of where I am; my mind conjuring up a fantasy world that over rides reality.)

'I haven't got all day, mate,' the postie said.

I handed him the card. And as soon as I did, I was glad I'd written it.

Now I wish I could be there to see her open it. To see her smile. To see the pink flush of desire creep from her cheeks to her collar.

To hear her say, 'I want you too.'

Wednesday

Woke up with a headache and wet sheets. Just before going to sleep I read my favourite scene from *Tara Lies Awake* again—the one where Tara and Luke screw in the changing rooms at the sports centre, their bodies reeking of chlorine from the pool. I must have read that scene twenty times already. I wonder if this scene is pure imagination or based on a real event? The most noteworthy thing that ever happened to me in a sports centre was catching a verruca.

It's class tonight. I can't wait, though I feel as nervous as hell. I ought to go to work, but I don't think I can face it. I'm going to call in sick.

Just did it—Jackie, my supervisor, sounded strange. Well, stranger than normal, the uptight bitch. She is the archetypal little Hitler. A small fish in a tiny pond, poisoned by power. She's been watching me closely recently because my stats are down. Last week, I took 14 per cent fewer calls than the average employee, and had more toilet breaks than anyone else, apart from cystitic Sharon. Employing her favourite cliché, Jackie told me I needed to buck my ideas up or risk being sent to see Martin, the big boss. Ooh, I'm scared! But I'm not going to let her get to me. There are far more important things in the world.

Like tonight. Like seeing the woman I . . .

Oh go on, Alex, admit it.

The woman I love.

There. I said it. Or wrote it, rather. I love Siobhan. I love her I love her I love her! God, that feels good. I want to do what they do in all those tacky songs: shout it from the highest mountain top, proclaim it from the top of the tallest building. I feel it fizzing inside me, a Catherine wheel spinning and shooting colours. A piranha gnawing at my stomach lining. Bubbles inflating and floating upwards, making me light, making me dizzy. All these things. Because:

I LOVE HER!

I got there early, without meaning to. I didn't want to risk arriving to find Siobhan already there on her own so I hung back in the car park, crouching behind a bush, until I saw Barbara and Jane go in. Then I made my way towards the classroom, flashed them a smile and sat down.

Everyone else arrived, and then Siobhan. She looked us over, focusing on me for an extra second, I noticed. I expect she was embarrassed about losing my number. She wasn't wearing her sexy outfit tonight: instead, she wore a black polo neck jumper and jeans. She still looked good, though, her sweater hugging her breasts, her bottom shapely in her jeans. I felt so hot from looking at her that I had to open a window, which made Barbara grumble.

Siobhan looked at her watch. 'We'd better wait for Brian.'

But he didn't appear. After five minutes, during which Siobhan chatted with Kathy, she said, 'Well, I think we'd better get on.' She looked a bit worried; perhaps she gets paid by the student. Oh Siobhan, if I could multiply myself to help you, I would. But I wasn't going to miss Brian. Especially as I was now the only man in the group.

Though that didn't mean I was the only one with my eye on Siobhan. As the class went on, I noticed how much Kathy was looking at her. Every time Siobhan turned around, Kathy ogled her arse. And she was trying to leap into the limelight at every opportunity. Anyone would think this was fame school, not a creative writing class, and that we should all be wearing black lycra.

'Who would like to read out their piece from last

53

week?' Siobhan asked.

Straight away Kathy said, 'I will.' Bloody teacher's pet.

She said the guy in her story had just come to her, 'walked into her line of vision', as she put it. Siobhan smiled and nodded at that. He was lonely, she said, and wanted someone to care for him. He'd had a difficult childhood, and a worse adolescence, sitting in his musty bedroom. Now he had met someone who he had fallen for, but he was too shy to approach this person (a non-gender-specific person, I noted). In the scene she read out, the boy—Michael—was writing in his diary about how he'd just love to spend a day with his loved one: a day by the sea, eating candy floss and paddling in the cold English Channel. At night they'd sit and watch the pier lights ebb on the surface of the sea. At the end of this, Siobhan looked tearful, her eyes moist, and I wanted to shout at Kathy, say, 'See what you've done—you've upset her.'

But then Siobhan said, 'That was beautiful, Kathy.'

My God. Was this more competition? Not just the man who left her house (if he is a competitor) but Kathy as well? Reading Siobhan's novel, knowing how sexual she was, I could imagine her wanting to experiment; or perhaps she was a full-blown bisexual. And I was certain this dyke fancied my Siobhan. Who wouldn't?

I wished I had something to read out myself. Something more beautiful—something like I'd written in Siobhan's card. Barbara went next, and her piece was bloody awful, quelle sur-fucking-prise, but I wasn't really listening anyway. Her words were drowned out by the buzzing in my ears.

And beneath the buzzing, I was thinking. About

how, very soon, Siobhan will realise that, apart from her, I'm the best writer in the class. And she'll ask me to read to her in bed, with our mingled sweat still drying on our skin. And as I read, she'll stroke me. She'll do all sorts of wonderful things to me with her hands and her mouth.

I found it even harder to concentrate after that.

At the end of the lesson, I hung back. Siobhan had given us more exercises to do: she wants us to put our characters into a severe weather situation. I think I'll be good at that, once I've come up with my central character. I got away without reading aloud this week—fortunately, Jane had written so much and went on at such length (I think she's cheating and that it was an extract from her novel-in-progress) that we ran out of time—but my good luck won't last forever. Funny how listening to someone read out a seven-page description of their back garden can be classed as good luck.

Siobhan said something to Kathy on her way out, then began to pack up her stuff.

'That was a good class,' I said.

She looked up at me, eyes wide and bright. 'Hi Alex.'

'I'm really enjoying this class,' I said.

She smiled. 'That's great.'

'And I learned a lot today about the flora of north London.'

She appeared confused for a moment then got it and laughed. I think she must have felt guilty though because she put her hand to her mouth and stopped herself. I was glowing inside. I'd made her laugh!

'I loved your novel,' I said. 'I think it's one of the best things I've read in ages.'

Now it was her turn to glow. 'Thank you for the

lovely review. Shame I never got any write-ups like that in the press. You could have just told me you liked it though rather than go to all that trouble.'

'I didn't want to embarrass you in front of the other students.'

'Oh, don't worry. Praise doesn't embarrass me, I can assure you. Anyway, thank you again.' She picked up her bag and threw it over her shoulder. 'I'll see you next week.'

She took a step towards the door and I knew I had to act fast before the opportunity slipped away. 'Siobhan.'

She turned back. 'Hmm?'

'Would you . . . I wondered if . . . maybe we could go out sometime? To talk about your novel.'

She had her back to the open door. 'You're asking me out.'

I wasn't sure if it was a question or a statement.

'Well . . . yeah. I guess so.' I tried my best to maintain eye contact with her.

She cleared her throat. 'I'm sorry Alex. I can't. It's a college rule. Teachers aren't allowed to date students. I'm sorry.'

'But . . . who would know?'

She was clearly unhappy about this rule too—she looked a bit choked. Oh, poor Siobhan. I wanted to comfort her, but I was frozen by what she had said.

She mumbled something about how rules were rules and how she couldn't risk getting into trouble with the college. 'And it would be so hard to keep it quiet.'

Before I could respond, she said, 'See you next week.' She left the classroom, leaving me on my own. I reached out for her, but she'd gone.

Walking home, I thought about what was going on. She was afraid. But was she afraid of breaking the rules, or of love itself? Was she using the college rules as an excuse? Maybe someone had hurt her recently? I know from the way she looks at me that she wants me. But she's scared, like an animal that's afraid of people, either timid by nature, or a victim of cruelty. That must be why she hasn't accepted my Facebook friend request yet.

If I'm going to win her love, I need to get the balance right. I need to show her that she needn't be frightened, that that love is a bond, not a cage. I need to tiptoe and whisper rather than rush and shout. And I need to get to know her: the way she lives and feels and thinks. Not that that's going to be a hardship. It's going to be fun, researching this woman I love, because it will mean I'll have to get close to her.

But what if she rejects you? What if she doesn't want you?

The voice whispering at me sounded just like my mother. I wanted to punch her in the mouth, shut her up. Because, I whispered back to myself, Siobhan *does* want me; will want me. Cupid, that fat little angel, who changes our fate with an invisible arrow, has chosen us. Our hearts were his target, and his aim doesn't lie. Siobhan and I are meant to be together.

Live our lives apart? I'd rather we were both dead.

I needed a drink, so I stopped outside a bar. It

wasn't the kind of place I would normally go to. Too trendy. But the people I saw through the window looked so happy and luminous, and the damp, shining bottles of beer on the table were calling to me. And seeing all the couples leaning close and laughing didn't make me feel sick like it normally does.

I stubbed out my cigarette and went in, bought a bottle of Corona and took it over to a table in the corner.

Siobhan doesn't smoke—at least, I've never seen her smoke—so maybe I should try to quit. She might not like the smell of it. Or, more likely, she won't mind it on me. She might even find it sexy, mannish.

I took out my notebook and began to work on my exercise for next week. I wanted my hero to be masculine, strong, well-read and -travelled. A kind of modern day Indiana Jones. I thought Siobhan would like that.

I scribbled away happily, engrossed in what I was doing. The bar was pretty quiet, and the background hum was pleasant; quite soothing. I finished my beer and stood up to get another, and as I walked past the table next to mine, I saw a face I recognised.

It wasn't until I'd reached the bar that I worked out who it was. It was him—the guy I saw leaving Siobhan's house the other night. As I walked back to my table, I kept my head down, looking at him from the corner of my eye. Yes, it was definitely him. I recognised the cleft chin (like a bum) and the bags under his eyes. He was wearing the same denim jacket. But the skinny woman he was sitting with was definitely not the object of my affections.

I sat down, my back to them, and tuned in to their conversation. It wasn't easy because they were

58

talking quietly, so I missed some words. But I heard enough.

He said, 'I want us to give it another chance.'

'But I don't know if I can trust you, Phil.'

'Why not?'

'Because . . . (*inaudible*).'

'But Lynn, sweetheart, I swear. It's over between me and Siobhan.'

'(*Inaudible*) . . . since last week?'

'I swear. On (*couldn't make it out*) life. I haven't even spoken to Siobhan this week.'

I couldn't hear the next couple of lines at all. Their voices went really low and soft, and then they stopped talking altogether. I sneaked a look over my shoulder. They were leaning towards each other across the table, holding hands and kissing.

'I love you,' I heard the lying creep say.

'I love you too,' said the poor woman. 'Let's go home.'

'To celebrate?'

She laughed throatily. I think they must have exchanged saliva again, and then Phil said, 'Lynn . . . you don't think I'm rubbish in bed, do you?'

'Eh? What's brought this on.'

'I don't know. I just . . . you don't think I'm crap, do you?'

'No! You're fine.'

He must have been satisfied with this faint praise because the next thing he said was, 'Okay, let's go. I just need to go to the loo.'

He stood up and crossed the room to the Gents. And I followed, one hand lightly scratching my brow so it hid my face.

He held the door open, not looking at me, and went straight into a cubicle. There was nobody else in the Gents. Perfect. I heard him unzip his fly and let his jeans fall to the floor. He sighed as he sat down. I waited till I heard the first splash.

'Phil,' I said, through the cubicle door.

There was a pause. 'Who's that?'

'You don't need to know my name. You just need to listen. Actually, think of me as a guardian angel—though not yours.'

'What?' I heard him tear off a strip of bog roll. I needed to hurry.

'I know you've been lying to Lynn. I know you saw Siobhan the other night. I want you to stay away from Siobhan. Don't speak to her. Don't go to see her. If you do, I'll make sure Lynn finds out about the lies you've been telling her.'

'Who the fuck . . .?'

But before he could clean his arse and fasten his trousers, I was out of there: out of the front door and round the corner. Phil couldn't come chasing after me because of Lynn. He hadn't seen my face, so he would have no idea who had been talking to him. And it was true what I said to him: I am a guardian angel. And I'd just helped Siobhan remove an obstacle from her life.

*   *   *

When I got home, I was still excited and pleased with myself. More than anything, I wanted to hear Siobhan's voice.

I hit 151 first to withhold my number, then dialled Siobhan's. The phone rang six or seven times. I just had enough time to wonder if she was in the bath, which gave me a wonderful image, her skin made pink by the hot water, her nipples peeking out

60

through a layer of bubbles, when she said, 'Hello?'

I didn't speak.

'Hello?'

God, I love her voice. What a pity I had to put the phone down.

Thursday

Called in sick again. Jackie said, 'You will be coming in tomorrow, won't you?' I replied that I wasn't sure.

The house was empty, with both Si and Nat at work. I ate breakfast in the nude, then checked Facebook to see if Siobhan had accepted my friend request yet. No luck. But when I looked at her friend list again I noticed that Kathy was now listed. How sickening. Siobhan had confirmed that lezzer's friend request but not mine.

Furious, I stormed into the bathroom and had a wank to calm myself down, unable to stop myself picturing Siobhan and Kathy in a Sapphic clinch. After I came I got dressed and collapsed on the sofa and watched some crappy programme on daytime TV. There was a phone-in about relationships: mainly women calling and complaining about how unromantic their husbands were; about how they never took them out or bought them flowers any more. That gave me an idea.

I headed down to the market. The flowers were so expensive.

'Have you got anything cheaper?' I said.

The bloke behind the stall rolled his eyes a bit and said, 'I've got these lilies. They're a bit limp, but you can have them for a quid.'

They looked alright to me. I decided to take them straight round to Siobhan's. My plan was to leave them on the doorstep, with a little note. I checked my bag for my pen but it wasn't there, so I wouldn't be able to leave a message. Oh well—it would add to the romance, anyway, if Siobhan thought her flowers were from a mysterious admirer.

I reached Victoria Gardens and paused at Siobhan's gate, which stood wide open. I could hear music coming from inside the house: something I didn't recognise. I wondered which part of the house she was in. As long as she wasn't looking out the front window, I'd be okay. I wasn't meant to know where she lived.

Heart beating fast, I headed up the short path to the front door. I was about to lay the bouquet on her step when I saw a bunch of keys hanging from the keyhole. What was this? An invitation? Turn the key and come straight in, Alex. But no, she didn't know I was coming. Was she expecting someone else? I was confused. But then I realised it was a sign, and I had another idea.

Taking the keys from the lock, and still clutching the flowers, I turned and ran back towards the main road. There was a heel bar there; I'd passed it on the way up. A sign outside said, 'KEYS CUT WHILE U WAIT'.

I only had to wait five minutes, then I headed back to Siobhan's house, creeping up to the front door again to replace the keys in the lock. My own copy of her front door key sat snugly in my pocket. Now I would be able to enter her territory and find out more about her at my leisure. I was so excited at this thought that I could hardly walk or breathe. I was tempted to hang around, hide somewhere until

62

she went out, but in the end I thought it would be best to come back another time. Before I went, I left the flowers on her step. Keys and flowers. A gift for both of us.

7

Siobhan

Thursday

Class went well last night. I think I'm finding my stride—well, I think we all are. I heard some really promising work. Kathy's was fantastic. It never ceases to amaze me, how the beauty of words can grip me in the gut and pull me—she read out this piece about yearning, and loneliness, and love, and I really felt choked. She talked about candy floss as 'tiny threads of twisted pink longing', and the bone-chilling ache of cold sea water turning her character's ankles numb.

It reminded me so much of my (one and only) holiday romance, when I was sixteen, with Colin the Glaswegian. We had to communicate in sign language because his accent was so thick. And body language. I wonder what happened to all his letters? I don't think I have them any more. Kathy's piece brought it all back, how I felt when his mum wrote that note to say he'd died in a car accident. Life is so harsh. I often wonder if he and I would have ended up together. I know we were only kids, but I really felt something for him. I can't picture his face any more, just that great mop of wind-swept curly black hair, those blue, blue eyes, and the clammy feeling of spending too long in a wet swimsuit. Coming back to the hotel at the end of the day all horny and sandy—that's what reminds me of Colin. I don't think I've felt that passionate about anybody since.

It really makes me think that if love does come along, you have to seize it with both hands and not let it go.

Anyway. Back to the class. Brian didn't turn up, which gave me a horrible feeling that maybe it was him who sent that card. Phil's still Number One suspect—and God knows how Brian could have found out my address—but I suppose it is possible. Surely not though . . .

Talking of my various admirers, Alex asked me out. Maybe the card is from him? He must like me. I said no, although I did give it a moment's thought—it's not that he's bad-looking, or anything. It's not even that there might not be a spark, if I let there be. But there's just something . . . I don't know what exactly . . . which unsettles me about him. Maybe just his own weird energy.

He seemed cool about me turning him down, though, so I'm sure he'll just move on to his next conquest. He probably doesn't even like me all that much; probably is just impressed that I'm a 'faymuss awfor'. Or, rather, an 'awfor'.

I noticed that he's sent me a friend request on Facebook, which I hardly ever go on. Kathy sent me one too, which was nice. But I am not going to confirm Alex because there are various shots of me on there in my bikini in Malta last summer with Phil. Don't want one of my male students perving over them, do I? Though maybe I shouldn't have accepted Kathy either . . .

And bloody Phil has unfriended me on there! I know because I tried to visit his profile to see whether he was still listed as 'in a relationship' and I couldn't get onto the page. Guess I must have hurt his feelings more than I thought.

Friday

Dead flowers. Phil has actually left a bunch of dead flowers on my doorstep. I can't believe it. That's a really horrible thing to do to somebody. I don't blame him for feeling fed up—he's been rejected by me *and* Lynn—but how could he stoop to something so cowardly and pathetic?

It must be Phil. All these weirdnesses can't be coincidence. Has he totally lost it? It's so unlike him. There was the graphic postcard. Then hang-ups when I answer the phone, six or seven times in the past couple of days. And now the dead flowers.

The more I think about it, the more angry it makes me. He knows I hate lilies. And these have got brown spots all over the petals, and slimy stems. They stink. What's that sonnet where Shakespeare talks about how bad lilies smell?

Just looked it up, it's:

'For sweetest things turn sourest by their deeds;
Lilies that fester smell far worse than weeds.'

That just about sums it up, Phil, you nutter. I feel like going into his office and ramming them up his –

Maybe I'll just ring him instead. Tear him off a strip on the phone. It's not worth the energy I'd expend in going down there myself.

I stuffed the lilies into the bin under the sink, snapping the stems in two, trying to cram them in without letting any of the woody ends rip the bin bag. All the petals immediately dropped off, and that atrociously sticky pollen fell all over my hands, the kitchen floor, the top of the bin. By the time I'd cleaned it all up (which took ages because at first my attempts just left yellow swirly smears everywhere, and I had to practically bleach all the surfaces) I was in such a rage that my best being-rude-to-estate-agents voice came completely naturally:

'Phil Harmony, please.'

'Sorry, he's on holiday. Can I put you through to his secretary?'

This somehow made me even more furious. I can't bear idiots who give you the wrong information on the telephone. Of course he wasn't on bloody holiday, his holiday had been cancelled. That receptionist always had been dim.

'Hello, Siobhan,' said Diane when I got through to Phil's office. 'He's not here, I'm afraid. He's on holiday.'

Oh—well, of course, he'd have already booked the time off. I felt bad for mentally slagging off the receptionist. She wasn't to know. She wasn't to know I'd mentally slagged her either, so I suppose I didn't need to feel guilty. I invited the anger back.

'Don't worry, I'll try him at home,' I said, about to hang up.

'He's not at home,' Diane said, sounding half-puzzled, and half-impatient; sort of, what part of 'on holiday' do you not understand? 'He's gone to Portugal.'

Suddenly the hand I was holding the phone with began to shake a bit. I'd been chewing gum at the time, and shock made it slide towards the back of my throat, giving me a moment's panic. I had to suck it back into my mouth again. I grabbed it and pulled it out of my mouth, then rolled it around between my finger and thumb, feeling it change consistency, becoming harder and smoother, like a small lump of fear personified, sticking to my skin.

'When, exactly?' I asked, having a weird feeling that the gum was still in my throat, choking me.

'They—I mean, he flew out yesterday morning. He rang me from the airport.'

'They? He went with Lynn?'

There was a silence.

I sagged against the back of the sofa, nearly dropping the phone. I didn't give a stuff that he and Lynn appeared to have got back together—let them baby-talk their way around the Algarve, Philly-willy and Lynny-winny—but my mind was racing, and even while part of me was in denial and trying to figure out why he was still ringing me and hanging up from Portugal, with Lynn there too; or how the flowers could have turned up on my doorstep today . . . another more cognisant part of me realised where the fear was coming from.

Because if Phil went to Portugal yesterday, he couldn't have left the lilies. And if he didn't leave the lilies, then he most likely didn't send the card. Or make those silent phone calls.

But if it wasn't Phil . . .

Who the hell was it?

*   *   *

67

I don't know. Maybe it's my hormones. I've got that weird, slightly unreal feeling that I sometimes get with PMT, like I'm inhabiting a parallel universe; one not dissimilar to this, but hazier, more painful. More frightening. A universe where I want to curl up and sleep and let someone look after me. I keep losing things, too. I lost my keys again, turned the place over looking for them (although 'turned the place over' isn't really the right expression. 'Picked up, looked, and replaced neatly', would be more apposite. Dr Bedford said I have issues with cleanliness and tidiness. I disagree. I think it's more to do with growing up in a big messy household that nobody could ever find anything in. I never could stand that, even as a little girl).

But the weird thing about the keys was that I'm sure the first thing I did when I realised they were missing was to check the front door, and they weren't there. I suppose I was a bit distracted, trying to stop Biggles from running out into the street again, but I definitely checked. Went back upstairs, cleaned out the fridge, fed Biggles, checked again to make sure—and there they were, dangling from the lock. It was bizarre. And that was when I found the flowers.

I'd been thinking what a wuss Phil was, to leave the flowers and run away without telling me that my keys were sticking out of the front door—I mean, anyone could have let themselves in!

But the horrible truth is that it wasn't Phil. Someone else must have seen those keys. Someone else. The same someone who sent me that card, telling me he wanted to fuck me? The same person who keeps calling and hanging up. When I thought it was Phil it was just irritating. But now . . .

68

Oh God. What if I'm not alone now? What if someone's standing behind one of my doors, perhaps this one . . .?

*　　　*　　　*

I'm all out of breath. Have just run up and down the stairs with the poker, opened all the doors, looked in all the cupboards. Put on *Combat Rock* at full blast—The Clash make me feel brave. Biggles is disgusted with me. He was chasing up and down the stairs after me with his tail out like a brush. At first, being paranoid, I thought that he could sense something strange. Then I thought, yes of course he can: me, charging around like a maniac with a poker while listening to music loudly enough to make his fur stand on end.

Naturally there was no one here.

I still don't understand how I didn't notice the keys the first time I looked, but it doesn't really surprise me. I'm getting so scatty now that by the time I'm fifty I'll probably be completely barking. It happened to that great-aunt of my mother's. She died in an asylum. God, that kind of thing is hereditary, isn't it?

I suddenly really wanted to talk to someone. I rang Paula, but one of her flatmates—I never can tell the difference between them—said she's not back from Thailand till Sunday.

Then I tried Jess, but she wasn't in either. I didn't leave a message. Things have been a little strained between us since she had Tom. I know I'm a crap godmother, but really, you'd think she could cut me a little slack here. She lives miles away—how am I expected to go and coo at him on a regular basis?

I think she just wants a free babysitter. Anyway, we haven't spoken for a few weeks, and I didn't want to leave a whingeing message.

Probably just as well she's out, on reflection. She'd only have banged on—about Tom's chesty cough and his mustardy nappies—urgh, babies. A cat is more than enough for me.

Eventually I rang Mum, and she was out too. Dad answered, but I didn't feel like running through the whole rude card/hang-ups/dead flowers thing with him, so I just asked him to get her to ring me later. I'm sure if I talk about it out loud then we'll come up with some logical explanation. Or at least it might help me figure out who it is and what's going on.

In the meantime I think I'll do some work. Try and take my mind off it.

8

Alex

Thursday

I felt happy this morning. Really happy, endorphins fizzing and popping in my bloodstream. I could feel Siobhan's key in my pocket; the metal warm where it touched my leg through the thin cloth. I kept stroking my pocket, a silly smile on my face, not caring what anyone thought of me, ignoring the looks I got on my way to work. I was so far over the moon I was about to collide with Venus.

So why did they have to fuck it all up?

I was just thinking maybe it wouldn't be too bad,

talking to customers today. I mean, sometimes I do have a laugh there. Although you only ever remember the bastards, 95 per cent of the punters are alright. Of course, it isn't my ideal job, but, I realised as I strolled from the tube to the office, it would suffice until I wrote my novel and hit the big time.

As soon as I got in, I knew something was wrong. Across the floor, I saw several people look at me then look away. As I walked towards my desk, the carpet tiles felt spongy and vast, and Jackie—mein call centre Kommandant, old Hitler-with-halitosis herself—stepped into my path.

'Martin wants to see you.'

'Is this about my sick leave?' I said. 'I was only off for two days. I was genuinely sick. I can get a doctor's note.'

The vicious expression on her face was replaced by something that looked very much like pity. She told me to just go and see Martin.

So I did.

Martin is only a year older than me, but he's managed to become the biggest fish in this cramped tank. This is despite being dumber than the average football player. A triumph of ambition over talent, rather like Victoria Beckham's career. He often treats us to jokes that he picked up at Sunday's rugger game and we all pretend to be amused. I guess you could say I don't have much professional respect for him. But he's the boss, so I have to try to stay on his good side. Because of our similar ages and the fact that we're both in possession of a penis—well, I assume he is—he often affects a fake bonhomie with me, asking me if I watched the footie at the weekend and pretending he's heard of the bands I like. Our conversations make me want to weep with despair.

'I was only off for two days,' I said as soon as I sat down in his office. There was a picture of a golden retriever on his desk. His best friend.

He shook his head slowly. 'This isn't about your sick leave, Alex. Everybody's entitled to go off sick from time to time. Even I had a day off last year, when I had that infection.'

I waited. I was starting to get a bad feeling.

He folded his arms, a classic defensive gesture. Bad news was coming. The kind of news that made him fear that I might attack him. Even just seeing him then, this 'oh isn't it awful being a manager when we could be great mates on the outside?' look on his stupid face, I did feel like slapping him. Punching his fucking nose through the back of his head.

'We've had a report from the IT department that you broke one of our most important rules, Alex. We know that . . .' he closed his eyes, as if the very concept of what he was about to say, this thing that I'd done, was too awful for him to bear. 'We know that you looked up a customer's personal records.'

I didn't speak.

And I don't even want to recount the rest of it. I don't want to have to write about how a random spot-check had revealed that I had taken an unauthorised look at a customer's details. How the call-monitoring computers confirmed that this customer hadn't called that day. How the IT department recorded every message that we sent from our email accounts and that they knew I had pasted this customer's details into a message and sent it home.

How he had no option but to let me go. With

72

immediate effect.

And I certainly don't want to recount the details of how I asked him, as he sat there with his arms still folded, unable to meet my eye, what the hell I was supposed to do to pay the bills now. How a cold sickness crept through me at the thought of being jobless and having no money. I couldn't believe that I'd been caught on the spot-check . . . It wouldn't surprise me if Martin had told IT to monitor everything I did because of my recent poor stats, so the bastards would have an excuse to get rid of me.

But I have to face it. How will I pay my rent? How will I eat? The only bright spot is that—thank God—I paid for Siobhan's writing classes up front.

I left Martin's office and pushed open the double doors to the main office, feeling, once again, all those eyes burning into me. Jackie avoided my eye too. What is it with these people? Why are they so gutless? Suddenly, I was an embarrassment, something that made them feel awkward. I was a failure and they wanted me gone.

I pulled open the drawer of the pedestal beneath my desk and began clearing out the contents. There wasn't much in there. A couple of books, a computer magazine, scrappy paperwork, stationery. I found a carrier bag and scooped this pitiful selection into it. Then I turned round to find Sally, the girl who sat next to me, staring at me.

She asked me what had happened. I told her.

'They just wanted to get rid of me, and this was their excuse, this cock and bull story.'

'If you didn't do it, you should fight them. Surely it's unfair dismissal?'

I sighed. I didn't want to tell her that it was all true. I was too ashamed.

73

I picked up my carrier bag and left, suddenly desperate to get out of there, not able to bear any of it, hearing my mum's voice in the back of my head, saying, F-A-I-L-U-R-E—that's what you are and what you'll always be.

Fuck her. Fuck the job. Fuck them all. I don't need them. I'll show them. Because I've found somebody to love now. That will give me strength. And think how much more time I'll have now! This is a blessing. Sure, it's pretty heavily disguised, but that's what it is. It's another sign, isn't it? A sign that I should devote more of my time to my own happiness. And to Siobhan.

My head was whirling when I left the building, handing in my pass to the security guard on the way out. All these terrors and emotions spiralled through my mind: money, revenge, bitterness, relief, confusion, anger . . . Spin, spin, lifting me up and slamming me down, making me dizzy and nauseous. And emerging from all this mental noise was a single thought:

I wanted to see Siobhan. I wanted to be close to her.

I was like a moth that had been battered by the weather, and was bewildered and lost. But one thing was clear—the urge to follow my instinct. To head towards Siobhan's light.

I put my hand in my pocket and felt the key: solid, warm, like a talisman. It gave me strength. It made me feel safe.

*　　　*　　　*

I didn't go straight towards Hampstead, though. First, I came back here. I needed coffee and

74

cigarettes. And there was stuff I wanted to take care of first.

I called Simon's name as soon as I came through the door, knowing that I was going to have to break the news to him. On the way home I'd stopped at the bank and checked my balance. I had enough to see me through a month and that was it. I'm so crap at saving. There'd been the new computer (and I can't sell that; I need it to write this journal and my pieces for college, for Siobhan) and my half of all the bills . . . and the rent here is so bloody high and my wages so pathetic that it didn't leave me anything to save anyway.

Simon wasn't in, which was a big relief. I came straight to my room and sat down at the PC, logging straight onto the Internet. First, I subscribed Martin to a load of hardcore porn sites. I found these really disgusting coprophagia sites and added his email address to their mailing lists as well. I added Jackie's too, for good measure. Well, they enjoy crapping on people, don't they? I felt it was apt. Even if I did make myself feel really sick.

I tried to think of something bigger I could do— something that would really fuck them up . . . and then realised I couldn't be bothered. The sick subscriptions were enough—for now, anyway. What's the point in trying to get further revenge? It will make me feel good for a few minutes, and then it will fade and I'll still be in the same place. I felt really mature and virtuous coming to that decision. Siobhan would be proud of me.

I wish I could have been there to see her face when she saw the flowers I left her. She must be so intrigued. I can imagine her talking about it with her girlfriends, excitedly wondering aloud who her mysterious admirer is. But she's so clever, I'm sure it won't be long before she works it out. And by then she'll be hooked. She'll be mine. But before that, I can't risk telling her how I feel; can't risk her rejection. Not that it matters too much. Because in the meantime I can still be close to her.

*   *   *

I've just had a horrible thought. What if my employer—or should I say former employer—contacts Siobhan to tell her I looked up her records? I'm pretty sure they wouldn't want a customer to know that their details were not 100 per cent secure. But there's a chance they might. They might have a legal requirement to do it, to warn her.

Maybe I should talk to her first. Explain why I did it. Because if they tell her it will make me look bad and she might kick me off the course.

I left the flat and headed towards her light. London felt so grey and cruel today, a dry wind blowing between the buildings where all the drones laboured away, chained to their workstations, and for what? I'm not a drone any more—and, thinking that, I felt liberated, momentarily free of my worries. The sky may be dim, the buildings may be bleak, but there's beauty in this city. And I was going to be near it.

I didn't know exactly what I was going to say to Siobhan. I thought I might tell her that I looked up her address because I was originally planning to send the review of her book to her house, but that I'd decided that would be a breach of her privacy and that I really regretted looking her up.

But then something happened:

I went into a newsagent's to buy some fags. And just as I was about to open the door to leave the shop, I saw her. Siobhan; coming down the road towards me. Her eyes were downcast, and she didn't see me, so I hid behind a card rack until I felt it was the right moment to come out. But when I did, she was gone. She had been heading down the hill, away from her house, towards Camden Lock. Suddenly, I had a decision to make. I could either follow her down the road, trying to stay out of her sight. Or I could go towards her house—where I might be able to check if she'd received any messages about me.

I pushed open the newsagent's door and headed up the hill.

I was sweating by the time I reached Siobhan's house. There was a guy with a black dog coming along the road towards me. I stopped just before Siobhan's gate and pretended I was trying to find something in my pocket. After he'd passed, I had one more look around then went up her front path. My palms were damp and the key almost slipped from my grasp as I pushed it into the lock. I didn't want to look furtive, so I didn't look around again. More aware of my heartbeat than ever before, I turned the key and went through the door.

It was utterly silent inside the house. I couldn't even hear a clock ticking. Which was why I jumped when my footsteps made the floorboards creak.

I laughed; the noise very loud in the silence. I guess it was just my conditioning—a voice telling me that this was wrong. But really I knew I wasn't doing anything bad. I was just checking out Siobhan's territory, exploring the place where she lives. Pretty soon I knew she would be inviting me inside anyway (oh God, I like the way that sounds: inviting me inside), so, telling myself this, I relaxed. There was a Modigliani on the wall inside the front door, a dark-haired woman stretched languorously on a bed, naked, gazing out intently at the artist and the viewer. Looking at the curve of her breasts and the shadow of her pubic hair, I felt myself become aroused. Why had Siobhan put such an erotic picture just inside her door? What did it signify? I held my hand up in front of me, yearning to touch the glass that screened the print. I held back. I didn't want to leave any marks.

I looked up the stairs. I wanted to go up there, see where Siobhan slept, but I had to hold myself back again. I wouldn't find what I was looking for up there. Instead, I went into the living room. It was quite small, but filled with light. More pictures on the wall, though I didn't recognise the artists. And the place was so neat—astonishingly so. It looked like a hotel suite just after the chambermaid's been round. No, it was even tidier than that. There were no magazines or papers scattered on the floor: instead, they were stored neatly in those boxes you get in Habitat. The carpet was spotless—I felt like I ought to take off my shoes. What a contrast to my room, with the stacks of books on the floor, the underwear over-spilling the drawers, the ashtray that I always forget to empty.

There was no sign of the flowers I bought her, nor the card. I imagine the card is tucked away in a special place—under her pillow, maybe, so she can get it out and read it at night when she can't sleep. Maybe she touches herself as she reads it. I like to think that—my words helping her come.

I crossed over to the sofa and sat down, rubbing the fabric beneath my palms. This, I thought with a tremor of excitement, is where Siobhan sits and watches TV. I could almost see her shape in the upholstery. Could smell her; a clean, sweet smell. I put my face to the fabric and inhaled. Delicious.

I stood up and moved towards the back of the room, where a computer sat on a desk. It was a small laptop; a very sexy little MacBook Air. She hadn't turned it off, which made me worry a bit—was she intending to return soon?—but I couldn't stop myself from sitting on her desk chair and running my hands over the keyboard, the instrument with which she wrote her fiction. The keys that knew the feel of her skin so well; that had felt the soft press of her fingers a million times.

I needed to check her emails to see if there was anything from Bookjungle. I opened the Mail program and scanned the list of messages received. Nothing. But what if one had been sent since Siobhan had last polled her emails? I pressed 'send and receive'. A new message arrived. I sighed with relief—it wasn't from my old company. Instead, it was from a woman named Patricia Collins. I recognised the name, though it took a few moments for me to realise where I knew it from. It was on the Acknowledgements page of *Tara Lies Awake*: Huge thanks to my wonderful editor Patricia Collins.

I read her message:

Dear Siobhan

We haven't spoken for a while. But you know how sometimes opportunities arise out of the blue? I've just returned from business in Amsterdam and while I was there I got chatting to someone from your Dutch publisher, Mareliese van der Zee. She asked after you and wanted to know if you had a second novel in the offing.

The interesting thing is that, as you know, Tara Lies Awake *was something of a cult hit in the Netherlands. And a radio station over there recently broadcast a serialisation of it, which has reawakened a small amount of interest in the book. She asked if you'd like to go over to Amsterdam to do a couple of signings. Nothing huge—but I think it would be good for you to get 'out there' again.*

Of course, you might prefer to put TLA behind you for good and concentrate on the next one. It's up to you. But her email address is mareliese@ mareliesevanderzee.ne

And please do contact me when your new book is ready. I'd love to see it first.

Best wishes
Patricia

I stared at the email for what felt like a very long time. Amsterdam? I had this awful image of Siobhan going out there and deciding to stay! Or even if she didn't stay, how long would she be gone? Days! The thought of her being so far away from me made my guts churn.

I had no choice but to delete it. Besides, she was bound to think it suspicious when she noticed that the message had already been opened, when she hadn't read it herself.

I logged off and then spotted something beside the laptop: a credit card. I picked it up and held it by its edges. I had an idea. I reached down to the printer, took out a sheet of paper and copied down the number, expiry date and three digit code on the back. I folded up the paper and slipped it in my pocket.

Next, I went back into the hallway and checked her phone for messages. Again, there was nothing. Thank God for that.

I walked into the kitchen. Here was her oven, her fridge, her washing up. There wasn't a single dirty piece of crockery on display—in fact, there wasn't any crockery anywhere to be seen. I opened the cupboard above the sink and there it all was, gleaming and spotless. I reached up and took a mug down: a plain white one. I lifted it to my lips and kissed the edge.

Something went thump in the hallway.

I dropped the mug. It landed on the worktop, rocking on its base, thankfully not smashing. I swivelled towards the hall, my stomach freezing, my heart forgetting to beat. I expected to see Siobhan coming through the front door.

But it was a ginger cat. It must have jumped from halfway up the stairs, the crazy creature, and now it was padding towards me. It was pretty fat, and heavy-footed for a cat. It came into the kitchen and started to rub round my ankle, purring.

'Hello. Do you want some dinner?' I said.

I opened a couple of cupboard doors and found a box of cat biscuits. The cat's purring grew louder and I crouched down, sprinkling a few of the biscuits on the floor. I stroked it as it ate. 'I'll be your daddy

81

soon,' I whispered.

I put the biscuits away and looked out the back door at a small garden. Washing was pegged out on the line. A couple of T-shirts, a pair of jeans, a jumper. A black bra and several pairs of knickers. I leaned closer to the window to get a better look. The T-shirts looked a bit worn, the bra was fading and the knickers were quite tatty-looking. I couldn't help but feel that she deserved better. If only I could afford to buy her nice new clothes; lingerie that would feel like silk upon her skin; that would flatter her and make her feel sexy. But now that I'd lost my job there was no way I could spare the money.

I felt sad. And I was very aware that I had to go.

I said goodbye to the cat, who was still munching on his biscuits, and headed back towards the door. I had no doubt that this had been an important event. I now feel as if I know Siobhan much better. I can hardly wait for my next visit. I wanted to go upstairs, to see her bed, to visit her most private place, but perhaps, I thought, it would be better to save that pleasure, to deny myself now so that it will be even sweeter when it happens.

*   *   *

I opened the front door slowly and looked out through the crack. As I stood there, looking up and down the road, making sure I wasn't going to be spotted, I felt a movement by my feet. The cat pushed past my legs and squeezed through the gap in the door, bounding down the path towards the road. Shit. I closed the door and followed the cat. But it ran across the road and disappeared into someone else's garden.

I'm sure it will be okay, though. And as I walked home I stopped worrying about it, and everything else too—I'd already forgotten all about the loss of my job.

I was too excited to fret. I was going to show Siobhan that it wasn't wrong to be a little self-indulgent. It seemed obvious that she didn't know how to treat herself, and that it was up to me to do it for her. After all, isn't that what lovers do?

9

Siobhan

Thursday

OK, now, something very weird is going on. Either Biggles has suddenly developed prehensile abilities—which he's hiding from me—or else I'm going crazy.

No matter how hard I rack my brains, I can't think of any logical explanation as to how he managed to get a handful of Go-Cat out of a packet in a closed cupboard. It was fresh Go-Cat, too—I checked it to make sure that he hadn't perhaps previously ingested it and puked it back up again, but it wasn't remotely soggy. It still had that dusty feel to it, like when it comes out of the box. And I can't figure out how he was outside the house when I got back from the gym—I'm sure I left him asleep on the sofa. He must have scooted out with me, I suppose.

And more strangely, I can't think how he could have climbed up on the kitchen counter, got a mug down, and left it there . . .! It's got a big chip in the base, which definitely wasn't there before. The mug wasn't there before. I never go out without leaving the kitchen tidy—mostly because I don't want Biggles up there padding around leaving cat hair in my tableware, or worse, licking stuff. I know that cats are clean—I wouldn't have one if they weren't—but still, I don't like the idea of his paws all over my surfaces. What if he'd just been raking his litter tray?

I assume I must have left the mug out, although how did I not notice that I'd chipped it? I don't like this feeling at all. I hate not being in control; it's like being on a fairground ride, when you can't tell them you want to get off. Oh God, please don't let this be the start of me losing my marbles; I couldn't bear it. I wonder if I should ask Paula what her thoughts on voluntary euthanasia are—I'll need someone to help me put a pillow over my face if it all gets that dire.

I can't wait for Paula to get home. I'm dying to tell her about Phil and the dead flowers and the filthy postcard. I've been thinking about it a lot, and I've come to the conclusion that maybe it was Phil after all; some kind of macho screwed up way of proving his masculinity, or something . . . I don't even want to go there. I'm sure if I don't respond then he'll stop bothering. It must have really got to him, to go to the lengths of asking somebody to leave dead flowers on my doorstep even while he's in Portugal. What is it, some kind of special branch of Interflora? Maybe he used one of those 'prank' agencies you see advertised in the backs of magazines, offering to carry out practical jokes for revenge. Wilted lilies for jilted willies. It almost makes sense.

If it was just the postcard, I'd suspect Alex—after all, he did ask me out, and he put a pink ribbon around the review—but there's no way he'd leave dead flowers, is there? Unless he's angry with me for turning him down? But he didn't seem angry, or at all upset. And besides, like Brian, he's got no way of finding out my address. The college would never give it out, and McGowan is a pretty common surname.

Monday

Paula's back; I rang her. Annoyingly, she was so jet-lagged that she couldn't understand what I was going on about, when I tried to tell her about Phil, etc. She just wanted to talk to me about her holiday, which sounded exactly like the stuff of my worst nightmares: slumming it in those cheap and atrociously dodgy guesthouses in Phuket, no toilet paper, mosquitoes in swarms, constant stomach upsets and the runs—and she calls that a holiday? It's my idea of complete hell. Still, she's only 24. She'll learn.

Tuesday

Well, dementia is clearly encroaching fast. I got a package this morning, special delivery: a beautiful box with the most delicious underwear in it; a slinky dusky purple body with teeny little spaghetti straps and ivory lace, in the sort of silk that's so smooth it feels like it's not even there, resting like an invalid in layers of fat white tissue paper.

But my delight at receiving such an exquisite package was ruined when I found the bill in the bottom of the box. £75.00, on my credit card—Lady Alzheimer is surely calling . . . I must have ordered it and then forgotten about it, or made some stupid blunder on the Internet. I can't think how it happened. I suppose it must have been when I was browsing through those fashion websites ages ago, the ones whose addresses Paula wrote down for me. They do brilliant reductions on last season's stuff, from all sorts of different designers. I must have accidentally clicked on BUY at some point. I *was* quite drunk that night. I don't understand how it works—would they be able to tell my address from my credit card details? Maybe it's the same as that One-Click thing I've got set up for when I buy books and CDs on Bookjungle. I'll ask someone more *au fait* with these Internet things—Dennis Tennis might know.

I'll have to send it back. I can't afford seventy-five quid at the moment, not until I get some articles accepted. I've still got four out with editors who should all have got back to me by now (must chase them).

It's so beautiful, I can't stop stroking it. The silk is so cool, and I can imagine how it would feel on my body. What a shame. I wish I was rich! But fortunately I seem to have ordered a size 10, and I can tell just by looking that it would be far too tight. It'd be up the crack of my arse in two seconds flat and I'd be uncomfortable all day, dying to hoik it out and not being able to unless in the privacy of my own home. Let's be pragmatic here—ten minutes of that sort of torture and I wouldn't care how soft the bloody silk was.

Wednesday night

Something horrible's just happened. I was walking home from the pub where Kathy and I had a drink after class (I'll write about that later, when I'm calmer). I'd cut across the swimming pool car park and was nearly at the far side, when suddenly I was sure I could hear footsteps behind me, secretive sly little steps. I glanced round, but there was nobody there. After what happened when I was fourteen, this is the one thing guaranteed to freak me out more than anything else. I instantly lost the ability to breathe properly, and started to kind of huff. I sped up, and just before I reached Colne Road—I am NEVER going to walk across an empty car park at night again—I spun around a second time. This time I did see someone, a dark figure pressed up against the wall by the disabled parking spaces, trying not to let himself be seen. I started to run, flat out, trying to clutch my bag close to my side in case he was a mugger, trying to figure out how accessible my clothes were in case he was a rapist.

I don't think I've ever run so fast in my life. I ran so hard that all I could hear was my footsteps banging on the pavement and my own panting—but just as I got to the gate, I turned round again and, oh God, he'd run after me. I saw him, I just didn't see his face but I swear it was the same man, lurking again at the end of the road, watching me.

He knows where I live. He knows where I live. He knows where I live. Who is he?

I need to talk to someone.

Tried Mum and Dad, and Paula, but they both had their answerphones on. M&D must be asleep, and Paula's probably out. It's only midnight, early for her. Better keep writing. Maybe I'll feel better if I get it all out, get the terror down onto paper and then it will just be little black letters and white spaces; nothing scary about that.

*   *   *

I hurled myself inside the house, bolted the door, and ran around yanking every single set of curtains closed, making sure that the back door and all the windows were locked, shaking so much that I could barely get my fingers to work. Then I poured myself a huge gin and tried to sit down in the armchair, but I couldn't sit still, even when Biggles jumped on my lap and wanted stroking.

I tipped him on to the floor and paced up and down, dizzy and fidgeting with fear. What did the man want? Was he outside the house now? Had he been after my bag, or worse? What if he tried to get in? I didn't know whether I should phone the police or not. I wished Phil wasn't in Portugal. I had a sudden urge to call Kathy, but of course I didn't.

*   *   *

I've been sitting in my bedroom for ages, peering through a tiny slit at the side of the curtains, scanning the road until I got a draught in my eyes and I was beginning to imagine dark shapes behind every garden fence. But whoever it was has—I hope—long gone. It's late now; well past two o'clock but I can't sleep so I'm just going to keep writing.

*   *   *

I've suddenly had a really, really appalling thought ... What if this is all linked? What if someone's broken into my house and that's how come the mug was there and Biggles got out and maybe somebody's got my credit card number, and maybe that's the same person that has just followed me home. It could be the same person who sent me flowers—not realizing they were dead?—and wrote that card. Oh God, oh God.

*   *   *

I've just run downstairs and checked the back door again. No sign of a break-in. Still locked and bolted top and bottom. Front door chained and Chubbed. Window locks all still in place.

*   *   *

It can't be that. It's impossible. I'm obviously just freaked out about that walk home. I'll have another drink ...

*   *   *

Had three big drinks. Bit pissed now. Keep writing.

*   *   *

This would never have got to me so much if it weren't for what happened when I was 14. That time, when I looked around, he hadn't pressed himself against a wall and tried to hide. Instead, I'd seen him clearly under the streetlight, running at me. He was young and skinny, with wiry hair and tight jeans. He wore a cheap vinyl bomber jacket with a bobbled elasticated waist—tonight, I hadn't even been able to tell if the man was black or white.

That time, I'd felt two hands pounce heavily on my shoulders, the way people at school did to one another when they wanted to scare them. I'd jumped, and actually half-laughed, trying to twist my head around again to get a better look at him.

It must be someone I knew, I'd thought. I waited for him to release me and announce himself. Perhaps he was that fifth year who went to swimming club with Donna, the one Donna said fancied me. But he didn't speak, and I didn't recognise him. An arm snaked out and pinned my neck in an arm lock, so my head was forced back against his chest. I wasn't choking, because the crook of his elbow had left a breathing space in front of my Adam's apple, but I couldn't move either.

'What are you doing?' I remembered trying to say. I remember how my voice was all small and spluttering. I could smell his breath in my ear, sour, heavy, more man than boy.

I felt his other arm move in front of my body, his fingers searching for the opening of my duffel coat beneath the bottom toggle. His hand shot inside and clamped itself between my legs, under the bulk of my Laura Ashley dress and over my cream woolly tights. I remember exactly what I was wearing; that awful green flower-sprigged Laura Ashley smock

90

thing. The tights were too small and had got dragged down a bit when I walked, and I felt his thumb brush against my bare stomach above the waistband, and it was the sensation of skin on skin which snapped me out of immobility. I tried to struggle, but he was holding me too tightly. His hand moved, a steel claw grabbing at me coldly, somehow dispassionately, and I felt pinioned, ready for dissection. It was almost like he was scratching an itch for me, but too roughly. Without my permission.

I made more of an effort to shake him off with my shoulders, flailing at him with my arms and hands. I managed to jam an elbow into his rib cage, and he gasped, but didn't let go. He was still clawing at me, mechanically, painfully, as if we were locked in a brief silent dance, a back-to-front waltz of lust and disbelief. I grabbed his wrist and tried to pull him off me, but his hand appeared to be super glued to my crotch.

I tried stamping on his foot, which unbalanced him, and we toppled together towards the alley wall. I was in front of him and so I connected with it first. I felt a horrible scraping, ripping sensation down the right side of my face as the rough bricks grated my skin, and then a stinging heat followed by a trickle of blood down my cheek and into the neck of my duffel coat.

*   *   *

Bloody hell. Where did that come from? I think I must have held my breath the entire time I typed that, it still stresses me out so much. I was 14, and twenty years later I still go to pieces if I even think someone's creeping up on me. And I'd been

91

lucky—I got away. I wasn't even raped, just 'sexually assaulted', as the policewoman said, when I gave a statement. But at least my assailant didn't know where I lived.

*　　*　　*

It's four o'clock. I must go to bed. I'm so tired and drunk now that I know I'll sleep.

Thursday

Really, really knackered this morning. Two rejection letters from editors—well, at least that's saved me the bother of chasing them. One said that the Botox thing had been 'done to death', and the other just that they aren't taking any work from freelancers at the moment. I wonder if I should bite the bullet and try and get a proper job somewhere. I could read manuscripts. I could maybe get a job working for a literary agent. Although probably all the failed writers in the entire world—and Lord knows there are enough of us—think the same.

Perhaps I could just run away somewhere remote, and hide. Me and Biggles. Safe where nobody can follow us or leave dead flowers.

Friday

Have just realised I forgot to write about class on Wednesday night—I was too freaked out by what happened afterwards.

It went well, I think, I'm really getting a good picture of their strengths and weaknesses. We did another sensory exercise and they were all much more attentive this week, now they know the drill. Not nearly so much fidgeting and scratching.

Speaking of fidgeting and scratching, Brian wasn't there, for the second week in a row. I feel somehow uneasy about his absence—I mean, I know it's not school and he's free to come and go as he pleases without a note from his mum—but what if he's too embarrassed to come in because it was him who sent that card?

Anyway, Kathy read out another really excellent piece of writing. Last week's exercise was about the character and their reaction to noise, and she'd done a brilliantly funny thing about roadworks. Her descriptions were so vivid that I knew instantly where she was talking about—they've been digging up the road by the park for ages—so when we got chatting afterwards, I asked her if I was right. Turns out that I was, and she only lives a few streets away from me.

We ended up walking home together, and just as we got to the George V, I mentioned what a great pub it was, and she said, 'I know, it's my local. I live across the road here. Shall we, then? I'm parched.'

Before I knew it we were inside the pub, looking around for an empty, non-sticky table, and draping our coats over the back of two spare armchairs.

'It's funny,' I said, feeling momentarily flustered, like I'd suddenly been asked out, 'but I've had to turn down two invitations for drinks with other students, on the grounds that it's against college regulations.'

She laughed. She's pretty when she laughs—her

eyes crinkle and her chin goes really pointy. I always feel so fascinated by lesbians. I instantly start wondering if they fancy me, and then feel affronted when they don't. I suppose that's how most men are, around pretty women. I like the idea of a 'lesbian experience', although I'm not sure I'd have the nerve to go through with it.

'Male students, I take it. Well, not difficult to guess which ones, since we only have the two.'

I tried to bluff it out, pretending that I'd meant the students were from other classes I'd taught, and not this one. It would have been a bit indiscreet. But I'm sure she wasn't fooled.

We got comfortable in the two big tatty armchairs near the fireplace with our drinks—vodka and tonic for me, Jack and Coke for her, and, just for something to talk about, I started telling her about the underwear delivery. I was laughing, saying how batty I've been lately, but she looked at me a bit strangely.

'There's no way you could have bought that off the Internet without noticing,' she said.

'Well, I must have done. It's on my credit card.'

'You would've had to type in your address, approve the amount, enter your card details, and then the site would almost certainly have confirmed your purchase with an email afterwards. They do that, to stop fraud.'

'Then how . . .?'

She shook her head. 'I've got no idea. Unless you were really drunk—or you were really losing your marbles.'

Yeah, thanks Kathy.

I sighed, tempted for a moment to pour out my heart about all the other weird things which had happened over the past two weeks, but instead we

94

drifted into a conversation about writing, and then publishing—Kathy used to have an agent, but the agent dropped her after failing to find a publisher for her first novel—so we had a lot in common. I told her about the *TLA* fiasco, and she sympathised, which made me feel worse. There was a time when people were impressed that you'd been published, not sympathetic. I can't stand being a has-been.

I was about to say goodbye and go, when Kathy got up. Her legs in jeans were inches away from me, and I suddenly wondered what she'd do if I pressed my face into her. She has nice legs, like a Barbie doll's. All the men in the pub looked at her when she stood up.

'Another drink?'

I checked the time on my phone—ten-thirty—although my decision wasn't time-dependent, since I'd already decided I wanted to go home. 'Better not. I'm a bit wrecked, to tell you the truth.'

'Want a lift? My car's just across the road. It wouldn't be a problem.'

I laughed—how ironic, in retrospect. Why did I not just accept? 'No, it's fine, thanks. It'll only take me five minutes to walk.'

There was a moment's awkward hovering at the door of the pub. I didn't know whether to shake her hand, or kiss her cheek, and it seemed that nor did she. In the end we grinned at each other and waved self-consciously.

'See you next Wednesday, then.'

'Yeah. Thanks for the drink, neighbour. Bye.'

Kathy vanished round the corner, pulling on her coat and simultaneously fishing around in the pocket for her keys as she walked. She strikes me as a multi-tasking kind of person. I wondered if, once the course was over, we could be friends and decided that it was quite possible. It would be nice to have a mate—I nearly said 'girlfriend'—living locally, none of my other friends do.

* * *

Then I began to walk home, across the swimming pool car park, and that's when I got chased.

Oh God, what if it is the same person who sent the card, and the flowers, and the underwear? That means he's been in my house. What do I do? Should I tell the police? Have I got a stalker? I don't know whether to be embarrassed or flattered. I know for sure I'd be terrified, if I really believed I had. No.

It's just not possible.

10

Alex

Wednesday

Seeing them together tonight made me feel sick. The way they were laughing, leaning close together across the table, looking so happy in each other's company. It was bad enough seeing that she'd accepted Kathy as a friend on Facebook while ignoring my request, but this was a more visceral disappointment. It should have been me in there with Siobhan, having a drink with her, telling her about myself, swapping smiles. It should have been me! She told me a lie; that she wasn't allowed to socialise with students. That hurts more than anything—maybe even more than the fact that she chose Kathy over me.

Why do the people we love always have to disappoint us so?

I hope Siobhan isn't going to go off with Kathy and embark on some crazed Sapphic affair. I don't think Siobhan's a lesbian. I've seen the way she looks at me—it's a look that says 'I like men', even if she hasn't realised exactly how she feels about this man yet. But I still feel so betrayed. After following them from the college to the pub, I looked in through the window and had a clear view of them. My stomach lurched and I only just stopped myself from vomiting.

*   *   *

After they'd said goodbye I followed Siobhan for a little while, just wanting to be near her. Needing to gain strength from her proximity. But she almost saw me—I had to duck into the shadows—and then she ran off.

Oh, Siobhan, I don't hate you now. I still love you. I still want us to be together. So no, my sweetheart, my angel, I don't blame you. Of course not. It's that bitch Kathy. I blame her. She persuaded you to go to the pub with her; maybe even coerced you, nagged you until you felt you had no other choice.

I wonder if you were wearing your new underwear tonight, Siobhan. Kathy didn't know about that, did she? About the delicious silk you were wearing beneath your clothes. That was our secret. You and me.

I can picture you taking it off: slipping off the shoulder straps in front of the mirror, your breasts buffed to even greater softness by the smooth touch of the silk; then sitting on the bed and pushing down the rest of it, kicking it aside, a wicked look on your face. And I'm there with you, like a shadow. You can't see me, Siobhan, but you can feel me. You open your arms and I fall into your embrace. We kiss and you run your hands down my back and you're moaning, saying my name, 'oh Alex, please, I want you,' and you pull me towards you, and you're already wet, so wet, and I slide into you and . . .

Kathy could never give you that.

Thursday

I've got a terrible headache and feel as if somebody's removed all the blood from my veins and replaced it with sand that's been soaked in lager and dipped in an ashtray. I've just read what I wrote last night before I passed out. There's an empty vodka bottle beside the bed which I shouldn't have bought. I can't afford it.

I vaguely remember going on the Internet last night as well. Did I order more stuff?

Ow . . . my head. Need water. More sleep. I want to write more but it hurts too much so I'm going back to bed. At least I don't have a fucking job to go to.

*   *   *

Afternoon. After returning to bed this morning I didn't wake up again until four. I staggered out to the kitchen looking for water. Simon and Natalie were there. They both raised their eyebrows at me.

'Have you been asleep?' Natalie asked.

I grunted in the affirmative.

'Haven't been on Monster.com then?' said Si. He'd promised me that he wouldn't hassle me about finding another job, although I'd assured him that I would do everything I could to find one quickly. He was actually really good about it when I told him I'd been sacked. He said he could cover the rent for a month until I found something new. So I don't know why he suddenly started going on about job-hunting today. Maybe Natalie had been nagging him about it—worried that he might have less cash to spend on her, no doubt.

'I looked on there yesterday,' I said. 'Total waste of time.'

Simon tutted but didn't say any more, picking up his iPhone and manipulating the screen with his thumb. Natalie came over and touched my shoulder. 'It's difficult to find a job, I think,' she said kindly in her sexy French accent. Her hair was messed up—I think she and Simon had thrown a double sickie today to be together. Natalie smelled faintly of sex. It was too much.

I had to get out. I bought a few cans of beer and went and sat down by the Lock. I had some thinking to do. And the fresh alcohol helped make me feel better; oiled the engine of my mind.

Seeing Siobhan with Kathy last night has made me realise that I should be her friend, and that it is possible because, clearly, there isn't really a rule about socialising with her students. I want to ask her why she lied to me, and I want her to know how I feel. Or do I? Oh . . . I don't know. I know from experience that it's best to be friends with women first, and that you shouldn't try to go beyond that

99

stage too soon. But what if Siobhan only has room for one new friend right now?

Kathy.

Room for Kathy and none for me.

By the time I'd finished my last can of lager I knew that I was going to have to do something about Siobhan's new friend.

I walked up past the college to the pub where I saw them having their cosy drink, the George V, and looked in through the window. No sign of Kathy. So I came home again, buying more cans of beer on the way home.

I'll go back tomorrow, even though I don't know what I'm going to say to her or what I'm going to do.

Oh fuck. Being in love like this is killing me.

Sunday

Went to George V again. Still no sign of Kathy.

Read *TLA*. Twice.

Googled Kathy and tried to find out where she lives but no joy.

Kissed Siobhan's picture. A thousand times.

Monday

Oh.

Oh fuck. What a . . .

My hands are shaking so much I can hardly type. I don't even know if I should be writing this down. What if . . .? But I need to get it out. I need to rid myself of it, like being sick when you've drunk so much you feel poisoned.

*   *   *

The day started like this:

I was woken by the doorbell. I turned over and it buzzed again. Opening one eye, I looked at the alarm clock. Half eight—Si would be at work. I half-fell out of bed and went to the door, wearing just my boxer shorts. It was the postman.

He looked me up and down and raised an eyebrow. 'Parcels for Siobhan McGowan.'

'Eh?'

'I've got two parcels for a Ms Siobhan McGowan. Have I got the wrong address?'

'Oh, no . . . No. She lives here but she's not in.'

He handed me the parcels, gave me another look and turned around. I shut the door and studied the parcels, both of which were soft and squidgy, with TheBoutique.com written on the packaging. I opened them and found myself holding a black skirt and a low-cut top, both with a Prada label. That's when I remembered: the other night, when I got home after following Siobhan, I'd been online, and I must have bought these using Siobhan's credit card. Except this time I'd made a mistake and put my own address down.

But seeing the clothes made me feel really cheerful. I don't know a huge deal about fashion, but even I could see that this was top-notch clobber, and exactly the kind of clothes that would really suit Siobhan; the type of stuff that for some reason she never buys for herself. She could wear this over her new underwear. Wow, she'd look hot.

This time, I wanted to see the look on her face

101

when she saw them.

I put the skirt and top into a bag and, after getting dressed, made my way towards Victoria Gardens.

As usual, the road was pretty much deserted. There was a pair of magpies sitting on Siobhan's roof. Two for joy: what a good omen. As I watched, one of the magpies stretched its wings and flew away. Damn. Still, it's the initial sighting that counts. I think.

I went up Siobhan's front path, took the clothes out of their bag and lay them carefully on the doorstep. Then I rang the bell and ran back down the path as quickly as I could. I crouched behind a car, ensuring that I had a good view of the door, and waited for Siobhan to emerge and find the clothes. How excited she would be: my card, the flowers, the underwear, and now this. It must feel like Christmas nearly every day!

I waited, but Siobhan didn't emerge. She must be out again, I thought.

I counted to ten then stood up. I'd had another brilliant idea. I didn't want to leave the clothes on the step all day in case some dishonest passer-by saw them and nabbed them. My new idea meant that I wouldn't get to see Siobhan's face when she found her new glorious garments, but I decided that was a price worth paying.

I walked back up her path, took out my key, scooped up the clothes and went inside. She must have gone out before the post, because it was lying on the floor. I picked it up and put it on the side table.

I really like Siobhan's place and can't wait till she invites me to move in, but I didn't have time to hang around. I didn't know if she'd just popped out to buy some milk or something. I went straight through to the kitchen and looked out the back window. There was the washing, hanging on the line. I unbolted the back door and went out into the garden. There were high walls surrounding the garden so I was confident nobody would see me, and I quickly did what I'd come to do. It was time to replace some of those scruffy old clothes that Siobhan slobbed around in with these new, flattering items. I pulled down an old pair of jeans and a misshapen T-shirt with I-♥-NY emblazoned on the front and pegged the Prada skirt and top up in their place. I noticed that the underwear I'd sent wasn't on the line. Maybe she was wearing it that very minute. I would have liked to have gone up and looked through her chest of drawers to check, but I was worried about time. Before I left, though, I noticed a little gate set into the wall in the corner of the garden. I looked over it—it led out to an alley. I made a mental note.

Taking the jeans and T-shirt with me, I went back into the house, bolted the door behind me and hurried out through the front door.

When I got onto the road, I heard a *miaow*.

I turned. It was Siobhan's cat, standing on the wall. Had it followed me out of the house? I hadn't even seen it. It jumped down from the wall and ran across the road, stopping on the kerb and looking back at me.

Then I had another idea; maybe I could get Siobhan's cat to deliver a message to her. I fished in my pockets and found a piece of paper and a pen. I wrote 'I love you' on it and crossed the road towards the cat. I was going to wrap the piece of paper around its collar.

As I neared the feline it tiptoed away, stopping

just out of reach. It must be a girl, I thought, amused. It was a little tease.

'Come on,' I said, making little cooing noises. 'Come to your future daddy.'

It blinked at me.

I crept closer, holding out the piece of paper, making little kissy noises now. Thank God there was nobody around to see, although I could hear a car coming down the street. I paused and stretched out my hand towards the cat, which was now washing itself.

'Come on, you little . . .' I said, and at that point I sprang, throwing myself towards it, aiming to grab its collar.

I missed. I made contact with the fur on its back, but the cat slipped out from under my grasp and ran at top feline speed into the road—straight into the path of a car. Through the fingers I thrust in front of my face I saw a blur of ginger fur, a flash of silver, heard a screech of tyres and then:

BANG.

I opened my eyes and removed my hands from my face. The cat was nowhere to be seen. But the car . . . oh shit! The car had swerved and smashed into Siobhan's front wall, sending bricks and dust flying. I saw a face through the car window, turning towards me: a woman, looking dazed and scared, but thankfully still alive, and with no sign of blood.

And what did I do? I ran. I got the fuck out of there, still clutching the carrier bag containing Siobhan's old clothes. It was only when I got home that I realised that I must have dropped the piece of paper that said 'I love you'.

*　　*　　*

104

But that wasn't the worst thing that happened today.

It was only mid-morning when I got back here, and I hung around the house all day, fretting about what Siobhan would think when she saw the demolition job that car had done on her front wall. It would probably lessen the thrill of seeing her new designer gear. And what about the cat? Had it been hurt?

I had this awful flashback to that time when I was a kid. Annette had a new hamster, called Chips. I loved that hamster, wishing I was allowed one, but I wasn't allowed to play with him. One day, everyone went out, leaving me alone in the house, and I rushed upstairs to get Chips out of his cage. He ran up and down my arm a few times, then I got bored and went to put him back. But the cage had a spring-door—and as I was putting Chips through the gap, I let go of the door and it snapped shut on his leg. He froze, I froze. I didn't know what to do. Chips was lying completely still in my palm, this grimace on his little face, his teeth sticking out.

I put him back in the cage and hoped that maybe he would recover. I sat by the cage all day, talking to him, pleading with him to get up and start walking round the cage, maybe run on his wheel. But he didn't. He just lay there giving me reproachful looks.

Mum's reaction when she got home and they saw him . . .

All I can say is, thank God he lived, even if he did limp for a long time. I don't know what she would have done if he'd actually died. And that's how I felt this afternoon, worrying about Siobhan's cat. Because if Siobhan thought I'd hurt her cat, it would be all over between us. And he was a nice cat too. Much nicer than a lot of the people I know.

By teatime I'd worked myself into such a frenzy of anxiety that I had to get out of the house. Si and Nat had come home and they kept asking me to 'sit still for God's sake'. And maybe because it was a habit I'd developed over the last couple of days, I made my way towards the George V. I could do with a drink even if Kathy wasn't there. I wasn't thinking clearly at all: I didn't know what I would do if I saw Kathy. But walking to the pub I was reminded of how sickening it had been to see her and Siobhan chatting like bosom buddies. If only she would disappear, leave the class and never come back. Thinking about it made my stomach hurt.

When I got to the pub it was half-empty. Ten seconds later, so was my first glass of beer. I sat and drank while the pub began to fill up around me, growing steadily noisier, the tables around me becoming occupied as people stopped off for a swift half after work. For many of them, that swift half became a slow whole, the alcohol deadening the disappointments of another day in the office. I almost pitied them. How they would envy my freedom.

I was contemplating this, tearing up a beer mat, when I heard a female voice.

'Alex?'

I looked up and saw Kathy. She wore a puzzled expression.

'What are you doing here?'

'I often drink here,' I said.

'I've never seen you here before.'

'I usually come during the day. And I haven't been for a while.'

106

She narrowed her eyes and studied me for a moment. She looked around, probably trying to see if there were any other tables free. There weren't.

'Do you mind if I join you?'

I told her of course not and she went off to the bar to buy herself a drink. I was feeling much calmer now, the booze washing through me, tranquillizing me. Kathy came back to the table and sat down and said, 'This is becoming a habit—drinking here with people from my writing class.' Then a worried look crossed her face, just for a split second. Maybe Siobhan had told her about the lie she told me about socialising with people from the class. She didn't say any more about it.

For the first hour or so we talked about the class, about the other students. Kathy did a great impression of Brian. I found myself really enjoying the conversation, mainly because it gave me plenty of opportunities to say Siobhan's name. I noticed that whenever Siobhan's name was mentioned, Kathy got this look in her eye. But it didn't stop me from enjoying myself. I almost forgot that I wasn't supposed to like this woman: that she was my rival. She was funny and very intelligent. I knew how much Siobhan liked Kathy's writing, and that irritated me, but then Kathy bought more drinks, and after we'd finished those I bought another round and by then I was feeling pretty warm and fuzzy. I even felt a bit sentimental, as if I was mourning something that hadn't actually happened yet. It was a strange feeling.

Then, after I'd mentioned Siobhan for the twentieth time, Kathy said, 'You like her, don't you?'

'Eh?'

'You fancy Siobhan, don't you? Come on, you talk

about her non-stop. Siobhan this, Siobhan that.' She laughed throatily. 'If I didn't like her myself I'd be thoroughly bored.'

'You like her?' I said.

'Don't sound so worried. I don't mean I like her in that way—just as a mate. I've got a feeling Siobhan and I are going to be really good friends.'

That worried me enough, but then she said, 'Siobhan told me you asked her out for a drink.'

I gulped. 'Did she say anything else about me?'

'No, not really. She didn't slag you off, if that's what you're worrying about. Actually, I don't know if we should be talking about this.'

And then it all came pouring out. I couldn't stop myself. It's one thing being able to write down how I feel about Siobhan, but I suddenly had an unstoppable urge to talk about it, to tell someone else. I told Kathy that I thought I had fallen in love with our teacher, that I couldn't stop thinking about her, and that I wanted to tell her how I felt but that I was scared of rejection. I even told her about sending her the card and ordering the underwear for her. Kathy just sat there and listened to me, her eyebrows raised.

Suddenly, I felt ill. I told Kathy I needed the loo and went off in search of it. In the Gents, I locked myself in a cubicle and was immediately sick into the toilet. And as I wiped my mouth with a piece of shiny toilet paper, my mind cleared. Oh fuck, I thought. What have I done? Kathy's going to tell Siobhan—she'll probably put her own slant on it as well. She might make me sound like some obsessive nut. And they'll talk about what I was doing in the George V in the first place. God. I sat on the toilet and put my head in my hands. Why was I such a moron? I had wanted to talk to Kathy, get to know her, find out how I could remove her from the scene in the same way I got rid of that twattish bloke, Phil. And I'd made a hash of it.

Shit.

I came out of the cubicle and splashed my face with cold water at the sink. I looked at myself in the mirror. What a state. I desperately wanted to go home, to crawl into bed and hide from the world. But I couldn't. I had to undo the damage I'd done.

I went back to the table. Kathy said, 'I was just waiting to say goodbye. I ought to get home. My head's spinning.'

Home. So she could phone Siobhan, tell her what I'd said, twist it into lies.

'Whereabouts do you live?' I asked.

She told me she lived just across the road, in a block of flats.

'Do you really have to go?' I said. 'I was enjoying myself.'

She looked at her watch, then at her empty glass. One thing I'd figured out over the last couple of hours: Kathy had a thirst on her. 'Well . . . I guess I could be persuaded to stay for one more. But you'll have to pay. I've got no more cash on me.'

I took out my wallet and looked inside it. There was a ten pound note tucked inside, but Kathy couldn't see it from where she was sitting. 'Shit,' I said. 'Neither have I.'

That was when Kathy gave me a long, appraising look. 'I've got some booze at my place.'

My heart started to beat quickly. 'That sounds good.'

'You know I'm not interested in you like that though, don't you? You know I'm gay.'

'How could I forget?'

That made her laugh, and she stood up, pulling her jacket on. I followed her out of the pub and across the road to a block of flats. She unlocked the door and we went inside, Kathy pressing the button by the lift. She staggered as the lift began to ascend and almost fell into my arms. 'God, I'm really drunk,' she laughed.

'Me too.' But really, I felt sober. Stone cold sober.

She lived two floors below the top flat. We entered her apartment and she went straight over to the fridge while I crossed to the window. She had an amazing view, right across north London, the lights of the city shining and pulsing in the night. Kathy came up and handed me a bottle of beer. 'Great view, isn't it? A lot of people feel sorry for me when I tell them I live in a block of flats, but they change their opinions when they see the view.'

'It's awesome.'

She laughed. I found myself picking at the label on the bottle of beer. I felt incredibly tense, all the muscles in my back cramping, sweat gathering in my armpits. I still didn't know what I was going to do. I didn't really even know what I was doing there.

'The view's even better from the roof. You can see all the way to Canary Wharf,' Kathy said, swigging from her own beer bottle. She really did like her booze.

'The roof?'

'Yes. You can get to it by climbing onto the fire escape. What do you reckon? Do you fancy it?'

'Is it safe?' I said.

'Well, it's a bit of a clamber, but I've done it a few times and I've always been alright. You're not going to wimp out on me, are you?'

I hesitated. There were all sorts of ideas in my head.

'Come on then,' I said, and she led me through the flat to a window that opened onto a balcony. From there, a metal fire escape led up to the roof and down to the garden. A long way down to the garden. The fire escape didn't look very sturdy. I looked down again and had a sudden attack of vertigo. My palms were wet with sweat. Half of me wanted to go home. But there was a voice in my head telling me what I had to do.

'Are you alright?' she said, turning to look at me, a silly pissed smile on her face.

I nodded.

Kathy stepped up onto the fire escape and I followed . . .

*   *   *

I can't write any more. It's too much. Too much.

I ran all the way home.

And I know that when I close my eyes tonight all I'm going to see is her crumpled body on the patio. All I'm going to hear is the way she cried out.

And how it sounded like the first syllable of my name.

11

Siobhan

Monday

It's too much. First, the card, the flowers and the underwear ... and now the weirdest thing yet has happened. Even more bizarre than that stupid woman in her car destroying most of my garden wall.

If it was happening to someone else, I'd think it was quite funny. I came back from Sainsbury's this morning and was just putting the fish fingers into the freezer when I heard a few spots of rain tap against the window. It was at that point I remembered I'd left the washing out, so I went into the garden, and there, hanging demurely on the line, were these clothes which weren't even mine!!!! At first I felt sick, and upset because whoever left them had nicked my favourite NY T-shirt and my vintage Levis. All these paranoid thoughts went streaming through my head, about sexual predators and freaks spying on me with binoculars—until I realised that *a*) nobody could see into my bedroom, and *b*) it was unlikely that any sad pervert would spend the kind of money which had clearly been spent on these clothes. They were Prada! Cotton jersey; a black skirt and a sort of slinky T-shirt, with the tags still on them. I unpegged them and scrutinised them. They felt lovely, that really smooth, thick, good quality jersey material.

My first thought was: I want them. I took them

inside. They looked like they'd be a perfect fit. But thinking about what they were doing there was too much—it made my head hurt. I needed some air, some space to think, so I hung the clothes in my wardrobe—might as well look after them—and closed the door on them. If it's all some great big mistake, I might not have them for long. Part of me was hoping that they'd be gone when I returned home; that the Prada Fairy or whoever the hell brought them would take them away in the time it took me to walk down the road to buy a paper. A bigger part of me hoped they'd still be there when I got back. Which of course they were.

I did make a few tentative phone calls, just to see if anyone I knew had left them there as some sort of joke, but got no joy. I even tried Phil—left him a message which he didn't return. I'm sure it wasn't him, though, he's not talking to me. I've called him a couple of times—he must be back from Portugal by now—but he isn't getting back to me. I think I must have really upset him.

Well, I'm sure I'll find out soon enough who left the clothes there. Nobody would spend that much money on me and want to remain anonymous for long.

Thursday

Police were called to Beulah Mansions in Grove Road, Camden on Monday evening, where the body of a woman had been discovered in the grounds of the building. She was later identified as 31-year-old Kathy Noonan, a resident of Beulah Mansions. There were no witnesses, but the police report states that

113

Ms Noonan had fallen to her death from the roof of the building. A police spokesperson said that Ms Noonan had been out drinking that evening, and that there was no suspicion of foul play. 'It seems that she tried to climb on to her roof via the fire escape and must have slipped,' the spokesperson went on. 'It's a popular spot for residents of the building.'

The Ham and High *spoke to another resident of Beulah Mansions, who told us,* 'The young people at the top of the building are always climbing up there. I've warned them it's dangerous, but they never listen.'

There was no suicide note, and Ms Noonan's parents tell us that they had spoken to their daughter earlier that day and she was in good spirits. The funeral will be held at St Peter's Church, Highgate, on Friday 2nd October at 1 pm.

Friday

Haven't written this diary for ages. Two weeks—that's awful. Haven't done anything much for two weeks, actually, what with all the crap that's been going on. I cancelled one writing class out of respect for Kathy—they weren't very pleased, at the college, but I was in no fit state to teach—and then it was half term. I haven't felt like writing anything, not even this. But I suppose I should write it all down, otherwise I'll forget it.

*   *   *

I thought it appropriate that I should go to her

funeral. After all, she was a friend—nearly—as well as one of my students. What I didn't anticipate was how much it would upset me. I suppose I'm lucky, having got to the ripe old age of 35 and having only been to two funerals in my whole life, both of which were for octogenarians; but this one was horrible, in a totally different league of awfulness to Granny's and Auntie Dot's. The church was packed with young people, and everyone—including me—was crying. Sobbing, mostly.

I will never forget the desolation on her parents' faces, a drab-looking couple in their sixties, who seemed bewildered, horrified and grateful by turns at the huge gay turnout. I hope for their sakes that they already knew Kathy was gay—I'm sure they must have done. She did like to broadcast it. I remember her so clearly at that first writing class, saying 'I'm Kathy and I'm gay', with a really proud, defiant expression on her face like it absolutely was a celebration for her, something she wanted to shout from the rooftops.

Bad choice of expression.

The service was so, so moving. Kathy clearly had a lot of friends, and they were so shocked at her just suddenly . . . being dead. There was as much disbelief as grief in people's eyes. I don't believe it was anything but an accident, and nobody else believed it either . . . but whenever something like this happens, you can't help but wonder if it wasn't an accident. There's this little voice that says 'What if she jumped?' But really, so what if she did? She's still dead.

The four or five people who stood up to speak, their voices trembling, clearing their throats and swallowing back tears constantly, talked of her lust for life, her adventurous spirit, her desire to excel.

No, there's no way she'd have thrown herself off her roof.

One woman in particular could barely get the words out at all. Poor thing. She said she and Kathy had been best friends since childhood—I remembered Kathy mentioning her, briefly, in the pub. She was quite pretty, in that rather gummy sort of way. I thought she'd probably look a bit horsy when she smiled—although since I didn't see her smile, I wouldn't know for sure. She got about two sentences into her speech and just kind of crumpled. The church was completely silent, a deep heavy intense silence that even people's quiet sobbing didn't seem to dent, and we all waited for her to finish, like the agonising seconds spent willing a stammerer to get his words out; but she couldn't. Her face turned redder and redder and eventually she shook her head, and fled back to her seat. It was awful.

The whole bloody thing was awful.

But there was one little part of me that—and I'd never admit this to anybody—felt oddly jealous. Imagine, being envious of a dead woman! But the love that all her friends felt for her was so completely palpable, and all the wonderful things that they said of her. I suppose everyone says nice things about you once you're dead, but Kathy clearly was a very special person. It made me wish that I'd had more time to get to know her. It also made me wonder if people would say the same kinds of things about me, if I died.

As we all filed out at the end (family and close friends only were going on to the crematorium), they played 'I Just Don't Know What To Do With Myself' by Dusty Springfield, because it had been

116

one of Kathy's favourite songs. At that moment I think every single person in the church felt the same, that now Kathy was gone, none of us knew what to do with ourselves, and that, even if we hadn't known her well, nothing would be the same again.

Then I heard a voice at my shoulder. At first I didn't register that it was Alex from the writing class; I was crying too hard.

'Isn't it terrible?' he said. He looked a state too; really white-faced and red-eyed. I didn't realise he'd been matey with Kathy. I nodded, trying to get myself together but feeling the corners of my mouth pulling right down for another batch of tears. He handed me a clean tissue, and sort of twitched his fingers, as if he wanted to reach out and comfort me. I was glad he didn't though—if anyone had touched me then, I think I'd have collapsed entirely.

'It was nice of you to come,' I said, then regretted it. It sounded like I was hosting the damn event or something. We stared at each others' ravaged faces, and suddenly I felt relieved that he was there. I didn't know anybody else, and couldn't face going back to the house for drinks; her father had hesitantly invited everyone.

'Do you want a lift somewhere?' I asked, wiping under my eyes with the tissue and wishing I'd thought to wear waterproof mascara.

'Thanks,' he said immediately, not saying where. 'That would be great.'

Later, in the car, once I'd calmed down enough to drive, Alex said that he and Kathy had had a drink after class a couple of times, and had met for lunch too. I thought it was odd that she hadn't mentioned it, but I suppose that she probably didn't really feel it merited a mention, him being a bloke,

117

and all. He seemed edgy, biting his nails and staring out of the window, and then surreptitiously studying me when I was driving, as if he thought I couldn't see him.

Turns out he lives quite close to me. I hadn't heard of his street, but he said it was only about ten minutes' walk away. Before I knew it, I found myself saying, 'Come in for coffee, if you like.' I thought that if I went home alone, I'd only sit and cry all afternoon.

He nodded, like one of those toy dogs who sit in the back windows of cars.

'What happened to your wall?' he asked, climbing over the pile of rubble to get to my front path. I hadn't told him which house was mine, but he just headed straight for it, no hesitation. At the time I thought it was strange, but I was too strung out to dwell on it. I should've called him on it. I should never have let him into the house. I'm a fool.

So, as weird as I thought it was then, that he knew which house was mine, things started to get even weirder when we got inside. I showed him to the sofa and he sat down on the very edge of it. He still seemed really jumpy, but I put it down to the emotion of the funeral. I made some coffee, and took the mugs into the living room.

There was a long silence. Alex looked so strange then that all these thoughts starting running through my head: if he knew where I lived, was it him who followed me home that time after class? I'd suspected him of sending the card and leaving the flowers, but now I felt more certain. Perhaps he'd only come to the funeral because he guessed I'd be there! Maybe he bought the clothes too—he must have got such a kick out of seeing me wearing the damn things—I wondered why he kept staring at them. I hadn't meant to wear them, not until I knew where they were from, but when I'd opened my wardrobe to try and find something suitable for a funeral, there they were, just perfect with my black jacket over the top . . .

I got up from the armchair and went over to lean— casually, I hoped—on the windowsill, willing Mrs Roberts over the road to be in her usual chair at her own living room window. At least that way if he tried anything, it would have to be in view of Mrs Roberts' beady old eye. My hands started shaking, and a splash of coffee spilled out onto the carpet. I was really upset—my pristine carpet!—but I didn't dare get up and get a cloth. I didn't want to leave the safety of the window. I thought longingly of the Stain Devil under the sink, and then almost laughed. This guy is a potential nutter, and I'm worried about a tiny splash of coffee on my carpet? It would take the application of several dozen Stain Devils to get my life blood out of the same carpet, if Alex really did turn out to be a psychopath.

But somehow I thought that, however uneasy he was making me feel at that moment, he probably wasn't dangerous. Probably . . . Although I was clearly in denial.

And then he said what he said, staring at the stain, not meeting my eyes, muttering almost coyly into his own coffee: 'I'm glad to see you're wearing your new clothes.'

My heart almost gave out. Even though I'd suspected him, it was a huge shock to hear him admit it. 'What?'

'Those clothes.' He stopped, and smiled at me then, a big, ingenuous beam of pride, like I was his mother and he was waiting for me to say, ooh, what a clever boy you are. 'They're from me. I left them on your washing line as a surprise.'

I lowered my coffee mug onto the windowsill, spilling some more out. Then I reached back and grasped the glossy white sill with both my hands, to steady myself and to try and stop them shaking. I wished I could rip the sill off, and bash him over the head with it, because at that moment I realised that it had all been him: everything—the card, the flowers, the man who'd followed me home; it was maybe even him who was responsible for the underwear that I thought I'd accidentally ordered myself . . .

'Was the underwear from you, too?' I said, sounding as if I was being strangled.

He nodded proudly, blushing like a schoolboy. I closed my eyes.

'Then—how—come—it was bought with myowncreditcard?' The last words came out in a huge rush, because I wasn't at all sure I wanted to hear the answer.

He looked at the floor now, guilty again. 'I just wanted you to have some nice things,' he muttered.

I noticed the way his eyelashes fell on his cheeks, lazily, softly. I think it was the eyelashes that made him seem like a little boy. And it was that feeling of power, dominance over him, which made me temporarily forget my fear, and allow anger, boiling and acid, to roll up inside me like vomit and spew out all over him. For about ten seconds I no longer cared if he was dangerous, or about the fact that he was five inches taller than me and probably much stronger. Right then, I could've crushed him like a bug.

'Don't tell me that I paid for these fucking clothes too,' I hissed, sticking my face into his face, almost spitting at him with fury.

He stood up then, lifting one arm, appearing to tower above me. As quickly as it had risen, my rage vanished and fear washed back over me again.

'I care about you, Siobhan,' he said, reaching out and drawing a soft line with his index finger down the left side of my face. 'I want us to be friends. That's why I sent you the card, and the lilies. I wanted you to know that I like you. I really do. I'm sorry if the card was a bit strong, you know, so soon, but I couldn't help it. You're so beautiful.'

I backed away from him, my knees trembling so hard that it took all my strength not to sit down, then and there, on the floor. It felt as if someone had removed my kneecaps.

'Please leave. Now,' I managed. 'Or I'll call the police.'

He looked scared at that but didn't move.

'GET OUT!' I wanted to push him, but I still had this knee-less problem. We just stood staring at each other, hackles up, tails bushy. Then he seemed to droop.

'I'm sorry,' he said, almost inaudibly. He turned and walked out of the room, and I heard the front door close quietly behind him.

12

Alex

Friday evening

I had been so happy to see Siobhan in her new clothes—and I was right; they did suit her; they made her look like a princess, all in black, a princess of darkness?—that I thought it must be another sign. She had invited me back to her house. She was wearing my clothes. She might even have her new underwear on. I thought this was the silver lining to Kathy's cloud.

But then . . . I pictured Siobhan's angry face. She looked really sexy when she was angry, her neck and face flushed pink, pupils wide, the air around us crackling with tension. Anger is closely related to passion, after all. Oh God, I wonder how long it will take her to calm down.

What if she calls the police, like she threatened? What if . . .?

*   *   *

Bang bang bang.

It was probably the police. A nice cop and a nasty cop, with suspicious eyes and minds and all sorts of questions.

And how did you come by these credit card details, sir? Where were you the night Kathy Noonan died?

It wasn't the police. It was a girl, asking for Natalie: 'Ah, hi. Have I got the right address?'

122

'Who are you looking for?'

I wondered for a split second if she might be a plainclothes policewoman—a honeytrap from the Met, sent to get me to 'fess up. She was a little overweight to be a honeytrap, perhaps, but she wasn't unattractive. Her eyes were blue and bright with amusement. She seemed a little flustered too—perhaps she's one of those people who mirrors the actions of the person they're talking to.

'Natalie Sauvage.'

'Oh no. I mean yes. Natalie does live here—sort of. Her boyfriend, um, does.' I was having an attack of the Hugh Grants.

The girl smiled at me. Probably a Hugh Grant fan, then. 'Is she in?'

'No. She's at work, I think.'

She looked at her watch. 'Oh yes, of course. It's just that I was in Camden and thought . . . well, anyway, can you tell her Emily called round?'

'Emily. Okay.'

And she walked away, looking over her shoulder at me and smiling again before I closed the door.

I lay on my bed for a while, waiting for my heart to slow down. When I closed my eyes, Siobhan's face swam up in front of my eyes.

I wanted to call her, talk to her. I needed to make her understand. I had a knot in my gut, a bubble of dread floating inside me. Had I screwed it all up? I don't pretend to understand women but I do know that they like underwear (as long as it isn't scratchy and crotchless); they love all sorts of flowers; and they're all totally obsessed with clothes. So why was Siobhan so angry? Sigh . . . maybe I should have sent her chocolates instead.

I suppose I shouldn't be surprised—Siobhan isn't

like other women. She's unique. Okay, I made her angry. I made some mistakes.

But there has to be some way to make it right. I need to know more about Siobhan, to really get inside her head, her most private spaces. That's it. Once I've seen into her soul, I'll know exactly how to win her heart.

Later . . .

I've just got in after going out with Si and Nat. They came home at about seven this evening; I was asleep. Must have been worn out. Don't think I dreamt about anything, though. Certainly nothing memorable. Simon knocked on my door and asked me if I wanted to go out for a drink.

I said I wasn't in the mood, but he insisted. 'It's time you came out of your bedroom, mate,' he said. He doesn't realise that every time I leave my room, something goes wrong. But I wasn't in the mood to argue with him. Plus I had no alcohol left in the house and I needed a drink to quell the tremors that kept running through me.

We went to a pub behind Camden High Street, a favourite haunt of Simon and Natalie. It was a cosy place, with an elderly clientele, the Irish barman's political sympathies tattooed in green on his forearms.

We sat and drank our pints. I was worried that Si might start asking me how the job-hunting was going, so I was tense. Plus I kept thinking about what happened the last time I visited a pub. Somebody died. Luckily though, we chatted about everything but job-hunting: football, telly, music, all the usual stuff that stops us having to talk about anything serious. It's one of the reasons Si and I get on: we don't ever go near weighty or emotional subjects.

Which was why I was so surprised when Simon started saying how he was worried about me.

'Why? What do you mean?'

He and Nat exchanged a look.

'Well, mate, you hardly come out any more, just sit in your room tapping away on the computer. You've lost weight, you're smoking twice as much, you hardly talk to us any more. I was amazed when you said you'd come out tonight.'

'I haven't been able to come out because I haven't got much money. I've been worrying about finding a job.'

'How is that coming along?' said Nat, but Simon raised a hand for her to shush. (He was quite drunk by now—he wouldn't have dared shush her if he wasn't.)

'I know that, mate. But you were like this before you lost that shitty job. And it was a shitty job, wasn't it? It used to depress me just seeing you come home after a day there. You're an intelligent bloke. You should be doing something different, better. I mean look at me . . .'

He went into a speech about how important and well-paid he is, writing copy for dog food adverts and tag lines for tampon commercials. Natalie nodded along. But beneath the waffle, he had a point. I knew that. I've spent the last ten years of my life drifting along, from crap job to crap job, going travelling when I could afford it, never having any money in the bank, approaching my thirties without a whiff of a career or a family. Not that I fucking want either of those things. I just want . . . well, what do I want? The only answer to that

125

question is 'Siobhan'. She's my only desire. Alright, there are other things I want—to write my book, have a little money, to not be so bored all the time. But if Siobhan and I get together, everything else will fall into place. She and I will be able to live together, writing our books, kind of like Iris Murdoch and her husband, but hopefully without the Alzheimer's. Although if Siobhan did get sick I'd care for her. I'd like that, in fact. And I wouldn't let anything go wrong like it did with Chips the hamster.

Simon had trailed off and he and Nat were gazing at each other in that way that made you want to say 'get a room'. Actually, thinking about it, they'd been shagging a lot less recently, or more quietly anyway. I didn't think I'd be so lucky tonight. Knowing that I needed more alcohol to knock me out, I stood up to buy a round. Si was drinking Guinness. I pointed at Nat's glass. 'What is that, vodka and orange?'

'Just orange juice, please.'

I had to wait ages at the bar, and when I got back there was a girl standing by the table talking to Nat.

'Hello,' she said, looking at me.

It was the same girl who'd knocked on the door earlier. What was her name? Emily. That was it.

'You didn't tell me Emily called earlier,' Nat said.

'Oh . . . sorry. I forgot.' I smiled apologetically at Emily, who smiled back then went off to the bar to buy herself a drink, after Natalie had invited her to join us.

As soon as I'd sat down, Simon said, 'Oh shit, I forgot to tell you something too. Your mum called.'

I went cold. 'My mum?'

'Yeah. I was surprised, because I've never known her call before. Not like my mum—on the phone every other day.'

I couldn't speak for a few seconds. 'Did she say why she was calling?'

He shook his head.

'Well, what did she say?'

'She just asked if you were there. I told her you weren't. And she said, "Can you tell him I called?" and put the phone down. Must have been the day before yesterday.'

I stood up. All of a sudden, I didn't want any more to drink. The pub felt too hot, too packed. I couldn't get any oxygen into my lungs. I said, 'I've got to go.'

Simon didn't get a chance to protest, because I turned swiftly and headed towards the exit, bumping into Emily on my way out. She went to say something but I swerved around her and pushed my way through the door, gulping down the cold night air and heading back here to the safety of my room.

Sunday

As soon as I woke up this morning I knew I had to see Siobhan. If I didn't talk to her and try to make her see how good we would be together, then everything Mum used to say would be true. Gutless wonder. Coward. All that stuff. I still don't know why she was calling me, and I'm not going to ring her back to find out. Maybe it was good news, though. Maybe she was calling to tell me she had a terminal illness.

I had a bath and shaved, nicking myself in a couple of places, having to press tissues against the spots to stem the flow of blood. Standing in front of the mirror with the Bic disposable in my hand, I imagined that it was actually a cut-throat razor and that Mum was standing behind me. I'd turn and there'd be blood on the bathroom floor.

After shaving, I sneaked into Si's room and borrowed some of his aftershave, wincing as it stung my sore face. I put on my best jeans and my favourite shirt and looked in the mirror. I scrubbed up pretty well. A little thin, maybe, like Si said, but I'm no monster.

On the way to Siobhan's I wondered if I should take her a present, but decided that the last presents I'd bought her hadn't been very successful. It was best just to present myself. That little thought made me giggle as I walked up the hill.

There was no sign of her cat. I hadn't seen him after the funeral either, but Siobhan hadn't said anything so I assumed he must be okay. I felt clammy with nerves as I approached the front door, but as I wavered I heard Mum's voice in my head and forced myself to do it. I rang the bell and waited.

She didn't come.

I rang the bell again, and knocked, just in case the bell wasn't working. Still no answer. For a writer, she seems to spend a hell of a lot of time out of the house.

I was about to turn away, when I became aware of something hot in my pocket. It really did feel as if the key was trying to burn its way through the material. I felt it calling out to me: use me, use me. I took it out of my pocket. It was like a cigarette, begging me to smoke it, even though I knew it was bad for me. I couldn't resist.

I unlocked the door and slipped inside. And this time I knew where I wanted to go. Towards the inner sanctum. Up the stairs. Where I could learn more about her.

There were a number of framed photographs on the wall beside the stairs. Like before, I wanted to touch them but resisted. They were black and white pictures of a very beautiful woman, wearing clothes from the twenties or thirties. I realised this must be a relative of Siobhan's—she had the same eyes and those kissable lips. But I knew how dangerous it was to touch. When I ran out of Kathy's flat, terrified that someone would see me leaving, I'd been worried about fingerprints. I'd taken the beer bottle with me so there was no sign that somebody else had been with Kathy that fatal evening. The only way they'd find that out would be if they dusted for fingerprints, and they'd only do that if they suspected foul play. I was incredibly relieved when I saw the newspaper report, with its reassuring words. A drunken accident; nothing suspicious.

I reached the top of the stairs. There was a framed copy of the cover of *TLA*; paperbacks were stacked on a table. There were three rooms leading off the hall: a small room which I looked inside, finding that it was piled high with junk (cardboard boxes, old teddy bears, more books, an old record player and accompanying vinyl; the debris of Siobhan's childhood?; stuff that she can't use but can't throw away either); a bathroom, and a master bedroom. It was all very neat—even the junk room had a certain orderliness about it—and tastefully decorated. I wondered if Siobhan got lonely living here on her own. Had Phil ever lived here with her? I hated to think of him fouling the air; it was like thinking of a burglar invading this sacred space, violating it. I was so glad that my warning had worked and that he hadn't been back. I'd done two women a big favour that day.

I went into the bathroom first. Again, very tidy, spotlessly clean. The mirror gleamed—not like the mirror here in my flat, with its layer of dust and specks of shaving foam and toothpaste mottling your reflection. I had to deliberately slow down my breathing when I saw the bath. There were candles around it, all the wonderful lotions and potions that most women seem to have: bubble bath, several varieties of oil and bath soak and Japanese crystals, whatever they were. This was where Siobhan spent her most private, naked moments. I put my hand into the bath and stroked the plastic. There was a hair on the side—one she'd missed when cleaning the bath. I ran it between my fingers, then rolled it into a small ball and put it in my pocket.

I opened the bathroom cabinet and looked inside. Headache tablets, assorted pills in small brown plastic bottles. Dental floss and tweezers; nail clippers and cotton buds. All the little things she used to make herself more beautiful. I moved onto the bottom shelf and found some contact lens solution. Next to that were a number of tubes. Savlon, for when poor Siobhan gets a cut or sore skin. Deep Heat, for when Siobhan gets muscular pains and doesn't have someone on hand to give her a massage. Preparation H for when . . . well, maybe Phil did used to live with Siobhan after all.

I closed the cabinet door and looked down at the toilet. It practically sparkled. Again, nothing like the toilet in my flat. I unbuttoned my jeans, pushed them down and sat on the toilet seat. Just for a few seconds. I didn't do anything, just sat there. Then I stood, pulled up my trousers and headed towards the bedroom.

It was a lovely room, the walls painted white, more Modigliani pictures on the walls: those naked women, stretched out, purring. And speaking of such things, Siobhan's cat was lying on the bed, blinking at me. I felt a whoosh of relief. He was okay, after all. I sat down beside him and stroked him, eliciting sounds of pleasure. A splash of dribble fell from his lips onto the quilt. Siobhan wouldn't like that. In fact, I was surprised she let the cat sleep on the bed, what with all that fur and the risk of fleas. Perhaps she was a bit freer in the bedroom. Perhaps the bedroom is where the real Siobhan emerges, a glorious sexual butterfly stretching her wings . . .

I got up from the bed and walked around the room, careful to stay away from the window. I loved the way light flooded into the room. Siobhan was very lucky to have this place. Now all she needed was someone to share it with. Somebody like me. I could imagine myself lying in this bed beside Siobhan, the cat at the end of the bed. I'd bring Siobhan breakfast and sit next to her reading the paper while she dunked soldiers into a boiled egg. Then she'd put her plate aside and gesture for me to put the paper down. 'I love you so much,' she'd say. And then she'd get that naughty glint in her eye and say, 'Why don't you fuck me?'

I moved around the bedroom. There was a huge wardrobe in the corner of the room. I opened it and saw how few clothes there were inside. There was no sign of the clothes I'd bought her.

I shut the door then turned back to the bed. That was when I saw a hardback book lying on the bedside table. I bent down to pick it up and realised, with a spasm of guilty excitement, that it was a diary. It had this year's date on the front. I sat down next to the cat. There was a fist clenching and unclenching in my stomach. Should I open it? I knew I shouldn't, but what if there something about me in it? There might be something in this book that told me how to win Siobhan's heart—that key that I'd been looking for.

I opened it at a random page and read the following passage. I can remember every word—it's seared into my memory:

I practically dragged him up to the bedroom and ripped off his clothes, and then there was the shock of the cold bedclothes over and under our hot flesh . . .

. . . and nothing had changed. The cat hair still made him sneeze. He squashed me under his weight. He moaned and grunted and thrusted, ripping at my hair and using his fingers in all the wrong places. I'd been really turned on for the first two minutes but then I just kept thinking, I want a real man. I wanted to be fucked, by a man with a dick like a truncheon, not this skinny little excuse for a penis. I want to come three times in a night.

I snapped the diary shut.

Beneath me, the front door had just opened and closed.

Somebody had come in.

13

Siobhan

Sunday

Have just got in from tennis. Dennis couldn't believe how well I was playing—nor could I, for that matter. It was as if I took all the fear and rage and confusion about this Alex business, packed it into a small green fluorescent ball, and smashed it at him, over and over, slamming it into the corners of the court, putting it over his head, squeaking it just inside the tramlines. I beat him, for the first time ever. 6-1.

The tennis was a brief and welcome break from the Alex situation, but I feel weirdly compelled to get as many different opinions as I possibly can. I was on the phone to Mum for hours last night. I was very calm (at that point!), but I think she was crying. Then I called Paula and we had a long chat, and after that, I even called Jess. She and I had our first decent conversation in weeks, and she only mentioned Tom's teething problems once. I even offered to do the godmotherly thing and take him out for an afternoon, which she fell over herself to accept; but mostly we talked about what had been going on with Alex. I 'philled' her in on the Phil situation too. (Tried to call him again last night but he never seems to be in, or else he's still sulking. Tosser.)

All of them—Mum, Dennis, Paula, Jess—say I must go to the police. Alex has been using my credit card. He's spent hundreds of pounds on it. I know they're right, but something's stopping me. After all, it's not as if he's broken into the house, or attacked me, or anything. He must have just taken my card out of my bag at some point, written down the number, and replaced it. I'm not condoning it, but at least he put it back. He'd have got access to the washing line by climbing over the back gate; and I'm sure it was me who left the mug out in the kitchen. I must have spilt the cat food, too. He's not Houdini, he can't have got into my house without forcing a lock or breaking a window—I'm so paranoid about security these days.

I don't know for sure that it was him who followed me the other week, and what else has he done? Nothing, except send me a card saying how much he likes and fancies me (OK, so that was a little inappropriate, but he's clearly embarrassed about that). He's sent me flowers (OK, so he didn't realise they were dead) and has bought me expensive presents (WITH MY OWN MONEY, Siobhan, you sap).

Anyway, I've decided how I'm going to play it. I've made it clear that his attentions aren't welcome . . . although a tiny part of me thinks what a shame. I just keep remembering the look in his eyes when he told me I was beautiful. It was one of those gorgeously longing looks, so full of affection. Phil never used to look at me like that.

Don't go there. The guy is probably a total freak. He scared me, and he's robbed me. Aargh, this is so confusing!

SO. I'm going to ask him for the money back, and if he doesn't pay up, then I'll go to the police. I'll keep the underwear, because it's too weird to give that back to him, 'specially since I've now worn it, although he might like that. (Happily, it fits me very well and doesn't climb up my arse at all.) I've worn the clothes too, obviously—which is another major reason why I don't think the police will listen to me—but I'll get them dry-cleaned, give them back to him, and he can sell them at one of those second-hand designer shops. Or he can wear them himself, or dress his blow-up doll in them, for all I care. Whatever.

What am I going to do about seeing him in class though? Jess and Paula both think I should get him kicked out; but then I've got to make a formal complaint and jump through all those bureaucratic hoops. I think I'll write to him instead. I've got his address in my student file. Yes. I'll write to him, tell him how much he owes me and that he can have the Prada back. And I will suggest that it's best that he drops out of my class of his own volition.

* * *

I'm writing this sitting on the bathroom floor waiting for the bath to fill up. I'm so sweaty—when I nipped into the bedroom to grab the diary from the bedside cabinet, Biggles was lying on the bed, and he gave me an 'ooh, you're smelly' look; that haughty expression that cats do so well.

This bath is so damn slow. I'm aching from the tennis, and I'm still disturbed by what happened with Alex yesterday, and Kathy's funeral, but despite all the confusion I feel oddly invigorated. Not just by the exercise. I don't know how to describe it, but it's a mixture of things: the catharsis of talking to good friends and family. The puzzle of figuring out a solution. The secretive buzz of having someone really fancy me, to the extent of buying me really expensive clothes. Yes, yes, I know—I paid for the damn clothes, but still. I wish Alex was less screwed up, or richer. He's not bad looking, and if he'd paid for the Prada himself, I'd probably be on cloud nine by now. I love men who buy me clothes. He scared me shitless yesterday, but I think that it was just the emotions of the funeral making me overreact. I can deal with the likes of him. The fact that he thinks I'm beautiful makes me feel strong, capable, dominant. And sexy too.

It's so nice to hear a man say that you're beautiful. Especially a younger man! Albeit a nutter . . . I've just peeled my damp tennis things off and stood in front of the big bathroom mirror, watching myself slowly turn into a ghost in the steam, trying to see myself through someone else's eyes. Through a non-critical person's eyes.

And I have to say: not bad. Firm enough. I'm no Cheryl Cole but at least I don't have cellulite or rolls of fat. Wish my tits were bigger, but they're still pretty perky, and I don't have to hide my body during sex any more, the way I used to feel I had to when I was younger.

Am now sitting in the bath writing this. I recently discovered that if I lean against the bath pillow, rest my diary on my knees, and keep my hands dry, I can carry on scribbling quite effectively. I adore big, deep, hot baths but unless you're reading a book or listening to the radio, it's such dead time, and writing this bloody diary is so time-consuming. I think I've spent as much time writing about Alex and the 'situation' as I have talking about it, i.e. HOURS. I wish I spent half as long writing fiction. I've got three novels' worth of words in my last two diaries alone. Shame my life is normally so boring—a confessional memoir would be a piece of cake, if I had anything worth confessing . . .

*   *   *

I can hear Biggles scuffling around in my bedroom—bless him, he never comes near the bathroom when I'm in it. He thinks I'm going to wash him. He hasn't quite been himself since the wall fell down. The woman in the car told Doreen next door that she'd had to swerve to avoid a ginger cat that ran out in front of her. I wonder if he's suffering from post-traumatic stress syndrome? Perhaps—

*   *   *

—What's that noise?

14

Alex

Sunday (continued)

I panicked, looking around the room, my instinct telling me that I had to hide. In a corner of my mind an image was illuminated: me, sitting on the bed; Siobhan coming home, smiling as she saw me, saying, 'Hi, darling', kissing me softly. But that was for the future. Right now, I needed to get out of sight. But where? Under the bed? No, there was no space. Behind the curtains? They were too short, and there was no balcony. The wardrobe was the only possible place. Watched by Siobhan's cat ('Don't tell,' I mouthed silently), I opened the wardrobe and slipped inside, crouching on the solid oak floor. It was like being inside a massive speaker, my heart providing the bass beat.

I strained to hear what was going on in the world outside the wardrobe. At first I couldn't make out a thing above my thudding pulse, but then I heard a creak and several quick footsteps. Siobhan (oh, my Siobhan) was coming up the stairs. I pressed my ear against the wardrobe door. She was heading in my direction—the tread of her pretty feet moving towards me. Here she came, right into the bedroom. I had a moment of amplified horror: had I remembered to put the diary back on the bedside table? Yes—yes, I had. Thank God. I heard her stop and say something to the cat: '(*Something something*) Biggles.' Well, now I knew what he was called. Quite cute, though perhaps reflecting a dodgy taste in literature . . . what the hell was I doing, mulling over the quality of Siobhan's cat's name? She was still standing in the bedroom, and I was terrified that she was going to open the door—not because I didn't want to see her, but I thought it might harm our relationship if she found me crouched in her wardrobe.

But she moved away out of the bedroom. Where had she gone? A few moments later my question was answered: I heard the shudder of pipes, the rush of water. She was running the bath. I took a deep breath.

Right now, just down the hall from me, in a room

where I had only recently stood, she would be taking
her clothes off, throwing them on the floor, dipping
a hand into the water to test its temperature. Maybe
pouring a little oil into the water, or some bubbles.
Oh God, she might even be shaving her legs or
armpits. Or would she do that in the bath? I've never
lived with a woman, never shared a bathroom with
any females apart from Mum and Annette, and I
never had any desire to watch *them* in the bath. I
used to sometimes fantasise about dropping a few
piranha fish into the water when Mum was in there,
but that was where my mother/bathroom interests
finished.

The taps stopped running; the water tank continued
to clank for a while, then suddenly fell silent. The
bath must be full. She would be stepping into it now,
her toes breaking the surface of the water, then one
ankle, and she would step in, slowly lower herself
into the hot, oily liquid, her skin flushed pink by the
heat . . . Oh, Jesus. I could picture her body; I knew
what it would look like: bottom like Kylie; stomach
like Angelina Jolie; breasts like Halle Berry. Flawless
skin, maybe a constellation of freckles on her
shoulders. Her eyes would close as she sank into
the water.

What was she thinking about?

Was she thinking about me?

One of Siobhan's dresses was hanging in front of
my face. I pulled it closer, against my mouth and
nose, breathing in her scent . . . then snapped out
of my erotic reverie. This was my chance to escape.
While Siobhan was in the bathroom, I could get out
of the house. As long as the bathroom door was
shut.

I opened the wardrobe door as quietly as I could,

blinking at the invasion of light. Slowly, I eased my way out of the dark space and stood up. I looked over towards the bedside table—the diary wasn't there! I checked the bed. I lifted up Biggles to make sure it wasn't under him. He wasn't pleased, and swiped at me, his claws scratching my hand. I had to bite my lip to stop myself from crying out. I watched the scratches turn red and sucked my skin. Biggles closed his eyes and went back to sleep, and I realised Siobhan must have taken the diary with her.

The bedroom door was open and, looking down the hall, I could see—oh thank you God—that the bathroom door was shut.

I crept down the hall.

The bathroom door had a panel of frosted glass which had steamed up from the inside. I stood just before the door. I trembled. The woman I loved was beyond that layer of glass, naked . . . a woman who wants to be fucked by a man with a dick like a truncheon. I didn't know if I would quite measure up to that, but I knew this: Siobhan was as frustrated as me; she was in need just like me. And I knew—I know—that she and I could help each other, could find what we're looking for in each other's arms; in each other's beds.

I stepped in front of the bathroom door and tried to look through the glass. All I could see were vague shapes, misty shadows that fed my imagination. I could hear splashing, rippling water.

My hand hovered over the door handle. All I had to do was turn the handle and push, and there we would be . . .

Siobhan would turn and smile, raise an eyebrow. Pick up the soap and hold it out to me. 'Don't be

140

shy, Alex. Why don't you come over here and wash me . . .'

I pulled my hand away from the door handle. I couldn't do it.

I walked past the door and went straight down the stairs—and as I descended I stumbled, missing a step, having to grab the bannister to stop myself from falling. My foot went bang on the next step.

I went rigid. I could see the front door below me. Above me, I heard a loud splash, the sound of a body emerging from water. Siobhan must have heard me. She would be frightened, wondering what the hell that noise was. Oh God, I didn't want to scare her; I hated to think of her being afraid. A wave of sickness crashed over me. This was a mistake. What was I doing here? It was all wrong. And I realised that I needed to do what I had come here to do initially: I had to talk to her.

I continued to the foot of the stairs. But instead of going out of the front door, I turned right and went into the living room. I sat down on the sofa and waited, sick with trepidation.

A minute later I heard movement on the stairs: she was coming down, slowly, my angel descending towards me. I combed my fingers through my hair, breathed into my cupped palm to make sure I didn't have bad breath.

I didn't have to wait long.

She appeared in the doorway just after I'd checked my breath for the third time. She was looking towards the kitchen at first, but then she turned her head towards me.

She jumped, clapping a hand over her heart. Her mouth formed an O, her eyes an umlaut above it. I tensed, expecting her to scream or at least cry out—but she remained silent . . . for a few seconds. Then she said, 'Alex.'

'Hello Siobhan.'

We looked at each other, neither of us saying a word. I could see her chest rising and falling rapidly. Excitement? Fear? Both, I thought—the blend of dread and exhilaration that we all feel before any momentous encounter; the same gut-churning sensation you get when you take your seat on a rollercoaster. She took a step towards me—she was wearing a blue robe; her bare feet had left damp footprints on the carpet behind her. She was unbearably beautiful—so beautiful that it was painful to look at her, like staring at the sun.

'How did you get in?' she said. Her voice was husky.

I reached in to my pocket and took out the key, holding it up towards her. She nodded slowly, a look of comprehension coming into her eyes. 'How many times have you been in here?'

I shrugged. 'Two or three. I . . . I wanted to get to know you better. To learn about you. I met Biggles and he seemed to like me.'

She came a step closer. She had her hands out in front of her, her palms towards me. She glanced towards the phone, which was over near her desk.

'You don't need to be afraid, Siobhan,' I said. 'I love you. I'm not going to hurt you.'

'No . . .' she said, very quietly.

'I promise, Siobhan. You wouldn't hurt me, would you? You'd never hurt someone you love or who loves you.' I almost added 'unless', but stopped myself.

'You don't love me,' she said. 'You think you do, but you don't, not really . . .'

'I do!' I stood up and she took a quick step backwards, fear flashing across her face.

'Sit down,' she said, her voice a whisper. 'Please.'

I did as she asked, wanting to obey her: to love, to honour, to obey. When we get married, I thought, I'll want to say those words—they'll be part of my vow. To love her until I die, to cherish from this day forward and . . . what else? For better, for worse, forever and ever and ever amen.

She looked at the phone again and seemed to think for a moment. Then she turned back towards me. 'Alex,' she said, 'you have to listen to me. You don't love me. You've . . . developed a crush on me, a fixation. You might think you love me but you don't really know me. This . . . this isn't how it's supposed to work. You're supposed to meet someone, go out for drinks, go to dinner, date, talk, kiss, go to bed, and then, if you're lucky, at some point down the line, you fall in love. I know you wanted to go for a drink and I lied to you, but that doesn't mean—I mean that doesn't give you the right to stalk me.'

Stalk? It took a few seconds for the word to sink in. I said it aloud: 'Stalk? You think . . . I've been stalking you?'

'I . . . look, it doesn't matter what you call it, but it has to stop. This is . . . this is wrong, Alex, this is fucked up. You should not be in my house! You should not have a key. I don't even know how you got it. But I now know that's how you got my credit card details.'

I didn't speak.

'What do you think the police would say if I told them about that? It's theft.'

I swallowed. 'Are you going to call them?'

143

She hesitated. 'Not right now. But I will—unless you pay me back the money you spent. All of it.'

I hung my head. 'I will.'

'And you're going to have to stop coming to the class as well. I don't want to see you there again.'

'But . . .'

'No. If you come, if I even see you lurking around outside, I'll call the police straight away.'

'But I like the class. I want to learn from you.'

'It's too late for that. You're not going to see me again, Alex. No more cards or flowers. No more presents. Certainly no more visits to my house. I want you to put the key on the sofa beside you and leave it there. That's it. Good.'

'How will I pay you back your money?'

'You can post it to me. You obviously have my address.' She took a deep breath. 'And now I want you to go, to leave my house. It's over, Alex.'

She fell quiet, folding her arms and staring at me. I stood up, leaving the key behind me. I walked across the room towards her.

I stopped right in front of her. There were just three or four inches between us. If I took another step that distance would increase, would keep growing with every step, until I was out of sight, out of her world. The thought made me feel so sick and scared. I knew I had to obey her—to move, to go—but my legs wouldn't follow orders. And there was something else, something that told me this was all wrong, that Siobhan was making a mistake: I could feel it—a current running between us. Electricity. Chemistry. She was trembling. I wondered if she realised what she was throwing away.

'Go, Alex,' she said again, and, finally, I went.

Out of the door. Out of her life.

144

When I got home I lay down on my bed and cried. But even as I felt myself sinking into a pit of despair, hot tears burning my eyes, I knew it wasn't over. No way. Fate wouldn't allow it.

PART TWO

PART TWO

15

Siobhan

It seems to be taking a long time, getting over the shock of finding Alex in my house like that. It's been a week, and I still can't stop thinking about it. About the way he looked at me; sort of greedy, ashamed, and defiant, all rolled together. I don't think I've ever felt as vulnerable as I did right then, standing dripping onto the carpet. I felt as if my dressing gown was invisible—he was staring fixedly right at my crotch and my nipples. At times he seemed as terrified as I was—although at other times he really frightened me.

What would I have done if he'd leaped at me, ripped my dressing gown off my shoulders, unzipped his jeans and jumped on top of me? Like that creep in the alley, but this time going all the way. I've often visualised how it must feel to be raped. The dry unwelcome thrusts, the pain, the humiliation. Wondering if you're going to escape alive, or be killed so you can't run to the police.

I don't know how I would have reacted; how much I could have hurt him back. I know what you're supposed to do—the poke in the eye, the knee in the balls, the screaming—but knowing and acting are two entirely different things, when you're standing there petrified and half-naked, like a teenage virgin on a sacrificial altar. Even thinking about it makes me feel as if my lungs are closing up, as if it's oxygen which is the invader, trying to force itself into my body while I rebel against it.

I'm quite proud of myself, actually, managing to tell him that he has to pay me back. I want him to know I mean business, so yesterday morning I looked up his address in my student files and wrote him a note, a brief but businesslike letter reminding him of the exact amount he owes me for the clothes (£524.98), and that he is barred from my class. If he shows up again, I will not only explain to the college exactly why I barred him, but I will also go straight to the police. Ditto if I don't receive the money within one month.

I've changed the lock on the front door too, just in case he had two copies of my key made. Coming home after my first post-Alex venture out, I convinced myself he'd got into the house again. Got in a bit of a state, actually. The air in the hall had that sort of occupied feel to it; an unnatural kind of stillness to the dust as it hung there, lit up by the sun through the stained glass panels.

Mind you, I thought I sensed it before I even opened the front door. I'd turned the key and crept in, really quietly, with my can of pepper spray at the ready in one hand (Jess bought it for me), and my tallest, most pointy stiletto in the other, ready to sink it into his head the second I saw him. But nothing. I tiptoed (well, as much as you can tiptoe wearing one stiletto and holding the other. I kept the other one on in case I needed to kick him in the nuts) round the whole place, but found nothing except a large spider in the bathtub, and Biggles, rolling his eyes at me, in the bedroom.

Actually, Biggles and I had a bit of a drama the other day. I'm sure this was Alex's doing too. I was just sitting at my computer, trying to think of something interesting that my characters might say to each other, when I heard from upstairs the unmistakeable and depressing sound of a vomiting cat. I ran up the stairs, two at a time, and sure enough, Biggles had chucked up enough of his guts to string a tennis racket. All over my bed. He was heaving and shivering, and he had that terrible ashamed look that they get. So of course we had to dash for the vet's, with him hawking and groaning all the way there. I was terrified that he was going to die, and that he had been poisoned. But the vet said that this was extremely improbable, and that it was more likely to be a virulent strain of cat flu that's going around. Or a bad mouse. I still have my doubts though, and I disinfected all Biggles's bowls and threw away his opened Munchies when we got home. The vet gave him the world's most expensive injection—the feline equivalent of Botox, costwise, cc for cc, and he seems fine now. It probably wasn't anything to do with Alex, but everything seems so . . . I don't know . . . amplified at the moment. I can't seem to help but jump to conclusions.

Funny that I haven't been able to write about it since it happened; not until now, that is. I haven't written anything for a week.

I think I know the reason though. It's just that I always leave my diary face-up on my bedside table, and when I came in from tennis that day, it was face-down. I've got a horrible, horrible feeling that Alex might have been reading it. In a way, that's almost as bad as rape. I mean, I know this diary is more Bridget Jones than Proust, but it's still totally private. The thought of anybody else reading it makes me feel violated and sick. Every time I've reached for it in the last week, I've seen it through the eyes of somebody else: flicking through the pages, noting all the banalities and shallownesses.

Ironic, really—being stalked is about the most bloody interesting thing that's ever happened to me. Was it Dorothy Parker who said, 'Only good girls keep journals; bad girls don't have the time'? Probably.

I shouldn't have the time to keep a journal. I should be hacking through the rainforest with a machete, or building clean-water wells in Africa. Or writing that novel. Or, at the very least, be run off my feet by a couple of small children and a weary but affectionate husband.

But I'm doing none of these things. I'm moping around self-indulgently, blowing up some relatively small incident—from which I emerged completely unhurt—into some giant event.

Still, look on the bright side. Everyone is being so supportive (apart from Phil, who's still not returning my calls. Well, sod him). Mum and Dad wanted me to move home, but I couldn't face it. They eventually stopped banging on about it after I got the lock changed, and Paula stayed with me a couple of nights after it happened. I even had lunch with Jess and Tom the other day, which was when she bought me the pepper spray. My godson is really sweet. He sits up in a high chair and bangs spoons now—last time I saw him, all he could do was loll around farting (not unlike Phil then, really. No wonder I wasn't much cop as a godmother). I'm definitely going to try harder to keep in touch with them, and Jess was all ears to get the latest in the Alex saga.

But apart from the thoughts of Alex buzzing like a bluebottle stuck inside my head, life continues the same as ever. I write about seventy-five words a day on the book. I play tennis with Dennis. I lock up the house like Belmarsh every night, get cabs home, rush to the post to see if Alex's cheque has arrived— but nothing. No hang-ups on the phone, no skulking outside the curtains. He's got a month to pay me back, then I really will go to the police.

I think.

Nobody questioned it at the writing class when I said that Alex had left. The life has kind of gone out of that class since Kathy died, anyway.

Although we had quite a decent session last week. My heart was in my mouth as I got out of the car in the college car park, but if Alex was there, he was hiding himself very efficiently in the bushes. I felt horribly nervous, going back into the classroom, but again, all was the same. Barbara still had her great big purple veiny calves sticking out from under her polyester skirt. Jane's phone still vibrated noisily in her bag until she turned it off and apologised— this happens every week. The worst thing that happened was my feeling of missing Kathy—it just seemed so weird that she wasn't there. Even weirder than Alex hiding in my house when I was in the bath, somehow.

Anyhow, I got through it. I burbled a lot about knowing when to write dialogue scenes, and when to use a narrative voice; that kind of thing, then we did an exercise, and then the time was up.

Frankly, I'll be glad when I can stop teaching this course . . .

16

Alex

I heard someone come home at about six-thirty this evening. I didn't really feel like seeing anyone; I just wanted to sit in my room and think about Siobhan and what the hell I was going to do next. Siobhan's letter—her invoice, I suppose you'd call it, with the amounts I'd spent on her card neatly totalled—lay on my desk. I had read it over twenty times, trying to take it in, desperately attempting to come up with a solution. How could I turn things around with Siobhan? By getting the money. How could I get the money? By getting a job. But how could I get a job when I felt like this?

I was fretting and rereading the letter when I heard a cry come from the living room: a high-pitched yelp followed by a gasp. I stood up. Were Natalie and Simon having sex in there? No, I had only heard one person come in and this hadn't sounded like a cry of ecstasy.

I ran out of my bedroom and into the living room.

Natalie was sitting on the sofa, leaning forward, her head between her knees. She was panting.

'Natalie?'

She looked up. Her face was awash with sweat, her eyes narrowed as if I was a brilliant light. She said something in French.

That's when I saw the blood—a trickle running down the inside of her leg, creeping down from beneath her short skirt towards her trainers.

'Fuck.'

I swivelled and grabbed the phone, pressing 999. I told the operator I needed an ambulance. They asked me questions: *What's the problem?* My friend's bleeding. *Is it an emergency?* Yes, of course it fucking is. *Calm down, sir.*

They told me the ambulance would be with us soon. I dropped the receiver and went over to Natalie, leaning down and touching her on the shoulder. 'It hurts,' she said. Her voice was like a little girl's.

I grabbed the phone again, punching in the number of a local taxi company. 'I need a taxi, now. To the hospital. Please.'

The woman on the other end was kind, concerned. She promised a cab would be with us within two minutes. I went and sat beside Natalie, putting my arm around her, telling her that it would be okay, that a taxi was on its way. She nodded, sweat dripping from her nose and chin. She looked like she was giving birth or something, and as I thought that, I realised what was happening.

I heard the taxi pull up outside, and ran to the front door, showing the taxi driver that we knew he was there. Next, I ran to the bathroom and grabbed a towel. Then I helped Natalie up off the sofa, not knowing if this was the right thing to do, just knowing that I had to get her to the hospital, all these horror stories about hour-long waits for ambulances floating through my head. I helped her to the taxi and put the towel on the back seat, worrying that the cab driver wouldn't let us in if he thought we were going to get blood on his upholstery. I was trying to think of everything.

The taxi sped us to the hospital. As it turned out of our street I heard the wail of an ambulance behind

155

us. Holding Natalie's hand, I thought about Siobhan, about how proud of me she'd be if she saw me now, helping my friend out. She had spoken to me as if I was a monster . . . a stalker, for fuck's sake. But I was just a boy in love, following a long tradition of people gripped by love, by the madness and passion invoked by that emotion, obsessed—I admit it—but dangerous?

I turned to Natalie, whispered, 'Hang on, hang on, it's going to be okay. Hold on, Siobhan . . .'

She leaned against me. She was warm, and I closed my eyes and imagined that this was a normal taxi ride home, that the girl leaning against me was in love with me, that we were going back to her room where she would undress and wrap herself around me, soothe me with kisses, her body a balm for my wounds.

'We're here,' the taxi driver said, and I was startled from my reverie, remembering where I was, who I was with, what I was doing. The taxi driver and I helped Natalie to the entrance of Accident and Emergency.

I grabbed a nurse and said, 'She's having a miscarriage.' And then she was swept away, down a corridor that stank of medicine and death and blood and life. They would make her better now. Make it all better.

I looked up and realised the cabbie was still standing there.

'Oh.' I reached into my pocket and pulled out all the money I had. £2.37. And a couple of furry bits of chewing gum.

The taxi driver tutted and shook his head. 'Forget it,' he said, and walked away.

I hung around in the waiting room for a long
time, watching the weak and the wounded trail
past, each begging in turn for help, the meek and
the belligerent, the accident-prone and, being
stretchered past, the just plain prone. I was amazed
how many drunks there were milling around,
demanding attention, breathing foul fumes over the
other patients, considering it was only early evening.
I wanted to go home, back to my cave to mope and
think, but I couldn't leave Natalie. I hadn't even
known she was pregnant. Maybe she and Simon
hadn't known ... Suddenly, I realised I hadn't
called him. Shit. The doctors might have called him,
but Natalie hadn't been in a lucid enough condition
to tell them his number, and they probably assumed
I was her boyfriend.

I waited for a Scottish drunk to stop shouting at
his wife on the only visible pay phone (he and I
must have been the only people there without
mobiles) then called Simon. The phone's mouthpiece
stank of stale whisky. It made me want to puke, but
at the same time made me think how nice it would
be to have a drink. God, I could taste it—bottled
oblivion, calling my name.

Simon arrived within fifteen minutes, his face as
pale as a hospital sheet, and he immediately spoke
to the receptionist and disappeared up one of the
corridors.

I waited a while longer, really craving that drink
now, thinking that maybe I'd end up here again
later, another ranting drunk who lost a fight with
his dignity. Then Simon came out and found me.
His eyes were pink and moist, and he put his hand

157

on my shoulder.

'Thank you for getting her here,' he said.

I nodded. 'Was it . . .?'

'A miscarriage. There was some medical term they used but,' he touched his head, 'I'm finding it hard to retain information right now. I was only just starting to get used to the fact she was pregnant. We were going to tell everyone about it this weekend.' He blinked at me. 'They said she was in danger . . . and that it was lucky she got here when she did. So, thank you.'

I thought he was going to hug me, but he just squeezed my shoulder again, his eyes shining.

'Do you want me to hang around for a while?' I asked.

He shook his head. 'No, it's fine. You can get going, if you like.'

'Okay.'

I turned to go, and he said, 'Alex.'

I looked at him.

'Thanks, mate.'

I nodded. 'No problem.'

*　　　*　　　*

I walked home, feeling strange and lightheaded, the adrenaline settling in my system. I wondered if there was some protocol I should be following right now. A card? Flowers? I decided to leave it. Cards and flowers usually got me into trouble.

I reached the flat and watched TV for a while. At about eight, Simon rang.

'How is she?' I asked.

'They're going to keep her in overnight, so I'm going to stay here for a while, until they chuck me

158

out. Look, I called to ask if you could do us a favour. Nat was supposed to be going out with Emily tonight and I don't have her number on my phone. Can you find it for me? It's pinned up on the notice board.'

'Sure.'

I went into the kitchen and located the scrap of paper that showed Emily's number. I took it down, went back into the living room and read out the digits.

'That's great.' He paused. 'Actually, you should give her a call yourself.'

'Who?'

'Who do you think? Emily.'

'Sorry? Why?'

'Because she likes you, brains. Listen, do you want me to send her round?'

'What? Now?'

He made an exasperated sound. 'Of course now.'

'No, no, it's fine. I . . .'

'Alex, I've got to go. I need to call Emily then get back to Nat. If you want to act on the info I've just given you, call her later. I can guarantee she won't say no.' He hung up.

Emily. Emily. I hadn't really thought about her much since meeting her; I had been too consumed by Siobhan. I didn't really know whether I liked Emily or not—I was just so surprised that she liked me. Shocked and flattered and excited and scared. And confused. I stared at the scrap of paper, where her name and number were written in blue biro. I ran the tip of my finger over the numbers. This girl liked me. Fancied me. I should ring her and then we could meet up and go for a drink, maybe go on a second date, do all those things that Siobhan was talking about when I was sitting on her sofa, all

159

those things that lead to love.

But this isn't Siobhan. This isn't the woman I want to be with. Oh Emily, why is your timing so bad?—I'm already in love with somebody else. If I call you now, I'll be betraying the woman I love. It will be like being unfaithful.

But Siobhan doesn't love you, whispered a voice in my head, a voice that sounded very much like Mum's. She thinks you're a stalker. She doesn't want you.

I was so confused. But staring at Emily's number, all I could see was Siobhan's face. Hardly realising I was doing it, I screwed the piece of paper into a ball. I walked into the kitchen and dropped it into the bin, looking up and seeing my reflection in the window, bright against the outside world, glowing like a ghost of myself in the dark.

I'd like to be able to say that the telephone rang at that precise moment—it would appeal to my literary sensibilities—but it didn't. I wandered around, ate a sandwich, drank a can of Simon's beer that had been lurking at the back of the fridge since the summer. I went to the toilet and then watched some more TV. I was feeling numb, and so worn out that I didn't have the energy to worry any more. I knew the anxiety would return tomorrow, or maybe in the middle of the night; I knew the yearning would come back. Maybe I would go to see Siobhan again. Try to persuade her to give me a chance. To try to get it through to her: we are meant to be together. Tell her about love and pain.

And then the telephone rang.

'Hello?'

'Um . . . hi. Is that Alex? This is Emily, Natalie's friend.'

160

'Emily.'

'Yes. Simon just called and told me what happened. Poor, poor Nat.'

'I know.'

Neither of us really knew what to say. Then Emily said, 'Alex . . . um, I was wondering if . . . well . . . God, actually I worry that this is in really bad taste, thinking about myself when my friend's just lost a baby . . . but Simon told me how you rushed Nat to hospital and how grateful he was and it made me start thinking about you and I couldn't resist calling . . .' She was really babbling; she sounded even more nervous than I felt.

She said, 'Would you like to meet up?'

There are times in our life when it seems easier to say no. Refusal is the easy option, even though you want to say yes. Sometimes, you know that agreeing will involve more effort, a risk.

But there are other times when you can't say no. When you can't think of an excuse. And maybe that's because you know there aren't really any excuses, not good ones, anyway.

I don't really know why I said yes when Emily asked me out. Maybe it was something about the way she asked me: she sounded so nervous, so sweet. And maybe, for a second, I forgot all about Siobhan. Whatever, I found myself saying, 'Okay.'

And Emily sounded so happy to hear me say that word that I said it again: 'Okay. Yes. Yes.'

We're meeting tomorrow. I have a date. And, despite everything, I can't help but feel really fucking excited!

Just woke up from a dream and can't get back to sleep. In the dream, I was in bed with Emily, but I knew somebody was watching us. I could feel their presence behind the curtain, even though we were on the second floor. I pulled back the curtain and there was Kathy, floating outside the window like the vampire in *Salem's Lot*. She grinned at me, and then floated through the window, her arms outstretched, waiting to take me in her corpse's embrace . . .

17

Siobhan

Sunday

I need to find myself another tennis partner. I don't want to play with Dennis any more, with his big grunty serves and quotes from the Bible. Not to mention his pursed lips whenever I swear. And his legs make me feel queasy, they're so hairless.

I can't get over what he said to me today. We were only chatting, as we always do in between sets, and I was just telling him about Alex poisoning Biggles, and how he still hadn't paid me my five hundred quid, and that I was really worried that everything going so quiet was a bad sign, that I'd come home one night and there Alex would be, with a carving knife and a roll of duct tape . . . and Dennis blurted out:

'Can't we talk about something else?'

I mean, what is his problem?

'That's not very Christian of you, is it, Dennis?' I said. 'Here am I having a major crisis, with this total nutter stalking me, and you want me to change the subject? Well I'm awfully sorry if I'm boring you.'

I thought that would shut him up, and he did say sorry too, but he sort of muttered it, and then got up and slammed half a dozen supersonic serves past me. Then he stopped and marched back up to me. He looked quite angry, it was weird. His eyebrows went almost white, and his face was brick-red, with a little ticking muscle in his cheek.

I frowned at him. 'What?'

'Siobhan,' he said. 'You have to stop talking about this guy. You had a shock, but that was over a fortnight ago. He's left you alone since then. You've got no evidence that it was him who poisoned your cat. I mean, I'm not sticking up for him or anything, what he did was awful—but you've got to move on. You can't let it mess up your life like this.'

The cheek of him! I couldn't believe it. I grabbed my racquet cover and bag, and headed for the gate, then and there, after we'd only been playing for half an hour. I hate not getting my money's worth on those courts, they aren't cheap, but I had no intention of letting that sanctimonious little prick talk to me like that.

'You men,' I said over my shoulder. 'You're all the bloody same. You make me sick—I thought you were my friend!'

'I am your friend,' he shouted, as I marched back to my car. I ignored him. Loser.

So I wasn't in the greatest of moods after that. Maybe it's my hormones. I'm due on any day now. I tried to ring Jess, and Paula, for a moan, but they were both out, so I left them long messages (which I did feel slightly guilty about. I hate it when people burble for ages on my answer machine, but it's just so tempting to pour your heart out on someone else's).

*   *   *

It was a beautiful sunny autumn day, so I decided to walk down to Angelo's and see if I could get a table outside for lunch, doing my usual trick of pretending to be waiting for a friend who doesn't show up (so much less embarrassing than admitting you're lunching alone). I took a notepad and pen, and thought it would be a good opportunity to eavesdrop and make a few character sketches for the novel. Not to mention eyeing up any cute men who might be out and about; maybe a nice rich divorcee taking his little daughter out for lunch— that's what I need. A new boyfriend, to take my mind off Alex.

Anyway, I got a perfect table, on the edge of the verandah, and sat there waiting for my Greek salad (I'd told the waiter that I'd go ahead and order, because my 'friend' was always late). There were indeed quite a few tasty men around, including said waiter. Not my usual type, really short and losing his hair, but flirtatious enough to cheer me up. I tried to make eye contact with two guys at a nearby table, but they weren't having any of it.

Gay, probably.

So, my salad arrived, and I'd had one forkful of feta when suddenly my already bad day got a whole lot worse: I spotted Phil and a girl, presumably Lynn. Phil-lynn. Sounds like something you have done at the dentist. And it was like having teeth pulled, seeing the two of them together. I clocked them from right down the street, arm in arm, nauseatingly lovey-dovey. She was even walking with her head leaning on his shoulder—I hope she got a stiff neck. I quickly put on my shades, and gave my salad some intense scrutiny, but to my horror they stopped. How dare he bring her here? This is where we used to have lunch together! And with me sitting there like Billy No-Mates. It was too humiliating.

They sat down two tables away from me, and instantly clasped hands with each other across the table as if they'd been parted for months. I noticed that he was growing a ridiculous little beardette thing, like a joke beard, or else something that he'd drawn on with a black felt tip. Prat. I leaned my elbow on the table and hid the side of my face nearest to them in my hand, but it was too late. I saw her look at me, then lean across and say something to him. He jerked his head up and towards me, with a look of such panic in his eyes that I was seriously offended—I mean, for God's sake, is seeing me really so terrifying?

'Siobhan,' he said in my direction, rather croakily, half standing up and then changing his mind and sitting down again. Lynn pressed her lips together in what I assume was intended to be a smile, but it was about as friendly as a tank full of piranhas.

Another couple came and sat at the table between us, but I thought, he's not getting away so easily, so

I stood up instead and went over to them. Might as well brazen it out, I thought.

'Hi!' I said, holding out my hand to Lynn. 'I'm Siobhan.'

'Yes,' she replied. 'I know. We met before, remember, at Phil's office.'

I didn't remember, but whatever. She was eminently forgettable—mousy hair, watery eyes, skinny and weak-looking. Even I, with my not-very-robust sense of self-esteem, thought *I'm much prettier than her.* Then I found myself thinking I could take her out, any day. I must really have PMT.

'So, how are you? Did you have a nice time in Portugal?' I chirped through gritted teeth.

'Lovely thanks,' said Phil.

'Really lovely,' added Lynn. Rub it in, why don't you?

Phil craned around me to look at the place laid opposite mine. 'Are you . . . with anyone?' he asked. He seemed really ill at ease. I was glad that I still had an effect on him; glad that he was jealous I'd found a new boyfriend. I temporarily forgot that in fact I hadn't found a new boyfriend at all.

'Yes—well, he'll be along later. Stuck in traffic— you know how bad the roadworks get around here at weekends. He went to visit his mother last night, you see.'

Phil looked even more terrified. What a complete pansy!

'Actually,' he said, giving the menu in front of him a nanosecond's scrutiny, 'You know what, Lynny?' (Lynny! Puke.) 'I don't think I really fancy any of this. In fact, I've got a bit of a yen for a Chinese.'

He laughed nervously and said to both of us: 'Yen! For a Chinese! Get it?'

166

'The yen is Japanese currency. In China it's the Yuan,' I said, standing over him with my arms folded, and noticing with glee that he had a bit of a bald spot.

'Oh well. Same continent,' he said. 'Ha ha.'

'Ha ha,' I replied.

Lynn was shooting daggers at me by now. She stood up.

'Yeah, I fancy Chinese too—let's walk round the corner to Ho Lin's. Nice to see you again Siobhan.'

They started to move away between the tables.

'Did you get my messages, Phil?' I called after them.

He half turned. 'No. I didn't.' And then they were gone, not even a word of goodbye.

I went and sat down again, with Angelo's horrible wicker chair scratching the backs of my legs, but I'd lost my appetite. My tomatoes looked half-cooked and soggy, and the feta had left an unappetising white juice all over the plate.

It's so odd, how you can be completely intimate with a person, and then they treat you like somebody who once ripped them off in a pub. That man has had his tongue in places that I didn't even know I had, and now he can't even be bothered to say goodbye, let alone return my calls? It's really depressing. I know I don't want to get back together with him or anything, but I can't help but feel jealous of what he obviously has with Lynn. Why can't I find a man who loves me like that? Why didn't Phil love me like that? What's wrong with me? I miss having a boyfriend.

*   *   *

167

I abandoned the rest of my salad, left a tenner on the table, and trudged up the hill back to my empty house. I suddenly felt that even finding Alex there would have been better than coming home to this . . . loneliness.

Loneliness, and a credit card bill for £631.80—my new tennis shoes, plus the money that Alex stole from me. Which he still hasn't paid back, the bastard. There's no way I'm letting him get away with it.

Later . . .

I've been working on the new novel, miraculously. It's the first time in ages I feel that I'm really beginning to get stuck into it. She's not a bad character, this Stevie woman—I'm actually starting to quite like her, whereas at first I actively disliked her. Fear, probably, if I try and analyse it. Fear that she, i.e. my creation, won't be good enough to get me another publishing deal.

Although I'm beginning to feel a tiny bit more optimistic about the prospect of future publication: I've just had an email from Patricia. She sounded a little sniffy, and said she'd been trying to get hold of me for a few weeks (well, she can't have been trying very hard. I get relatively few emails, and would definitely have seen one from her had she, as she claims, sent one before. Why hadn't she phoned?). Anyway, the good news was that *TLA* has, unbelievably, been selling very well in translation in Holland, and the Dutch publishers got in touch with Patricia to ask if I might be interested in coming over for a bit of an event: a reading, and some stock signings. A free trip to Amsterdam might be just what I need to take my mind off all this trauma.

I don't know, though. If I had a man to take with me, it would be different; I'd be there like a shot. Amsterdam is such a romantic city, with all those kindly windows and canals. I can see myself in a— what is the Dutch equivalent of a gondola?—well, in a boat, trailing my fingers seductively through the sunlit sparkly water as a beautiful man recites paragraphs of *TLA* to me . . . yes, I like that. He could be a fan. He's learnt whole pages of *TLA* off by heart, and he's lying there with his head in my lap, reciting them. Mmm, that would be blissful. Then we'd go back to my hotel and—

—I've got sex on the brain at the moment. I was writing a sex scene for Stevie earlier, when Rollo follows her home, lets himself into her house, strips off all his clothes and joins her in the shower. I know showers are rather a cliché, but there is something so damn sexy about being shoved up against a slippery tiled wall, him lifting her with his thrusts as they gasp to try and catch their breath, through the streams of hot water blasting off their bodies.

This is pretty sick, though—and God knows what Dennis Tennis would have to say about it—but when I was writing the scene, I accidentally typed Alex's name, when I meant Rollo. Twice! I suppose it was because I was still subconsciously thinking about Alex outside the bathroom door like that, with me naked inside. But if Alex had been a lover, it could have been extremely erotic.

So anyway, I haven't decided about Amsterdam. I feel so lethargic at the moment that frankly, I'm not sure that I can be bothered. I mean, a couple of signings and a reading to one bored punter whilst—in all probability—tumbleweeds blow through the empty bookshop? It's hardly going to make a difference, is it? Especially as it's the UK where I want to get another deal. I'll think about it for a while. I've emailed Patricia back to say that I'm not sure how my work commitments are going to pan out over the next few months, and provided there's no urgent rush on a decision, I'll let her know in a week or so.

Later still

Feeling down again. Have just been to Sainsbury's, and everywhere I looked there were couples cooing over the angel-hair pasta, or planning their next dinner party, or buying nappies. I haven't even got a boyfriend, let alone a husband or baby. And there's been all this stuff in the press lately about how, if you're not married by the time you're 35, then you only have a 13 per cent chance of ever getting married. And worse, if you haven't had your first baby by the age of 38, you only have a 3 per cent chance of conceiving! That's terrifying. I want a baby. Even though I hate other people's babies . . .

I want to be loved. I don't want to be alone.

There must be something awful the matter with me. Am I the sort of person who gets less appealing the more you get to know her? I mean, for heaven's sake, two weeks ago I had a man who was utterly obsessed by me. How ironic is that—even my stalker has lost interest!

Although that's probably because he's having trouble getting the money together to pay me.

No, I am so not going to feel sorry for him. I'm having trouble getting the money together to pay

170

my bloody credit card bill! Time is running out for Alex Parkinson, and I'm not going to let this drop. He owes me that money, and I want it back.

18

Alex

Thursday (the morning after!)

Emily and I had arranged to meet at Moulin Rouge, a wine bar not far from here. I have no idea why I agreed to go to a wine bar. I spent the whole of yesterday morning trying to work out what to wear, then trying to work out how to iron a crease into a pair of trousers, and finally trying to figure out how to get rid of said crease. After that, I counted my money.

£3.76. It wasn't going to buy the best bottle in the joint.

However, after turning the sofa upside down and sticking my arm inside, I no longer only had £3.76. I had £3.86. And a dead spider. And the oversized ten pence piece I'd found wasn't even legal tender any more. What was Emily going to think? Maybe I shouldn't even bother turning up: it was pretty obvious that when she saw how poverty-stricken and sartorially challenged I was, she would make an excuse and climb out the window in the Ladies.

Thinking about money reminded me of Siobhan's letter. I imagined myself going round to Siobhan's and handing her the cash. She would invite me in and tell me she'd had a change of heart. She didn't

171

care about the money. In fact, she was wearing the lingerie I had bought her and she wondered if I might like to see it on her; take it off her.

I feel so ashamed. I was thinking about Siobhan while I was on my way to see Emily. And I'm starting to wonder now if I should be writing this stuff. What if Emily sees it? Luckily I have this file password protected. I was worried before that maybe Si or Nat would come in and try to read my words. But I need this outlet for my feelings.

So, anyway: yesterday.

I got to the wine bar about ten minutes early. Emily wasn't there, but I didn't want to go in and buy a drink because then I'd have no money by the time she arrived. I hung around outside, smoking a cigarette and drawing snooty looks from the staff inside. I was really hungry. I'd felt so sick with nerves that I hadn't eaten anything all afternoon. And breakfast had consisted of two pieces of toast and marge. I really wasn't in the right state to be going on a date.

I looked at my watch. Emily was five minutes late. Maybe I should go home. I looked up and down the road, suddenly aware of how badly I wanted her to turn up. I didn't want to go home alone. Not again. Perhaps if Emily stood me up I could go round to Siobhan's so she could tell me I was a stalker and get the police to arrest me, throw me in a cell where I wouldn't be made to suffer by women any more. Maybe in prison I would discover the joys of . . .

'Hi! Am I late?'

'No. Well, not really.'

She had arrived in a cloud of Issey Miyake. The first thing I thought was, that's the same perfume Siobhan wears. I had seen the bottle in her bedroom, and the smell had stayed with me. Then I looked at Emily's smile and thoughts of Siobhan disappeared in a puff of Issey Miyake-scented smoke.

'What will you have?' Emily said, once we had gone inside. 'Shall we get a bottle?'

I hoped she couldn't see the panic in my eyes.

'What do you prefer?' she said. 'Red or white?'

'White.'

'Oh. That's a pity, I fancied red.'

Phew. 'Well, let's just get a glass. I'll have the house white.' I had already checked out the price list, and a small glass of house white was only £3.50. I was paying my way.

We sat down and Emily removed her coat. She wore a red sweater that stretched tightly over her breasts. Her large breasts. Actually, I had already noticed that most of Emily was quite large. She was the kind of woman that people describe as voluptuous; kind of like Kate Winslet when she isn't starving herself. I liked it. She looked soft. The only thing I didn't like about her appearance was that she was wearing quite a lot of make-up. I could see flakes of foundation on her cheeks, little blobs of mascara on her eyelashes. But she still looked good. Realising how good she looked made me feel more anxious.

'Are you okay?' she said.

'Yes, I'm fine. Just a bit nervous, I guess.'

She smiled again. 'Me too.'

We both examined the tabletop, embarrassed, but when I looked up she was still smiling. We lifted our glasses and took a sip.

'So how's Natalie? Is she okay?' She looked at me over the top of her glass.

'She's alright, yeah ... I think. She and Simon have gone away for the week. He's taken her to

173

Greece.'

'Oh. That's a good idea. It must have been . . .' She trailed off, shaking her head. Her hair fell over her eyes and she brushed it away. She smiled, as if to say, let's change the subject, and I strained to think of something to say.

'What do you do?' Emily asked before a fascinating subject had sprung to mind. 'I mean, for a job?'

I wondered what Natalie had told her. 'Hasn't Natalie already filled you in about me?'

She shook her head. 'Not really. She told me you used to work for an Internet company.'

'That's right. But I . . . quit. To concentrate on my writing.'

'You're a writer?'

'Well. An aspiring one.'

And a skint one. Who got chucked out of the local creative writing class. I could feel my cheeks burning.

'That's a coincidence.'

'You're a writer too?' I couldn't believe it. I'd just had my heart broken by one writer and now . . .

'No, no. God—I'm not that creative. No, I work for a publisher. I'm an editorial assistant.'

'Sounds cool.'

She smiled and I noticed little dimples on her cheeks. 'Yes. It's a nice job, most of the time. It can be a bit . . .' She screwed up her face. 'I don't know. It's very competitive and there's a lot of bitchiness and backstabbing. I'd rather work somewhere where everyone got on. Where people were nice to each other, y'know?'

I nodded, thinking about my old office. Those bastards. 'I'll drink to that,' I said.

We drank our wine and made small talk: I can't remember exactly what we talked about. But after a little while, Emily said, 'Oh, I feel a bit tipsy already.'

'Really?'

'I'm such a lightweight. It only takes one glass.'

'What would happen if you drank another?' I asked, temporarily forgetting that I only had 26 pence (and an out-of-date coin; I left the dead spider at home) in my pocket.

She raised an eyebrow. 'I'm not sure.'

I immediately felt myself stiffen. I couldn't remember the last time a woman had flirted with me, and the way Emily was looking at me was actually making me feel nervous—but also very excited. I heard Simon's voice in my head: She likes you. It was such a powerful feeling—or, rather, an empowering feeling. To have somebody want you. I was sure I was reading the signals correctly this time.

'Look, Emily,' I said, suddenly feeling the urge to be honest. 'I've got a confession.'

She looked worried. Some of the colour faded from her cheeks; her eyes lost a little of their sparkle.

'I'm skint,' I said. 'I came out tonight with less than four quid. I'm really sorry.'

And although I was expecting her to be appalled, she grinned. 'God, Alex, I thought you were going to say you had a girlfriend. Or that you were gay.'

'Well . . .'

'Of course you're skint. All writers are skint. Don't worry about it—I got paid today. Come on, let's have another.'

So Emily and I sat there and had another glass of wine, and we talked about . . . well, all sorts of stuff. Films. Music. Books. Normal stuff. This, I kept thinking, is exactly what Siobhan was talking about when she gave me that lecture about how relationships

175

are meant to proceed. That night she stuck a serrated knife in my heart and went *riiip*. I looked at Emily's soft, friendly face over the table and realised that this woman would never knife me in the heart. She would never use such cruel words. She didn't think I was a freak or a weirdo or a creep. She liked me.

She really liked me!

And after we'd been talking for a while, she leaned across the table and said, 'So . . . Natalie and Simon are away?' And the next thing I knew, we were walking back to my place.

We didn't hold hands, but as we talked she kept bumping into me, leaning against me and touching my arm. I felt as if my blood temperature had just shot up ten degrees; I felt vertiginous, heady. Everything seemed bright and sharp, as if all my natural senses were heightened: the streetlights dazzled me; I saw a fox dart from an alley into a garden, fur shining, eyes glinting.

When we stepped into my flat it seemed impossibly quiet. We stood in the hallway, breathing loudly.

'Do you want a coffee? Or tea? Or . . . water?'

'No wine?'

'Not unless you can perform miracles.'

She laughed and said, 'Water would be fine.'

She followed me into the kitchen and stood behind me while I rinsed and filled a glass with water. When I turned around she was standing really close. She moved forward, her face tilted upwards. I kissed her, and spilled water down her as my arms went around her.

'Oh, shit, I'm really sorry.'

She shook her head, frowning. 'Look what you've done!'

'I'm so sorry . . .

She smiled, letting me know that her frown was a trick. 'I guess I'm going to have to take this off now.'

I could feel my heart banging against my rib cage.

'Alex,' she said quietly. 'Don't look so scared. You must do this sort of thing all the time.'

'I . . .'

'Come on.'

She took my hand and let me lead her towards my bedroom. I still couldn't believe this was happening. This was going against the stuff Siobhan had talked about. This was still the first date, and here we were, heading towards the bedroom. Maybe, I thought, Siobhan is out of touch. She is a bit older than Emily and me, after all.

In my bedroom, I turned the bedside lamp on and sat on the bed. Emily shimmied out of her skirt, sat down and leaned towards me. We kissed. Her mouth tasted sweet and earthy.

'Let me put some music on,' I said, when we came up for air.

'Good idea. Have you got any Adele?'

'Um . . . No.' Shit, I knew I should have followed the crowd and bought that album. 'I've got Rumer's album though.'

Emily had clearly never heard of her, but she nodded. I found it on iTunes, clicked Play, then headed back towards the bed. Emily lay back on the sheets. 'I want you,' she said, and I gulped.

Emily watched as I unbuttoned my shirt, sucking in my stomach as I reached the lower buttons. At the same time, Emily hoisted her jumper over her head. Her navel was pierced, a pale blue stone winking at me. She was wearing a white bra, her nipples visible through the fabric. The bra seemed too small for her breasts: the flesh appeared to be

177

straining to be set free, and a moment later Emily obliged, reaching behind her to unfasten the garment.

Wearing just my boxer shorts I knelt on the bed and kissed her, moving my mouth from her lips to her neck, then taking a nipple in my mouth. She grabbed the hairs at the nape of my neck. We kissed again, our mouths wet, Emily reaching down to stroke my penis through the fabric of my shorts.

'Help me,' she said, looking down at her knickers.

I pulled them slowly down over her thighs, kissing her wispy strip of pubic hair as I did so, making her laugh. Her flesh was so pale, a few freckles dotted here and there. I could smell her, that sweet, unique smell, and I heard a sudden intake of breath as I stroked the inside of her thighs.

I moved upwards again and kissed her neck, feeling her hands go down to my shorts, pushing them down. All the while, I felt detached, as if I was watching myself do this, as if this wasn't really me. But it was me. I was wriggling out of my underwear when that thought really struck home: this is real.

Suddenly, I felt gripped by nerves. I heard Emily say, 'Have you got any condoms?'

'What?'

'Condoms. Rubber things.' She smiled in the half-light.

'Yes.' I pulled open the drawer of my bedside cabinet and groped through it. I had some Durex that I'd bought from a pub vending machine a few months ago, one night when I thought I might be able to find someone to come home with me. I found them and pulled a condom out, knowing as I did so that something had just gone wrong.

'Oh, shit,' I said.

'What is it? Did it break?'

'No.' I sat there, holding the condom in my hand, looking down at my penis. There was no way a condom was going to go on while it was in that state.

Emily smiled. 'Don't worry.'

'I'm sorry.'

'Don't be silly. And if you say this is the first time this has happened I'll be really offended.'

'But . . .'

She shushed me and leaned in to kiss me again. She opened her eyes. 'You're trembling. Are you cold?'

'No, I'm . . .'

'Come on, let's get under the covers.'

She pulled the quilt up over us. I felt so stupid. What the hell was wrong with me? Why did I feel so nervous? I felt wretched with shame. I wanted to get up, leave the room, ask Emily to go home, so I could go back to my sad, solo existence. I moved to leave the bed but Emily stopped me.

'Alex, it doesn't matter. Stop worrying and just kiss me.'

I did.

'And there are other ways to make me happy, you know.'

Her flesh was so warm and her voice was so soft. Even though my penis still wasn't behaving, I knew I wanted to be here with her: this close to someone, this intimate. I slid under the quilt and trailed kisses over her breasts and belly, down between her legs. I kissed her, then licked her lightly, circling her clitoris with my tongue. I heard her groan, far off in the distance, then I continued to lick her, feeling her thighs press against my ears, hearing the roar of the ocean as she covered them. She tasted salty and sweet. She tasted delicious.

When she came, she bucked so hard she nearly broke my nose.

We lay together in the darkness, the bedside lamp now switched off, Emily stroking my chest as we talked in low murmurs. After a while, I felt myself drifting off, having resigned myself to the fact that my stupid bastard body wasn't going to do what I wanted it to.

I don't know how many hours had passed when I woke up, emerging into a half-asleep state, my muscles fully relaxed. I could feel something stroking my penis—my hard penis.

I could barely see Emily, just feel her, her breasts and thighs brushing against me, her fingers stroking me delicately. Then she pulled herself on top of me. She was quite heavy, but it was a welcome weight, especially when she took hold of me again and guided me into her. For a second, as I stared into the near-darkness, I saw Siobhan sitting astride me, her eyes closed in an expression of bliss. But in the same moment, that vision disappeared, wiped out by a flash of light inside my head, a rush of colours.

'God . . .'

I was dimly aware that I wasn't wearing a condom, but it was too late to stop. The sensation was too sublime, the relief that I wasn't a flaccid failure too great. Emily came forward and kissed me and a moment later I came.

She kissed me again and lay on top of me for a while. Then I heard and half-saw her get out of bed and pad down the hallway to the bathroom.

'We didn't use a condom,' I said when she came back to bed, her body cool against mine.

'It will be okay,' she said.

*   *   *

And now it's the next morning, and Emily's just gone—she's going to be late; hope she doesn't get in trouble. We're going to meet again tonight. She said she'll bring over a bottle of wine, a DVD and a pizza. It's bizarre. It's as if . . . as if I have a girlfriend.

Something happened before Emily left that showed me that she really likes me. The phone rang and Emily answered it because I was in the toilet.

'Who was it?' I asked when I came out.

'I don't know. They hung up as soon as I said hello.' She looked suspicious. 'You don't have another girlfriend, do you?'

'No—of course not.'

She looked at me for a few moments, eventually saying, 'Hmm.'

Then she kissed me goodbye. And when she left I had to suppress the urge to run around the room punching the air. She had slept with me. She wanted to see me again. And, not only that, she had got jealous because she thought another woman had called for me.

I almost felt like calling Siobhan to tell her she didn't need to worry about me pursuing her any more—not now I've found someone who likes me.

19

Siobhan

Thursday

I'd been trying to work up the courage to call Alex all week. Rehearsing in my head what I'd say to make him give me back my money; whether I'd be calm and reasonable, or threaten him, or maybe even shout—although I'm not a good shouter. I feel like a faulty valve on a pressure cooker when I shout—once I start, I can't stop, and that terrible feeling of spiralling out of control always ends in tears. So, no, I dismissed the idea of yelling at him. Calm and reasonable with a hint of a threat would be best, I decided. A little reminder that his four weeks is almost up, and I need my money back. I've had the clothes, including the lingerie, cleaned, and I put them all in a bag—a nice Karen Millen bag with string handles, not a crappy Tesco carrier or anything—ready to hand to him in case he wants them back in exchange for the cash.

I was still dithering about whether to turn up on his doorstep (rape alarm in my hand in case he tried to grab me, of course), figuring that it would be less easy for him to fob me off if I was standing there in person; or whether to just phone. In the end I decided to drive down to his flat, call him from the car to see if he was in, and then ring the bell.

I looked up his address again in the register for the writing class and drove straight there this morning before I changed my mind. I remembered

182

him telling me that he wasn't working at the moment, apart from writing—ha, has he got some disappointment ahead of him—so the morning should have been a good time to catch him. I felt odd at the prospect of seeing him. Almost excited, bizarrely. It has been said that love is the closest emotion to hate, and I like the poetic notion of his love and my hate mingling to form something explosive and . . . God, did I really just say that? Get a hold of yourself, Siobhan. It's clearly been too long since you last had sex.

Anyway, I reached his house, a nasty 1940s semi with porridgy pebbledash and wonky crazy paving up the drive. You wouldn't think a house that small could be divided into flats, but there were two bells, and I knew Alex's was B. Was B ground floor or first floor? Upstairs, presumably. I parked a couple of houses away—not too far, in case I had to make a dash back to the car—and with a clear view of the (scabby) front door.

I dialled his number on my mobile. After two rings it picked up, making me jump. There was a short pause, during which I assumed an answer machine was about to click on, then a woman's voice. Sort of sleepy and smug-sounding. I was so surprised that I terminated the call immediately. But then I thought about it, and decided that she was probably just his flatmate's girlfriend. I'm sure that he told me he lived with a male flatmate that time we talked after Kathy's funeral.

Actually, I was pleased that she'd answered the phone. It gave me the courage to get out of the car and walk towards his front door, knowing that another woman was in the flat. He couldn't possibly try anything with her there—unless I'd stumbled on

183

a Fred and Rosemary West-type scenario, heaven forbid. I made sure that my finger was poised over the button of my rape alarm, and my pepper spray was in my jacket pocket for extra back-up. Despite my trembling hands, I felt brave. Look at me, I thought, confronting my fears, exposing my demons. I want Alex Parkinson to know that I am not a woman to be toyed with like a cat with a mouse. I can give as good as I get!

Just then I heard the front door begin to open— and my much-vaunted courage dissipated like steam from a kettle. Feeling foolish, I hurled myself behind a tree which was conveniently growing out of the pavement, pressing myself close to its tough urban bark. Its girth was just about wide enough to conceal my own.

A youngish, fattish girl came out. She looked flushed and slightly dishevelled, and her clothes were rumpled. Yesterday's clothes, I thought. You go, girl. Alex's flatmate's girlfriend must have stayed over last night. Her mouth was twitching at the corners, and then she broke out into a huge grin, which she tried unsuccessfully to hide by staring down at the crazy paving. I know a freshly shagged woman when I see one. I felt a pang of envy, and idly wondered if Alex's flatmate was in any way fanciable.

She turned and began to walk away, thankfully in the opposite direction to my tree. I was about to emerge from my hiding place, albeit with more qualms now that my potential back-up had left the building, when I heard a sharp knock from the upstairs window of Alex's house. The girl wheeled around, no longer trying to hide the beam on her face, and waved exaggeratedly. I followed her gaze up to the window, which was when I saw—Alex. Not

184

a flatmate at all. Alex!

Gone was the furtive and somehow downcast expression I was used to seeing him with, the one that made him look as if he was afraid of getting sand kicked in his face on the beach; the one that trumpeted 'I have a grudge against the world'. It wasn't even the intense, lustful expression with which he'd stared at me in my living room that time. His face looked so different—open and delighted. He waved back at her, then blew her a series of kisses, which I imagined pressing themselves through the glass and flying over to the plump girl, alighting on her hair and face like tiny white butterflies.

Unbelievable. There was no mistaking the sexual energy, even with twenty feet, a flight of stairs and a replacement double-glazed window between them.

Unbelievable!

I ducked back behind the tree, waited till Alex vanished behind the net curtain and the girl's exhilarated humming had faded into the distance along with the tap of her heels on the pavement, then slunk back to my car and drove home.

*　　*　　*

Four hours later, and I still can't believe what I saw this morning. The more I think about it, the more furious it makes me. I'm so angry that my hands are shaking and I've bitten nearly right through my lip. After everything he put me through! After him hanging around, breaking into my house, following me, professing his undying love for me, stealing my money, poisoning my cat—after all that, he goes out and gets himself a girlfriend?

Maybe he had one all along. Perhaps he's married

185

to her! Maybe he's one of these sick creeps who gets off on scaring women. Maybe he never gave a shit about me, it was all just some weird fantasy. Or worse, research for his crappy novel!

He just seemed so convincing. His eyes were so intense, that time he was in the house and I was naked except for the robe. The way he looked at me—I really believed that he did love me. Nobody has ever looked at me like that before. It was just a pity he's a psycho. And now he's a psycho with a girlfriend! Oh, the irony.

*   *   *

I rang Paula. The conversation went along these lines:

'Hi Sis, it's me.'

'Hi Siobhan, how are you babe?'

'You remember Alex?'

There was an audible groan from the end of the line. 'You're not still on about him, are you?'

What is it with these people? Don't they care about me at all? I can't understand why nobody seems to be able to accept that what Alex put me through has really traumatised me. Maybe I should make a few more appointments to see Dr Bedford. At least he listens to me—even if I have to pay through the nose for the privilege.

'Yes, Paula, I am still "on about" him. He broke into my house, remember? Amongst other things.'

She sighed this time, a downgraded groan. 'Yeah. I know. And I still think you should've gone to the police.'

Then—and not before time!—her voice sharpened into concern. 'What's the matter, what's he done?

He hasn't been back again, has he?'

That was more like it.

'No, thank God. But you know he owes me all this money still?'

'Ye-es.'

'Well, I gave him a month to pay me back, and he hasn't paid me back, so I went round there and—'

'You did WHAT?'

'I took my rape alarm. And the pepper spray.'

'Siobhan Alice McGowan, are you out of your tiny mind? What the hell did you do something as mad as that for?'

'I want my money back.'

She laughed mirthlessly. 'Right. So, that time my flat got burgled and they took my stereo and my holiday cash: by that logic, do you think I shouldn't have informed the police, but instead—had I known the guy's address—gone round there and politely asked for my stuff back? Only what you've done is worse, because this Alex was after you! You could have been in danger!'

Alex was after me. Alex wanted me. 'Well, he isn't after me any more.'

'How do you know? What did he say?'

'I didn't talk to him. He's got a girlfriend.'

'So?'

'So . . .' Suddenly I didn't know what to say.

'So that's a result. I'm made up for you—at least that means you've got him off your case for good.'

'But what about my money?'

She groaned again. 'For heaven's sake, Siobhan, forget the money. For a start, you've got some lovely clothes out of it. You look great in them, and you'd never normally have spent so much on gear. Look at it as if you've treated yourself! I know he's a freak,

187

but if you're not prepared to tell the police, then the only thing you can do is keep quiet, hang on to the nice clothes, and forget about the money.'

'I can't. It's the principle.'

'Then I'm not going to talk to you about it any more. You're behaving completely irrationally. I will say it one more time: you should have told the police. You chose not to. So change your mind and tell them, or get over it.'

I hung up on her. She tried to ring me back immediately, but I unplugged the telephone and went to sit by the window. I stared out into the street, stroking Biggles with the long hard squeezing motion that he likes best, not thinking about anything in particular except the fact that, deep down, I guessed that Paula was probably right. It was too late to go to the police now, so I should just let it drop.

But it wouldn't let me go. I could feel Alex, smell the potent mixture of his aftershave and my own fear, all the time. I wanted to punch out at him, hurt him, for having all that misdirected emotion; for getting it so wrong. How come he was so fucked up with me, and yet now seemed to be having a perfectly normal relationship with somebody else? It didn't make sense. The confusion of it all seemed to be fanning the sparks of my anger at him into something bigger and even more preoccupying.

I was beginning to worry about myself.

20

Alex

Saturday

Emily came over again last night. I spent much of the afternoon fretting that it was all going to go disastrously wrong, that we'd be clumsy with one another; the flame we had kindled snuffed out by post-first-date awkwardness. But I needn't have worried. Emily grabbed and kissed me almost as soon as she'd stepped through the door. Five minutes later we were in bed, and this time I didn't wilt. I was All Man. A rock. Eleven and a half stone of surging testosterone. We made love, and then we made love again.

It was incredible. Every time she smiles I get this weird feeling in my stomach. And she really makes me laugh. She says such silly things, and she's so sweet and naïve. She makes me want to protect her, wrap my arms around her and shield her from the harsh world. She was telling me about her childhood, about this girl who used to bully her at school, and I can tell she still feels hurt by the experience even though it was more than ten years ago. She told me she can't cope with confrontation, or aggression. If anyone's mean to her at work it can leave her feeling upset for days.

Now she's just kissed me goodbye, and I'm a bit delirious. I feel euphoric, a warm liquid feeling flowing through me like honey . . . but the silver lining has a cloud:

189

Siobhan.

While Emily and I were lying in bed, blissed out and post-coital, not caring about the damp patch beneath us (it's so nice to share a damp patch with someone after all this time!) I had a sudden, horrific realisation: Siobhan's letter, asking for repayment, was lying on my desk, face up and in full view of anyone who happened to glance down at the desk. Suddenly, I couldn't concentrate on what Emily was saying. What if she saw the letter, with its matter-of-fact summary of all I'd done? What would I say?

I'd already decided not to tell Emily about Siobhan. Not because I want to keep secrets from her but . . . well, how would I explain it? When I think about how I behaved, how stupid I was, I feel sick and have to try to push the memories away. I haven't forgotten about Siobhan—I can't just turn my feelings off, despite what's happened with Emily. But Siobhan rejected me, and I know I acted like . . . well, all I can say is that I'm not proud of myself. I thought I was in love with Siobhan, but I think it was just because I was so lonely. I was looking for someone to save me, and I really believed that Siobhan was the one. But I was so wrong.

It's as if Emily has cast a brilliant light that makes me see everything clearly, including the shadows. When I'm lying next to Emily and I think about the things I did to try to get close to Siobhan, I feel wretched. Look how simple things are with Emily; how straightforward. This is the way it's supposed to be. And maybe I'm just trying to excuse myself, but it's as if I was ill, and now Emily has made me feel better. It's like I've had an epiphany. And a chance for redemption.

So right now I want to be able to forget the last

few months, erase them as if I'm dragging a file into the trash, start afresh. But how can I do that? I can't forget it ever happened—not until I've paid Siobhan the money I owe her.

Every time I feel a ray of happiness warm me, I think about how I'm going to pay Siobhan back and I feel cold again . . .

After a while, Emily got up to go to the loo, and I shot over to my desk, stepping over the two used condoms, and hid the letter under a big pile of paper. I was just about to get back into bed when I heard a scream.

I rushed out into the hall and collided with a naked Emily, who was running back into my bedroom. She dragged me back into the bedroom, her cheeks pink.

'What is it?' I asked.

'I was coming out of the loo when the front door opened.'

'What?'

'Natalie and Simon are back from their trip.' She laughed. 'Poor Simon didn't know where to look.'

'God,' I said, 'you had me worried. I thought that maybe we had an intruder.'

'Hi Alex,' called Simon from outside the room. 'Hi Emily.'

Giggling stupidly, Emily and I climbed back under the covers. 'I bet he did know where to look,' I said.

'Oh yeah? Where?'

'Right . . . here.'

*   *   *

Later, after Emily had gone, I went into the kitchen where I found Si and Nat making lunch.

Simon raised an eyebrow. 'I don't know, we go

191

away for a few days and look what happens. From monk to lothario. What a transformation.'

I turned to Natalie. She looked well. 'How do you feel?'

She nodded. 'Better. Not one hundred per cent, but . . .'

Simon put his arm round her and they exchanged a look that, just a week or two ago would have made me feel envious, if not ill. But now, it made me feel all . . . God, I feel really embarrassed writing this, but it made feel all glowy.

Now, I understand what it feels like to be part of a couple.

It feels fucking great.

*　　*　　*

This afternoon, I decided it was time to find a job. A decent one. Something to keep me fully stimulated until my writing career takes off. I updated my CV and went out to buy the local paper to see what the employment world had to offer.

There were simply dozens of opportunities—if you want to work in telesales or as a care assistant. What a choice. Wiping arses or speaking to them. Still, I thought, tomorrow's paper might have some fantastic opportunity that will help me earn the cash to settle with Siobhan.

In the meantime, I decided to work on my short stories. I've written a few, mainly about my travelling experiences, and I was starting another one—about an unemployed guy who falls in love with two women—when Simon knocked on the door.

'Phone.'

It must be Emily, I thought, a smile broadening

to a grin as I walked towards the living room. What would we do tonight, I wondered? Maybe we could try out her bed for a change.

I picked up the receiver and said a cheery, 'Hi.'

'Alex?'

A snowball exploded in my stomach.

'Hello, Alex?'

It was a voice I hadn't heard for a long time. I was unable to speak; I felt my throat close up. I just stood there, holding the receiver, feeling as if I was going to throw up. She said my name a couple more times and then, finally, I spoke: 'Mum?'

I heard her inhale. Or maybe she was sucking on a cigarette—'my little crutches', as she used to call them. She said, 'Didn't you get my messages? I've been trying to get hold of you for weeks.'

'I . . .' I was trying to think how long it had been since I'd spoken to her. Three or four years. And here she was, talking to me as if we weren't strangers, her voice filled with that oh-so-familiar tone of indignation.

'I expect your friend didn't bother to tell you.'

'I think he may have . . .'

She interrupted. 'So how are you? How's London?'

'It's fine.'

She grunted. There was a long silence. Awkward was not the word for it.

'Well, anyway,' she said, inhaling again, 'I've got some sad news for you.'

I tensed, wondering what it was. Was she coming to visit me? I shuddered.

'Your Great Uncle Clive passed away.'

Who? 'Oh. I'm sorry.' I wanted to ask why on earth she felt the need to call me and tell me about the death of some distant relative who I'd probably met at some function or other but who I had absolutely no recollection of.

'Yes. It was very sad.'

There was another long, painful pause. I could hear the distant sound of laughter through the walls: Si and Nat in his bedroom. I started to chew my thumbnail, just like I used to until Mum made me smear my nails with a foul-tasting liquid. I could taste it now.

She cleared her throat. 'Anyway, I needed to talk to you because Uncle Clive left you and Annette some money. I've got a cheque for four thousand pounds sitting here with your name on it. So, assuming you want it, and I don't know why you wouldn't, you'll have to come and get it.'

'Pardon?'

'Well, I'm not going to send it to you. I don't know what kind of person you live with. You might not get it.'

'No, I meant, can you say that again? Uncle Clive left me some . . . money?'

She huffed. 'Yes—four thousand. It was in his will—he wanted his money to be divided up between all the family. Not that either of you kids ever bothered to go and see him. Just like you never come to see me.'

There was a pause, during which I visualised a cheque for four grand. Then I imagined myself having to venture into the dragon's cave to get it.

'It's perfectly safe for you to send it here,' I said.

I could picture her shaking her head, sending fag ash flying. 'No. You'll have to come here to get it. Is that really such an awful prospect?'

God yes. 'It's just that I'm really busy . . . '

She puffed. 'Look, if you don't want the cheque

194

I can always send it back to the solicitor.'

I started to speak and she stamped on my words: 'Look, the cheque's here. If you want it, you know where I am.' She hung up.

I walked back to my room, in shock. £4000. With £4000 I could pay back Siobhan, and still have a decent amount left over—enough to help me get by while I looked for a job. Of course I wanted it. I needed it. But having to go back home to get it— that fact turned the sweet news sour.

This was her way of maintaining her power over me. She need never have told me about the money— she could have spent it on herself, on fags and make-up and the live scorpions she enjoys eating for lunch (okay, that's an exaggeration—she only eats dead ones). But then she must have schemed up the idea of making me go there to get it. If only I didn't need the money—it would give me great pleasure to tell her to keep it, or give it to her favourite charity, the National Society for Cruelty to Children. But I do need it. It's the only way to sever my ties with Siobhan and get on with my life. It's been a huge stroke of luck for me to be left this money—it's the kind of thing that makes me wonder if I have some kind of guardian angel. It would be stupid of me to turn it down.

Sunday

I've just spent a whole night and day with Emily and for most of those hours I felt drunk. Now she's gone though, the anxiety is starting to creep back: I've decided I'm going to go home tomorrow, to pick up my cheque.

'That's such good news,' Emily said, when I told her about the money. We were lying in bed, her head resting on my chest, her hair soft and slightly tickly against my skin.

'I know. But I don't want to have to go there to get it.'

'Why?' She rolled onto her front so she could look at me properly. She smelled delicious and warm. 'Why do you hate your mum so much?'

I sighed and closed my eyes. It was so difficult to explain. How could I summarise it? Years of small cruelties, subtle abuses of power and trust. I said, 'Because she hates me.'

Emily looked taken aback. 'How can your mother hate you, Alex?'

'Because I'm too much like my dad, I suppose. Well, according to her, I am. I wouldn't know.'

She waited for me to continue.

'My dad left my mum when she was pregnant with my sister, Annette, who's two years younger than me. So he left her with a two year old and a bump. I don't remember him, of course—all I remember are the things my mother used to say about him.' I rubbed my eyes. Telling this tale made me feel tired. 'When I was growing up, I couldn't understand why she was so awful to me. Then I worked out that she blamed me for what happened. But even if you think about it logically, it doesn't make sense: why didn't she hate Annette? He hadn't left until she fell pregnant with my sister.'

'So she treated the two of you differently?'

'Definitely. It was as if the two of them were allies and I was some kind of enemy within. Maybe it was just because I was a man. Maybe I looked like him. Maybe I reminded her of when he was around. I

196

don't know. But my earliest memory is of her having a go at me because I'd knocked over a glass of blackcurrant; and Annette was there in the background, just a baby, laughing along.'

Emily stroked my chest.

'I suppose there were times when Mum was . . . a normal mother. If I got into trouble at school she would defend me, too vociferously sometimes, marching into school and shouting at the teachers, so they started to dislike me too. And I remember this time when I was really sick. I had this awful fever, hallucinating.' I laughed. 'You won't believe this, but I could see Tetley Tea Bag men climbing up the curtains.'

Emily smiled and said, 'Beats pink elephants.'

'Hmm. So . . . where was I? Um, so she was nice sometimes. There was another time, when I ate too many Creme Eggs and was really sick and she nursed me. But most of the time she was a cow. She wasn't really violent—not often, anyway. She would shake me; she slapped me a couple of times. Oh God, and once she caned me. Shit, I'd almost forgotten about that.' I paused, waiting for the memory to crystallize. 'I remember why she did it. I'd been running around in the playground at school and some kid had tripped me over. When I hit the concrete my trousers ripped—they were ruined. Mum said she was going to teach me a lesson for being so clumsy. She had this length of bamboo, and she made me hold out my hand, palm up. I was trembling; it was really hard to keep my hand outstretched. But she said that every time I snatched my hand away she'd add two strikes.'

Emily took hold of my hand and kissed my fingers.

'The thing is, that kind of cruelty was easier to

deal with than the day-to-day mental stuff. The insults, the piss-taking, the sarcasm. That wore me down, made me feel useless, pathetic. But I didn't know how to deal with her; she knew exactly how to control me. I just used to think, as soon as I'm eighteen I'll be able to leave home and then I'll never have to speak to her again. And I used to imagine myself becoming rich and famous so I could tell the world what a bitch she was.' I laughed mirthlessly. 'I have a lot of sympathy for Eminem.'

'And have you spoken to her since?'

'A few times. I saw her a few years ago. But I've spent most of my adult life trying to forget she exists. Which isn't easy. And now I've got to go back there, to see her. I'm still having to play her fucking power games.'

'Well,' said Emily. 'I think that you should go and show her what a wonderful man you've turned into.'

I kissed her. Having her beside me, I felt a lot braver. And maybe this will sound weird, but she makes me feel more normal. For years I've worried that I'm some kind of freak; that I was never going to fit in and be like other people. I felt like an alien. I suppose I took a perverse pride in it—I liked to think of myself as extraordinary. Now I know I'm not extraordinary—but Emily is.

What will I do if she changes her mind about me, realises that I'm not normal, or if she finds out about the things I've done in the past? She'll leave me— and I don't know if I could bear to lose her. Not now, when I'm just starting to feel better.

21

Siobhan

Monday

I'm looking at what happened this morning as material for the novel. I certainly don't see it as spying . . . although I hadn't intended to follow her like that.

I just went back to Alex's house again, that was all. Seeing as I chickened out of asking for my money last time. And now it's definitely been over a month since we agreed he'd pay me back. My credit card bill needs to be paid. I think I'm going to have to ask him for the interest on the payment too. I'm so not stumping up for it myself.

It was fun at first, actually. I wore shades and a scarf around my head, à la *Thelma and Louise*, even though it was a tad grey and parky to be out in sunglasses. I thought I'd drive over there, phone to see if he was in, then if either of them answered, hang up and wait like I did last time until he came out. I'd changed my mind about ringing the doorbell and confronting him directly in his house. I don't know—seeing him acting so normal with that woman made me think that perhaps he's more schizophrenic than I'd previously thought. (Or maybe it's just me who brings out the psycho in him?)

Anyway, I decided that it would be best to wait till he went out, then follow him and make it seem as if we'd just bumped into one another by chance. I don't want to make him angry.

But I didn't even need to phone—I was just parking the car when the front door opened and he came out, with that girl again. He didn't look quite as happy as he had the other day, though. He had a furrowed brow and a kind of nervous, peaky look about him. Ha. Perhaps his new relationship's on the rocks already, I thought—until they put their arms around each other and walked off down the street like they were practising for a three-legged race.

The girl was dressed in a knee-length grey skirt, boots, and a short cream jacket—smart clothes, but they looked terrible on her. The skirt was too tight, and showed her bulgy ass, and the jacket was clearly undone not out of choice, but because there was no way that it was going to stretch across those great melons of hers. The boots made her knees look fat. She was carrying an overnight bag, and I felt a stab of somewhat irrational fury at the thought that she must have stayed at Alex's over the weekend. Her hair was tied back in one of those big *Johnny Loves Rosie* silk flower hair clips, and she looked as if she'd just got out of the shower, shiny and overripe, like a past-it plum.

She looked innocent, too. I wondered if I should warn her—surely that would be the sisterly thing to do. She'd be horrified if she knew that only a month ago Alex had been stalking me. I disliked her on sight, but that didn't mean I wanted to see her get hurt. Alex was a dangerous man.

Once they were at a safe distance, I got out of the car and followed them. They took a left into Arcadia Road, and I realised that they were probably heading for the tube, so I sped up. I was intrigued. She was dressed for work and he was out of work, so where were they going on a Monday morning? It would be quite a challenge following them into the Underground without being spotted.

When I reached the tube, I lurked in the entrance until they'd safely gone through the turnstiles, into the corridor which led to the escalator. I bought a Zone 1–6 return ticket and dashed after them. By the time I got to the top of the escalator, they'd reached the bottom and were turning left into the southbound platform. I heard the sound of an approaching train, but couldn't tell which tunnel it was coming from, so I galloped down the escalator stairs, two at a time, barging past a group of Japanese tourists and a couple of skateboarders.

I charged onto the platform just as the train pulled in. Glancing frantically around, I saw Alex and the girl preparing to get on, one carriage down. That was OK—I could keep an eye on them from inside the train.

Then disaster struck. The doors opened, and in my dishevelled and panicked state, I propelled myself forwards too quickly into the carriage, feeling myself tilt towards the dirty corrugated iron floor of the train. Trying to regain my balance, I overcompensated and lurched back—right out of the train again! I landed on my ass back on the platform, with the faces of the other passengers gazing out at me in utter amazement. I felt myself begin to blush, but worse was to come—when I looked to my left, I saw that Alex and the girl still hadn't got into their carriage, and had witnessed the whole undignified scene! Thank God I was in disguise.

I was so embarrassed that I once more launched myself into the train, where I finally landed unceremoniously on my hands and knees—on the same dirty floor I'd only just prevented myself falling onto before. Bloody great private detective I'd make! I couldn't have drawn more attention to myself if I'd taken off all my clothes and run up and down the platform screaming, 'Look at my knockers, Alex!'

'Are you OK?' asked a bemused Indian woman, offering me her hand. I took it and struggled to my feet, although her hand felt so soft, and she was so small and light, that I nearly pulled her down with me first. Someone else handed me my shades, which had fallen off.

'Fine, thanks,' I eventually replied, mortified, regarding my ripped jeans and straightening my skewed headscarf. My right knee was bleeding, and my palm grazed—but my pride had taken the severest battering of all. All around me, passengers' lips were twitching and sniggers being suppressed. And then—then!—I looked through the glass window in the doors dividing my carriage from Alex's and saw both him and his fat girlfriend peering through at me, laughing hysterically!

I wanted to cry. How utterly, utterly humiliating. And what if Alex had recognised me? If he'd looked through two minutes earlier, he'd have seen me without the sunglasses.

I'm such a sodding failure.

At the next station, I got off the train—carefully—and walked past Alex's carriage as if heading for the exit. He and the girl were sitting near the door dividing their carriage from the one I'd just left, and they had their heads together. He definitely didn't see me, so I ducked back into the next carriage down, where I positioned myself with a clear view of them through the other door. Morning rush hour was well and truly over, so I had no problem getting the seat I wanted.

Seeing them together made me feel sick, and I realised I was shaking. Partly from the shock of my fall(s), but mostly I think with sheer anger, that I was reduced to following this little geek and his fat girlfriend around London, making a fool of myself in the process, chasing after money that he owed me. I wish I was a bloke. It would be so much simpler—I'd just kick his head in until he paid me back.

They got off at Kings Cross, and Alex didn't once look around as I followed them through the tunnels and up to the main-line station. It was much easier to slip along behind them in the wide crowded concourse—lots of bagel stands and coffee bars to lurk behind. People were looking oddly at me again, but compared to the humiliation in the tube train, it was nothing. Alex bought a ticket, and they walked slowly to a gate which said 'Milton Keynes' on the screen next to it.

Then they kissed; lengthily, disgustingly, pornographically. I wanted to heave. He was running his hands all over her back and blubbery buttocks, pressing himself against her as if they were going to get down and dirty right there on the platform. They both looked upset, as if he was going away somewhere for ages.

What if he was running away, to get out of paying me back? But he had no luggage with him, just a WHSmith bag which looked like it had a book in it. He couldn't be going for long. I decided to march up to him then and there, and demand my cash. I was just working up to it, my breathing shallow and adrenaline pumping through me, egging me on—when a whistle blew and Alex tore himself away from his girlfriend, waving behind him as he jumped into the train.

Damn, I thought. Now what? I felt at a sudden loss, all dressed up for battle and no one to confront. The girl turned away, a troubled expression on her chipmunk face, and walked right past me without seeing me. I felt like a ghost. Instinctively, I turned too and began to follow her. I was curious. Who was she? What was so fucking brilliant about her that Alex could just drop me and fall in love with her instead? I'm much prettier! I bet I'm more interesting and successful, too.

She got back on the Northern Line, and I sat down three seats away from her, hoping she wouldn't recognise me as the woman who'd fallen over. The whole time I toyed with the idea of going up to her and warning her about Alex, but something kept preventing me. I made little deals with myself: if the seat next to her comes free, I'll do it. If she uncrosses her legs, I'll do it. If that man leaves his newspaper behind when he gets off, I'll do it. But none of those things happened, and before I knew it she was getting off at Tottenham Court Road.

I followed her past the umbrella sellers (it was starting to rain) and the fake designer bag stall on the corner, across the road opposite the Dominion Theatre, and then right into a little side street past the YMCA. The streets looked weirdly shimmery through my sunglasses, which were starting to annoy me. I felt as if I was walking around in a fog. Then I realised that there was absolutely no reason I shouldn't take them off, since Whatsherface didn't know me from Adam. I whipped off both the scarf and the glasses, relishing the feel of the drizzle on my forehead and flat hair, watching as the girl walked into a newsagents' across the road. I crossed too, intending to loiter outside, reading the headlines of the papers in a Plexiglass cabinet on the pavement.

Another woman was just coming out, a tall, skinny, Cruella de Vil-type with the boniest knees I've ever seen. She was ripping the cellophane off a packet of Marlboro's, and she and the girl nearly bumped into each other.

'Morning, Emily, so glad you could struggle in for us today,' I heard her say to Alex's girlfriend. Emily—what a typical, mealy-mouthed wimpish sort of name. Emily blushed puce.

'Sorry I'm late, Pernilla,' she said. (Pernilla? That was even worse than Emily.) 'I had a doctor's appointment—I did email you about it on Friday.'

'I don't recall,' said Pernilla coldly, and I felt like cheering. I lifted up the flap of the newspaper cabinet, and pretended to scrutinise the front page of the *Daily Sport*. 'See you back in the office.' Emily nodded, bolting into the newsagents', and Pernilla began to teeter across the road on her spindly legs, sucking on a fag like it was a McDonalds milkshake.

On impulse, I whipped out my shades, put them back on, and hurried after Pernilla. I don't know what possessed me—and in truth, I'm not at all proud of myself, even though Emily had been laughing at me in the train—but I brushed past her, my heart thumping.

'Emily hasn't been to the doctor's,' I said out of the side of my mouth, like the spy I was. 'She's been with her boyfriend. I saw her.' Wincing at my sneakiness, I doubled back on myself, dashed away and hid around the corner before Pernilla could say anything in reply. I saw her turn round, mystified and shocked, but by that time I was already out of sight. She stood puzzled for a second, and then marched angrily up the steps of a tall Georgian building in Bedford Square.

(I changed my mind. So what if I get her into trouble? She laughed at me. They both did.)

Emily hurried out of the newsagents' a minute later, unwrapping a Twix and shoving a finger of it into her mouth as she went into the same building. I let a safe period of time elapse before sauntering past and noting the plaque on the wall by the door: Frazer Shaw Publishers Ltd. She bloody would work for a publisher, wouldn't she! Frazer Shaw are quite decent too—not one of the biggies obviously, but I think they do quite a bit of contemporary fiction. I began to regret talking to Pernilla, just in case she turns out to be an editor, and Patricia sends my novel to her. Perhaps Pat's so impressed with the 20,000 words I emailed her last week that she's already thinking about showing it to editors—it's going so well at the moment. So maybe this was a mistake . . . I know it's unlikely that she'd remember me, but you never know. Wouldn't that just be my luck?

22

Alex

Monday

The day started well. Emily came with me to the station after a wonderful night together, lying in bed, making love, drinking wine and eating Belgian chocolates in frilly paper cases beneath the quilt; it was like being in a little shelter, the two of us protected from all the missiles and bullets the world could throw at us. On the way to King's Cross we saw something really funny: a mad woman hurling herself on and off the tube train, for reasons best known to herself. She was a real Care in the Community case, by the look of her. Emily and I giggled about it all the way to the station, and our shared laughter helped alleviate my nerves about seeing The Dragon—although even as we were laughing I felt uncomfortable about how close I'd come to a breakdown in the past. It could so easily have been me entertaining the commuters on the tube. And now here I was, about to get on another train to visit the root—the living cause—of those problems.

Still, as we crossed London I kept looking at Emily and thinking how lucky I was, and how great it felt to be with someone. I put my arms around her to prevent her from being knocked into by strangers, even though the tube train wasn't all that full. Then, at Euston, I felt a great wave of emotion crash over me as I said goodbye to her.

'I wish you didn't have to go to work,' I said.

She kissed me. 'I wish I didn't too.'

We kissed again. 'But my boss is a real old bat.' Another kiss. 'She sacked the girl who worked there before me for having too many days off sick.'

The train was ready to leave. I lingered on the platform, clinging to Emily until the last possible moment, when the guard blew his whistle. I leaned out of the window, feeling like a character in a wartime movie, heading towards the blood-drenched fields of Europe, not knowing if I would ever return.

'Call me tonight when you get back,' Emily said as the train dragged itself into motion.

'Okay.'

'Good luck.'

As I went into the carriage to find my seat I saw a guy nudge his friend and roll his eyes at me, as if he thought it was a great joke that I had been leaning out of the window saying goodbye to my girlfriend. I felt a flare of anger, but immediately suppressed it. Why should I let someone like that get to me? I smiled sweetly at him.

The train was packed. I found the only empty seat, which was next to an old woman with an enormous bag of crisps on her lap. I think it must have been a magic crisp packet: it lasted her the entire journey, as if she was trying to suck every crisp to death.

The journey passed both quickly and slowly. Quickly because I dreaded getting there; slowly because I wanted to get it over and done with so I could return to London and Emily.

After our eventual arrival at Milton Keynes I went to sit outside a café opposite the station, to fortify myself with a coffee and a cigarette. I was terrified that I would see somebody I knew: an old school friend, for example. I didn't want to have to give a summary of the last ten years of my life.

I took the same bus that I used to take out to the estate where I grew up. I sat at the rear of the bus which was half empty, fortunately, so nobody noticed this sick-looking guy, trembling like a jellyfish on the back seat. When we reached the bus stop nearest to my mum's house (I almost typed 'my house' then: but it isn't my house; it never was) I nearly stayed put. Sod the four grand. I didn't need it. It wasn't worth it. But then I thought of Siobhan, and how I had to get the money to her, and forced myself to disembark.

I stood in front of the house, and before I had a chance to change my mind again, the door opened.

'Hello Alex.' She looked me up and down. 'Are you just going to stand there gawping or do you want to come in?'

She looked older. She'd put on weight since I'd last seen her, and the extra bulk made her look shorter. Her black hair was peppered with grey and her face was heavily lined—not so much crow's feet as raven's feet. Well, it suited her.

I followed her into the kitchen and stood awkwardly by the kitchen table. Some fossil of a DJ was wittering away on the same portable radio Mum used to listen to when I was at school, but apart from that the house felt uncomfortably quiet and still. It hadn't changed at all since I'd lived here—the same floral wallpaper, the same sickly-green paint, cracked tiles, dirty paper lampshades. I had this horrible feeling that I was eighteen again, that the last decade hadn't happened. A week ago I might have welcomed the chance to start my adult life again, see if I could avoid making the same mistakes

209

next time, but now I've got Emily—and I don't want to erase my life.

I couldn't shake the time-warp sensation. I felt my face to see if there were pimples on my chin. Annette would come through the door at any moment, her usual sneer making her look ugly. But it was just Mum now. Alone.

'Annette's already been round to collect her cheque,' she said, reading my mind. She caught my eye for a second then looked away. I could hear her breathing above the song on the radio.

'How is she?'

She shrugged. 'She seems alright. Living in Cheltenham with an electrician. Robert. She brought him down at Christmas. Can't say he electrified me.'

She laughed dryly, and said, 'Do you want a cup of tea?'

'Umm . . . okay, thanks. I just need to use the loo.'

I left her filling the kettle and went upstairs to the toilet. After washing my hands I stuck my head into my old bedroom, expecting it to be empty. It was almost exactly as I'd left it. My old quilt was on the bed; my posters of The Cure and Transvision Vamp were still on the wall. Seeing it sent a shudder through me. Why had she kept it like that? It seemed unnatural, creepy. It was as if I'd died or gone missing; the bedroom of a teenage murder victim whose mother can't bear to alter a thing. I rubbed my forearms, felt goosebumps rising.

Back downstairs, I went into the front room. A widescreen TV dominated the room. There was a photo of Annette at her graduation ceremony on the mantelpiece. And a picture of me when I was, what, five or six? I was holding our tortoise and grinning gummily. I picked up the photo and wished

Emily was with me to see it. She'd have laughed at my fantastic eighties haircut and the prized *Blue Peter* badge pinned to my hand-knitted tanktop. For a moment I felt aggrieved that Mum didn't have any pictures of me as an adult. But then, where would she have got any from? She'd have had to employ a private detective to follow me.

I went back into the kitchen and found a cup of tea waiting for me.

'It seems so strange seeing you here again,' she said. I didn't respond. I didn't know what to say. I got the impression that there was something she wanted to tell me, some speech she had rehearsed while awaiting my arrival. She kept opening her mouth to speak and then closing it again, the words catching in her throat. Instead, she lit a cigarette and, after hesitating, offered me one. I shook my head. Weird—I didn't want her to know I smoked.

We exchanged a few banalities about the weather, and then she said, 'Well, I suppose you want your cheque.'

She opened the cupboard above her head and took down what looked like a biscuit tin. Then she opened it and pulled out the cheque, handing it to me. There was my name, and the words 'Four Thousand Pounds Only'. Not really a figure to get a *Who Wants To Be A Millionaire?* contestant excited, but enough to sort out a couple of my problems. I took out my wallet and slipped it inside.

'Should come in handy, I'd think,' Mum said. 'I'm thinking of spending my share on doing up the kitchen. Maybe I'll have double-glazing fitted. Or I could go on holiday, I suppose.'

She turned and looked out the window and I followed her gaze, out at the dull road with its dull houses and cars and people. The sky was the colour of pale charcoal. No, I tell a lie: it wasn't even that interesting. It was a nothing colour.

I finished my tea and didn't know what to do next. All the muscles in my body were tensed; my shoulders hurt and I was aware that I been picking at the skin around my fingernails.

'So,' said Mum. 'Are you . . . seeing anyone?'

I realised with a shock that there was genuine interest in her voice. Actually, more than that: hope. Maybe she was hoping that, if I had a girlfriend, there might be a grandchild on the horizon—not that I'd ever let a son or daughter of mine near her. I almost lied; nearly told her I was alone—but I couldn't resist the urge to talk about Emily.

I told Mum all about her: basic biographical facts, like the fact that she was 27, worked for a publisher and originally came from Brighton; I told my mum how pretty Emily was, and that 'things were going really well'. I told her that I was in love.

She nodded, and although I had expected this news to make her smile, she was frowning, her eyes downcast. Maybe she knew what I was tempted to say: that Emily was the first woman I had ever loved (and yes, I know, I know, I used to think I loved Siobhan, and the others, before her, but I was never deluded when it came to loving my mother), and that it was her own fault. And in that moment I realised something: I didn't hate her. Not any more. I felt sorry for her, living here on her own, her children driven away, her son a stranger to her. It was a pitiful situation. I also felt a weight lift off me, the pressure of hatred dissolving, evaporating into the grey air.

'I'd better go,' I said. 'I need to get home.'

She nodded.

'Don't you want to stay for tea? I got a nice quiche in. It's from Marks & Spencer.' There were some cakes beside the bread bin. I guessed she'd bought those for the occasion too.

'I have to catch my train,' I said.

'Got to get back to her.'

'Emily.'

'Yes. Maybe you'll bring her up to meet me one day.'

'Maybe.'

All of a sudden I was outside. I walked towards the bus stop, not looking back. I wished everything could have been different. I wish I could have stayed and had a piece of quiche and the cakes she'd got in specially. But things weren't different. And it wasn't my fault.

*   *   *

The train was twenty minutes late and I stood on the platform listening to a furious gaggle of long-suffering commuters calling for the head of the Transport Minister, reminiscing about the good old days before privatisation and the electrification of the railways. When the train finally arrived, we piled on and found our seats. I felt emotionally washed out, itching to get out of this dreary dump and back to London. As the train departed I leaned my head against the window and felt the vibrations work their way into my brain. I couldn't wait to see Emily.

I fell asleep somewhere between Milton Keynes and Watford Junction. When I woke up we were pulling into Euston and I had a cold trail of dribble

213

running from my lip to my chin. I wiped it away, looking around surreptitiously to see if anyone had noticed. I felt rough, my head sore where I'd been leaning against the window, pictures from my mobile dreams still lingering: Mum, staring out the window; Emily, giggling as I kissed her belly and thighs. I wiped my chin again and noticed a girl smirking at me, but I didn't care. Thoughts of Emily had galvanised me; I would see her later, I thought, and we could crawl back into our bed-linen Anderson shelter.

I got off the train, heading for the tube. The cheque felt heavy in my pocket and as I waited for the tube train to arrive I allowed myself a small cash-based fantasy. The other day, Emily and I were talking about my writing ambitions: she read a couple of my short stories and told me they were 'incredible'. Of course, she's biased, but it made me glow to hear that. My dream has always been to write full-time; to be a writer, not a fucking call-centre worker. I'm sick of McJobs.

I remember Mum telling me once that it was stupid to have such unrealistic ambitions. 'You'll just come crashing down,' she said. Well, as far as I'm concerned it's better to try to fly than spend your whole life hugging the ground because you're scared. There was a poster on the wall behind me, a huge pair of star-shaped sunglasses from the cover of a debut novel looming over me. The author of that novel must have been in the same position as me once. It isn't impossible to fly. I decided right there and then that over the next couple of months, while I was looking for work and while the £4000 lasted, I would spend every spare minute writing.

I found a wrinkled copy of the *Camden Journal*

on the tube train and stuffed it into my bag, thinking it might be worth checking the job pages, just in case there was anything worth applying for.

As soon as I got home I called Emily.

'How did it go?' she asked.

'Hmm. Well . . . I'll tell you later. What time can you come round? Or do you want to go out?'

She hesitated. 'Do you mind if we give tonight a miss?'

'I . . .'

'I'm really tired. I need to sleep.'

'Oh.' My throat had dried up. 'Okay.'

She sighed, half-amused, half-exasperated. 'Alex, sweetheart, don't sound so down. It doesn't mean I've gone off you. I'm just really knackered and I wouldn't be good company tonight. I'll see you tomorrow, okay?'

'Okay.'

'And the other reason I need to get an early night is that I can't afford to be late tomorrow.'

'Why not?'

'Well . . . actually, it was really weird. I saw Pernilla outside the office and told her I'd been to the doctor. But then, a few minutes later, she came into the office and said that if I lied to her again I'd be back on slush-pile duty. She said she knew I'd been with my boyfriend. And I'm really bad at lying, Alex—I could feel myself blushing. I asked her how she knew and she said a little bird told her.'

'A little bird?'

'Yeah. And get this—she said, "I'm awfully pleased to hear that you've managed to finally lose your virginity, but if you don't shape up you'll have to make a choice between getting laid and getting paid".'

'What a bitch.'

'You said it.'

'Poor Emily. Pernilla's probably just jealous . . . and I bet she was just guessing, anyway. Maybe you've got the air of a well-satisfied woman.'

She laughed, a low, throaty chuckle that sent a thrill through me. 'The cat who got the cream. Actually, after she'd had a go at me I went into the ladies to check that I didn't have any love bites.'

We said goodbye and I went to my bedroom. I felt restless and bored, an evening without Emily stretching out drearily before me, the taste of the day's events still in my mouth. Sitting on my bed, I pulled the *Camden Journal* out of my bag and started leafing through it. And that's when I saw it: on page 8. There was a picture of a scowling woman, and underneath was the headline 'Woman Urges Police to Investigate Fall Death.'

I caught my breath; my heart started thumping like a techno track. I read on:

When Elaine Meadows returned home from a year-long backpacking trip around Asia last week, she was a woman with a mission. While she was in Asia she had been informed that one of her closest friends had died in a fall from the fire escape of her building.

'I couldn't believe it,' said Ms Meadows, 30. 'I know that Kathy used to climb that fire escape a lot. She was such a careful person, I find it really hard to accept that she just slipped.'

Kathy Noonan, 31, had, according to the official report, been out drinking in a pub near her home in Camden. That night she had attempted to climb onto the roof and had fallen to her death. The police said there was no suspicion of foul play.

But Ms Meadows decided to do some investigating of her own, unable to believe that her old friend had died in 'a stupid accident'.

'I went to the pub, the George V, where Kathy had been drinking that night and spoke to the regulars there. They remembered Kathy well. And one guy told me that he saw Kathy there that evening—with a man.'

Ms Meadows wants to know why the police have never tried to find this man and talk to him. She is calling for the police to reopen the investigation.

'I want them to find and interview this man. If he's reading this, I want him to come forward and explain himself. Only then will I rest. Only then will I be convinced that my friend was not murdered.'

If anyone has any information about Ms Noonan's death, the Camden Journal *has opened a confidential hotline. The number is . . .*

I threw the paper to the floor, trying to catch my breath, trying to calm down. Every hair on my body was standing on end. I thought I was going to be sick, but somehow I held it back.

I knew my hometown was cursed. My own mother is my bad-luck talisman. Just when it looked like everything was going to be fine, this happens.

Fuck. Fucking fucking fuck.

23

Siobhan

Wednesday morning

As I was halfway through chapter 8 of my 'novel', obliviously typing away, the telephone rang, heralding the end of my writing career. It was Patricia. I have put 'novel' in inverted commas, since she does not appear to think it even deserves the description.

And besides, now it really isn't a novel any more. When our interminably awkward call was finally over, I dragged the computer file into the trash folder on my desktop and emptied it, putting the lid back on the cyber-dustbin before I had time to change my mind. Then I took the memory stick containing the back-up, placed it carefully on the kitchen floor, and pounded it with a hammer until it splintered and shattered, destroying all my carefully thought-out words. Broke one of my kitchen tiles too. But who cares.

All that work. All that effort, gone, for nothing. My career is now officially down the toilet. Of course Patricia didn't put it that bluntly. In fact she was complimentary enough about certain parts of it—but basically she didn't think it was good enough yet to bring up at an acquisitions meeting. Which means she thinks I've lost it; I'm finished. There's no other explanation, when my last publishing deal was garnered on a mere six chapters of *TLA*. I'm buggered if I'm going to slave over 130,000 words of a new one and then get it rejected—no thank you very much, life's too short.

Once again, my judgement is totally screwed up. How can I be that deluded? I really thought the book had been going well, that I'd broken the back of it, and that it would be plain sailing from here on in. But no: Patricia didn't like the main character (I didn't tell her it was me—that would just have been too depressing), she said she was too unstable and paranoid to be appealing to readers. She doesn't know what she's talking about—or maybe she's just out to get me? She complained that something should really have happened after seven chapters, but that there was no action. What does she expect? Bloody '*Die Hard*—the Novel'?

And to make matters worse, I've since had an email from her, trying to be placatory, telling me to 'keep going' with it, and that she's sorry if she came over a little bluntly but that she really values my work, and is sure that the new novel will be 'splendid' when it's finished.

Bit bloody late for that now.

*   *   *

Oh God, what have I done?

I've lost it. I've lost my precious book, the one I was so proud of, the one I really thought would establish me as a serious novelist. What have I done? What have I done? What have I done?

Later . . .

Had a bath. Had a long, long cry. My eyes are stinging and my eyelids are so puffy that they look like two little *millefeuilles*. I cried even more than I did at Kathy's funeral, and to be honest this hurts far more. I feel bereaved, bereft. It's done now though. No going back.

And to top it all off, I've got the bloody writing class tonight. I can't hack it. I don't think I'll go.

*   *   *

The phone rang again. As I plodded across the sitting room to answer it, tipping a fed-up Biggles off my lap (thank God for Biggles, I'd be so lonely without him), I was really hoping that it would be a friend, a shoulder to cry on rather than a cat. I didn't have the energy to phone anyone myself, but it would have been nice to know that someone was thinking of me for once. Paula, or Jess or even Phil.

It was, of all people, Alex. He spoke in a hurry, gabbling quietly and nervously: 'Hello Siobhan, it's Alex Parkinson here. I'm really sorry for the delay but I just wanted to let you know that I've left a cheque at college for the money I owe you, I know you'll be teaching the class tonight. I didn't want to post it in case it got lost, and I know that you don't want me near your house again, so anyway I left the cheque at reception. Sorry, again, for everything. Bye.'

And he was gone, before I could even get a word in. I slammed the phone down in a rage. He'd been in love with me, and what—he couldn't even bear to talk to me now? Why are people so fickle and

220

untrustworthy? (Still, at least he didn't ask me for the clothes back. I've got quite attached to them now. And they wouldn't fit his fat girlfriend anyway.)

Oh bugger, that means I'll have to go to class tonight after all. I'd forgotten what a nice voice he's got. It's gentle—weirdly enough, for a freak like him. Wonder what he and Emily get up to in bed? I wonder if he ever thinks about me when he's screwing her—surely he must still find me attractive. I mean, you can't just switch off your feelings for someone, can you?

I still can't fathom what he sees in Emily. She's so—*brockety-looking*, as Mum would say. It fascinates me, and infuriates me. I want to know what she has that I don't. I can't bear it—I'm going to have to go and find out, now that I know where she works.

Midnight

Well, that's the last time I'm ever going to teach a writing class. What a day—both strands of my career now in tatters.

It was the usual sorry excuse for a group; only four of them left now. I got them to do an exercise—writing a story using each letter of the alphabet in turn—and while they were busy with that, I slit open the envelope which the receptionist had given me. The same receptionist who handed me the review that Alex had wrapped in that lovely ribbon; it seems so long ago. I hoped that Alex would at least have written me a nice card or something, perhaps another of his Klimt specials—but no. It was empty apart from a folded cheque for £524.98, the right amount. But as I scrutinised it, I saw something which made me so angry that I could've punched the wall—he hadn't signed it, the stupid, stupid prick. Now I'm going to have to send it back to him, and it'll probably take forever for him to return it . . . I wonder if he did it on purpose? Perhaps smug little Emily thought it would be a good idea, a hilarious way to wind me up. I bet that's it.

When I looked up, the four of them were staring at me and I realised that I may have been growling to myself, just a little bit.

'Right,' I snapped. 'Time's up, who's going to read their story first?'

Brian's hand crept up like a slug climbing a wall. I nodded and he began to stammer his way into the mess of words he'd written, something like: 'A Bayonetted Cavalryman Died Emptying Fireworks', or some such crap, until I couldn't bear it any longer.

'Brian,' I said, more harshly than I should have. 'Stop. That makes no sense. I asked you to write a story, not to fit a random collection of words together. It's writing, not typesetting, for pity's sake. And there's not even any such word as "bayonetted". You're not even using real words!'

'Actually,' said Barbara nervously as Brian scratched and shuffled like a schoolboy. 'I'm sure "bayonetted" is a word. I'm sure I've seen it.' She turned to the other two. 'Haven't you seen it written down? I have.'

That was when, I'm afraid, I really lost it.

I stood up and roared at them. Screamed. Can't remember the exact words because it's all a bit of a haze, but suddenly it all got too much for me: Patricia's rejection, Alex's rejection, Alex playing tricks on me with the cheque. Everything. Even Kathy's absence tore at my heart. We could've been friends, and she's gone. I have nobody.

Their faces! It was almost funny. I slammed my fist down on the desk, wanting to stop but not being able to. I recall shouting something about 'not wasting any more of my time with you losers' (oh, the shame) and 'the only one of you with any talent was Kathy' (not true: Alex and Jane are both tolerably proficient writers, but I was too far gone to mention it). And finally, predictably, with Alex's useless cheque burning a hole in my bag, I snatched up my jacket and stormed out shouting, 'I QUIT.'

Like I said—the end of my career in all ways.

24

Alex

Thursday

Waking up this morning, still drowsy, I heard Emily say, 'I'm going to take these in with me.' I think I must have grunted 'okay' or 'hmm'; I don't remember. I was still trying to cling to sleep, attempting to bury myself in my dreams, away from all the anxiety about Kathy and her crusading chum. Over the last few days that's all I've wanted to do: lose myself. In sleep. In sex. In Emily.

I heard the front door shut and, a little later, woke up.

Since reading the story about Kathy's friend, I've been living in a state called High Anxiety, a place bordered by Trembling Paranoia and Abject Terror. God, I don't want to go to prison. Just thinking about it gives me the shits: gruel for breakfast. The long hours of screaming boredom punctuated only by gang bangs in the shower room, some twenty-stone monster with halitosis having taken a liking to my pretty ass. A monster who'd call me Alexis and make me his bitch.

Or maybe I've seen too many American prison movies. And maybe I have nothing to worry about. After days of flinching every time I heard a police siren, nothing has happened. Nobody knows I was with Kathy that night. Okay, people saw us in the pub, but who's going to link me to Kathy? It's not as if my photo is on police files somewhere; no one's going to leaf through a book of photos and suddenly gasp, having seen my mug shot, 'That's him, officer. And come to think of it, he did look like the kind of guy who'd push a woman to her death.'

And here's a note to the police—if they ever arrest me and force me to tell them the password: I'm innocent! Okay? I didn't push her—she slipped.

Maybe I should relax. Let Kathy's mate run around trying to convince the cops that she was pushed. They've already decided that it was an accident. They won't want to reopen the investigation without hard evidence. I'm safe.

Safe as houses with dodgy fire escapes.

But anyway, having convinced myself that my ass was not at risk for the time being, unless Emily had any kinky plans for it, I peeled myself off the sheets and went to the kitchen to hunt down breakfast. The house was freezing, condensation on the insides of the windows, the tap water icy. I splashed some on my face, which jolted me into life and made me remember Emily's parting words.

What had she meant when she said she was going

to 'take these in with me'? What was she talking about? I went back into the bedroom and looked around. She had been standing by the desk when she said it. I scanned the desk surface: my short stories were gone.

I swore under my breath. She read the stories again last night, proclaimed them works of genius and jumped my bones. 'You're going to be famous,' she said as she straddled me, really seeming to get off on the idea, flushed pink from her throat to her chest. Of course, I liked the idea too, but I really don't think the stories are good enough to show anyone, not yet. They aren't polished. And I don't think I could stand being rejected at the moment, just when I've started to get used to being accepted.

I decided I would have to go to see Emily at lunchtime and get them back—hopefully, nobody would have looked at them yet. Emily told me that most submissions sit on their slush piles for weeks if not months. It would be easy for her to retrieve my work from among the other slush.

Then the phone rang.

I thought it might be Emily, calling me from her desk to say hi. She often does that in the morning, even when we've just parted. So I almost skipped towards the phone.

It wasn't my beloved.

'Alex?' Two slow heartbeats' worth of silence, then, 'It's Siobhan.'

My tongue was paralysed. Her voice was low, less melodic than I remembered. I always thought she had a lovely tone to her voice, even when she was telling me to get lost, but now, with just a few syllables, I could tell that something had changed.

'I suppose you think you're clever, don't you?'

225

When she said 'clever', the word wobbled, her voice trembling with the emotion she was trying to suppress.

I managed to speak: 'What?'

'I suppose you think you're clever. Or funny.'

'What are you talking about. Did you get the cheque?'

'I got it alright. And then I ripped it in two.'

'You—why?'

'Don't try to come across all innocent. I want you to write another cheque, and send it to me—you know my address, don't you? You've probably memorised my postcode.'

NW6 6BG, I almost said, biting my tongue before I could.

'I honestly don't know what you're talking about,' I said. My voice was trembling a little too.

'I'm talking about the fact that you "forgot" to sign it.'

'Oh shit. I . . .'

'Look, just send me a replacement today, alright? Signed, this time. And . . . and . . . stop trying to mess with my head. It isn't fair.'

The phone went clunk.

I held onto the receiver for a few moments, listening to the dialling tone. My hand shook as I replaced it. Maybe it was the aggression that Siobhan had fired at me. Maybe it was the knowledge that I'd made another mistake, causing hassle for myself and upset for Siobhan. Or perhaps it was just the sound of her voice that did it. After all, not long ago I was convinced that I was in love with her. Maybe a fragment of that delusion still lingers, somewhere deep inside me, in the place where my memories dwell. The sooner I could get another cheque to her and get her out of my life the better.

I went into the bedroom, which was warmer than the rest of the flat, and dug out my cheque book which, apart from the cheque I'd written to Siobhan, was completely unused. I wasn't used to writing the things—it wasn't surprising I made a mistake. I couldn't believe she thought I did it deliberately. What kind of person does she think I am?

I left the house and headed for the post office, where I paid a little extra to send the cheque by recorded delivery. I read the cheque over three times to make sure I hadn't written 'five pounds only' or signed my name as Mickey Mouse. I even asked the woman behind the counter to look at it for me and check I'd written the correct date. She gave me a queer look then said, 'It looks fine to me, love.'

Good. I walked out of the post office with my head down and collided with somebody coming in.

'Sorry,' I heard a vaguely familiar voice say, and when I looked up I realised it was Brian, the guy from Siobhan's writing class. I tried to scurry away but he had recognised me and his myopic eyes had lit up as if we were old, great pals.

'Alex,' he said. 'How are you?'

'I'm alright,' I said, wanting to keep my answers as short as possible so I could get away from him. He was wearing a *Star Trek* baseball cap. God, what if somebody cool saw us together? They might think he was my friend. I shuddered.

'You'll never g-guess what happened last night,' he said, pausing to see if I could in fact guess. When he saw that I wasn't going to bother trying, he said, 'Siobhan flipped out. She shouted at us and called us all rubbish writers and st-stormed out. It was really shocking. She had a real g-go at me about this exercise she made us do. Jane and Barbara were quite upset.'

I was interested now. 'So has she quit?'

'L-looks like it. She said she had, anyway. The college has said we can have a part refund for the course fees. It's a real shame—I was really enjoying the course. And I always thought Siobhan was so nice. But I suppose, well, writers are re-re . . .'

I waited a moment for him to spit it out.

'Renowned for being a bit volatile, aren't they?'

I said, 'Hmm,' thinking of Siobhan's phone call earlier.

'Why did you leave the course anyway?' he asked.

'Oh, I've been really busy at work.'

He nodded. 'We ought to have a re-reunion,' he said. 'The old class. Except, of course, poor Kathy couldn't come.'

'Yes, yes,' I said, suddenly wanting to get away again.

'Did you see that thing about her in the paper?'

My bad-news radar started bleeping. 'Yes. I did.'

'Well, I gave that woman a ring.'

I could feel storm clouds gathering overhead. A number 13 bus went past the post office. A gipsy came out and gave me the evil eye.

'You what?'

'Yes. Well, I wanted to offer her my condolences and tell her that I was a friend of Kathy's.'

A friend? In my experience, Brian had barely exchanged a word with Kathy. What the hell was going on? Was he part of some great conspiracy against me?

'She was really interested,' he continued. 'She said she was compiling a dos-dos . . .'

'Dossier?'

'That's right. On people Kathy might have met recently. So I gave her a list of the people in the writing class. She seemed very grateful. She . . .'

'A list? Including me?'

He was starting to look nervous and went into a huge spluttering fit of w-w-ws, and I quickly realised that I was being a moron: I didn't want to give the stupid twat any reason to wonder why I was so upset. I took a deep breath. He took a deep breath too. And after I'd counted to five, I said, 'So is she going to want to talk to us?'

'Yes—I think so. Just to see if Kathy said anything to you about meeting anyone that night—the night she died.'

I nodded, then blurted, 'She certainly didn't say anything to me.'

'Nor me.'

I could picture Kathy in the half-light, clambering on the fire escape. I could hear the noise her body made as it hit the ground. Suddenly, I had to get away. I said, 'Well, maybe I'll call this woman to save her the trouble of trying to contact me.'

Brian nodded and started to say, 'Bye-bye.' Before he could get to the second bye, I had gone, striding into the pedestrian flow on the High Street. What the hell would happen next? Why was Brian such a stupid freak? And then I thought, well, how is this woman going to find me? It's not as if Brian had a list of our phone numbers to give her? So what if she had a list of people who knew Kathy? She probably had a list as long as Park Lane. I needed to chill out.

And I needed to see Emily. After talking to Siobhan and then Brian, both of them torturing me with memories of the past, I needed to talk to the one person who represents my future. My Emily.

I decided to walk to her office, thinking I might just catch her in time for lunch. I could get my short stories back then have a bite to eat and a few soothing kisses. That was what I needed. Balm for my inflamed nerves.

Standing outside Emily's office, I called her on my mobile—which I've finally been able to replace, thanks to Great-Uncle Clive—to surprise her and tell her I was standing outside. An extraordinarily posh woman answered: I almost hung up, thinking I'd dialled the number for Buckingham Palace by mistake. I said, 'Um . . . is Emily there?'

'Emily? She's at lunch.'

I looked at my watch—it was one o'clock, later than I'd thought. 'Oh. Do you know where she's gone.'

'Maybe Aroma Therapy.'

'Eh?' Was Emily so stressed out that she'd signed up for lunchtime aromatherapy classes?

'It's a coffee shop.' She hung up, rather abruptly, I thought. Rude old bag. Maybe that was the famous Pernilla. Emily would often lie with her head on my chest, telling me about the bitchy things her boss had said to her that day, impersonating her fag-addled upper-class voice.

I stopped a passing suit and asked him if he knew where Aroma Therapy was. 'It's a coffee shop,' I said when he looked at me as if I'd just asked him the most abstract question ever.

'Oh. Try around there—there are a few cafes and things.'

I thanked him and walked around the corner. There was a florist and a pub, plus a swanky Italian restaurant. And there, just across the road was

Aroma Therapy, a pretty natty-looking place with a blackboard outside, no doubt advertising various flavours of coffee and the quiche of the day. I hurried across the road and looked through the window, trying to see if Emily was inside.

She was—sitting at a table in the far corner. She was sitting with another woman, who had her back to me. Emily seemed engrossed in conversation—it was nice watching her without her knowing I was there. She's my girlfriend, I thought, rather soppily. I was just about to go inside when the other woman turned her head to the side and I realised, with a thunderbolt of horror, who she was.

It was Siobhan.

25

Siobhan

Thursday

I wonder if I should go back to Dr Bedford. Or maybe just back to bed. No career, no boyfriend, crap friends, useless and unsupportive family. I'd almost forgotten what it feels like to be so depressed—the sleeplessness, eye-bags and pallor; the dark misery every minute of the day, so thick I feel like slicing it with a knife. Or slicing myself, after what happened today.

I'd got the tube into town, telling myself it was for a change of scene, a need to get out the house after last night's histrionics. I always feel so drained after a big emotional outburst like that. And to be honest

I'm fairly mortified at what I did—in class, I mean; although I'll get over it. It's the loss of the novel which still feels like bereavement.

Anyway, even though I kidded myself I was just going for a walk around Bloomsbury and a spot of lunch in a café, I knew where I would end up: lurking around outside Emily's office. Call it character research for a future novel—if I ever write another one—but I was still really curious to know what she's like, what he sees in her. She draws me like a car crash.

I followed my instincts and got there early. She's definitely the type that would have an early lunch break—she probably claims she gets hypoglycaemic if she goes without food for more than two hours—and I was right. At 12.33, she and another woman (not Pernilla, thankfully. Although Pernilla wouldn't have recognised me this time since I'd decided to come out without a disguise) came down the steps.

It had been raining earlier, and Emily was carrying a large furled umbrella, which she dragged along the iron railings as she walked past them, like a kid would. Clunk-a clunk-a clunk-a. She is like a little kid: awkward and clumsy. And stupid. I followed them. They were chatting and laughing and clearly knew each other well. They went into a cafe round the corner and sat down at a small table at the back, so I went in after them. To my irritation, a sweaty businessman and a harassed-looking woman beat me to the table right next to them, and so I had to sit at the next one along. If I strained my ears, I could just about hear Emily and friend's conversation—snippets of it, anyway.

Emily's friend was a bit of a wet weekend too. Mousy lank hair, sloping shoulders, no lipstick and cheap shoes, the sort that people used to call 'court shoes' for some reason (probably because the fashion police would have you up in court for wearing them). She was wearing a wedding ring, and I thought, blimey, who'd marry her? I tried to imagine her in a wedding dress, still with the greasy hair, unmade-up face and court shoes. She probably thought she adhered to the 'natural' look.

They appeared to be gossiping about work—the friend, who had her back to the door, kept half-turning as if she was worrying about being overheard, and I heard Pernilla's name mentioned a few times. On at least one occasion it was followed by a gale of guilty giggling.

How childish, I thought contemptuously. Then the friend said, 'How's Alex?'

At that moment of all moments, the waitress chose to come and take my order. I glared at her and snapped out my request for coffee and a bagel, then went back to trying to eavesdrop.

Emily said something I didn't catch, and then I heard: 'It was awful. He was really obsessed with her.' My heart jumped into my throat the way it does when somebody's talking about you without knowing you can hear them. I noticed the tabletop had a sticky mark on it, and I spat surreptitiously on my folded paper napkin and tried to rub it off, all the time listening avidly. My heart was beating too fast and I was holding my breath to see what she'd say next.

I couldn't believe it. Quite audibly, and looking towards me as she spoke, she said, 'He calls her "the old dragon", and she certainly sounds like one. She's made his life a misery.'

The friend tutted sympathetically. Emily paused

233

as the waitress placed a large sandwich in front of her, and a latte in front of the friend, before continuing. 'But I think he's finally getting over it now. I tell you, I feel like going up there and telling her what I think of her . . .'

I went hot and cold with outrage. The people at the next table started up a loud conversation, drowning out Emily's next words, but I did hear her mention something about a cheque, and then she said '. . . on the train . . .' and then I knew that it was true: Alex had told Emily everything. He'd definitely recognised me that day I fell in and out of the tube train. They'd probably lain in bed together laughing about it. How they must have roared to think that Alex had actually had a crush—on an old, unsuccessful harridan like me? Well, ha bloody ha. She won't be laughing when I've finished with her. If she wants a fight, she'll get one.

All my self-pity suddenly disappeared at that point. I stopped wanting to slice myself—I felt like slicing that horrible little tart instead. I mean, to actually catch her in the act of slagging me off! It was astonishing, the complacency with which she put me down. She knows nothing about me! How dare she? She's clearly found out that her precious boyfriend is in love with me, and she can't handle the jealousy. Well, she might have every right to be jealous, but I'm not going to stand for anyone bad-mouthing me around the place.

My coffee and bagel arrived, but I couldn't eat. The coffee was good though, hot and strong, and it helped calm me down. Sudden tears sprang into my eyes—must have been an overspill from yesterday's traumas, but I felt desolate. Furious, used, unloved. Vengeful, if the truth be told. I was about to finish my coffee and slink off home again, when two things happened which changed my mind.

First, the couple next to me looked at their watches, drained the froth on their cappuccinos and left, the man jabbering into a mobile phone and the woman putting on her jacket as she scurried off behind him. This seemed to remind Emily's friend of something, because she too looked at her watch. I heard her apologetic tone, although not the actual words, and then she too gathered up her things and walked out, leaving three pound coins on the table.

As soon as she was alone, Emily began to stuff the sandwich into her mouth, trailing bits of watercress and tomato. There was nobody between her and me. I hesitated. Then I leaned across.

'Excuse me? It's Emily, isn't it?' Emily smiled at me in a puzzled sort of way, raising her eyebrows. She had a big piece of cress on her front teeth. It was revolting. 'Yes. I'm sorry . . .?'

You will be, I thought. You will be. I beamed falsely at her. 'Don't worry—I can't remember where we met either. I'm very good at names, but not very good at places.' How we laughed. 'It's bugging me now,' I said, frowning. 'You weren't at Vincent Shaw's party, were you?'

She shook her head. 'Do you go to Cannons gym?' Another shake, making her cheeks wobble like a baby on a bus going over a cattle grid.

'Mind if I join you?' I nodded towards her friend's vacated seat, and Emily spread her palm towards it in invitation, smiling with her green teeth. I moved my coat and coffee, and sat down opposite her.

'You look familiar to me, too,' she said, her mouth full of sandwich.

Of course I do, you dozy cow, I thought. You've

235

probably seen my photograph in the back of Alex's copy of my book. This led me into a small dilemma—should I tell her my real name and freak her out now, when she realises who she's talking to; or should I soften her up a bit first? I decided on the latter.

'What do you do?' I asked, my head on one side in chirpy interrogation mode. Her umbrella lolled under the table between us, so I wiped my feet on it a few times. I felt quite pleased with myself for being such a good actress, when actually all I wanted was to pick up the umbrella and stab her in the throat with the spike on the end.

'I work in publishing,' she said. 'Round the corner. Nothing grand—I'm an editorial assistant.'

I slapped my hand to my forehead. 'That must be it!' I cried. 'I'm an author. We've probably met at the Book Fair or a party or something.'

Emily looked doubtful. 'I don't go to many publishing parties,' she said. 'Who's your publisher?'

'It was Penguin, but I'm between publishers at the moment.' I thought it would be better not to pretend I was with any particular publisher currently.

'What's your name?'

'Um—I write under the name Jessica Thomas,' I said, naming my mum's elderly next-door neighbour as the first person who came into my head. 'But I only had a two-book deal which expired a couple of years ago. My agent's about to auction my third.'

Emily's eyes widened. 'How fantastic. I've heard of you, you know, but I'm afraid I haven't read either of your books. You got brilliant reviews for the last one, didn't you?'

Silly, silly tart. I inclined my head bashfully. 'Well, I suppose they were pretty good, yes.'

She gushed on. 'Oh, I do admire writers. I'd love to be one myself but I can't even write a shopping list! I'd like to be an editor one day, though. I like working on other people's stuff. . . . My boyfriend's a writer, too, actually.'

'Oh?' I said, gritting my teeth. 'Published, is he?'

'Not yet. But I've just shown his short stories to my boss. I know she's going to love them—they're fantastic. He's really talented. It would be so brilliant if he got a publishing deal.'

My blood ran cold. This was a new and horrible prospect I hadn't even contemplated before—Alex, getting a deal when I had none! It was unthinkable. It was becoming harder to disguise my anger and contempt for the pair of them, especially when I thought again of what I'd overheard Emily saying about me just minutes earlier. I drained the lukewarm dregs of coffee and stood up.

'Well, must dash. I've got a meeting with my film agent—apparently Paramount are going to option my first novel. Nice to see you again, Emily. By the way, you've got spinach or something in your teeth. Bye!'

I walked unsteadily up to the cash register, paid for my coffee and bagel, and hurried out of the door, resisting the urge to flatten myself, panting, against the damp brick wall outside. I felt sick and upset, and at that moment I hated Alex and Emily with a vehemence that obliterated every other thought in my spinning, aching head.

26

Alex

Thursday (continued)

Siobhan. Siobhan and Emily. Together.

I closed my eyes for a second, praying that it was an hallucination. But when I opened them, the two women were still there. Talking to each other. Terror made me go cold; I felt a black dog snapping at my heart. This could be it: the end of Emily and me; the death of everything we had together. Siobhan could shatter our world with a well-chosen word. I peered through the window, half-hidden behind the window menu, one eye closed, as if that would make me less visible, wondering what they were talking about. Emily looked a bit confused. Not upset or angry, just bewildered. Then she smiled, looked happier (and even then, feeling that stressed, that scared, I noticed how lovely Emily is with a smile on her face).

God, I wished I could hear them; I would give anything to be able to turn myself into a fly so I could go buzzing in there and spy on them. Or to make myself invisible—stand beside them and hear exactly what they were saying. Was Siobhan telling her about the clothes I bought her? The time I—and it makes me sick typing this—hid in her wardrobe? She might even show her the card I wrote her. It's bad enough for any man when his current girlfriend meets the previous object of his desires. It makes it a little bit worse when the current girlfriend doesn't

238

know that her boyfriend was formerly a stalker. Because that's exactly the 'well-chosen' word Siobhan will use to describe me.

I had a sudden impulse to rush into the cafe and shout, 'Don't listen to her. It's all lies.' But then I pictured Emily turning to me, brow furrowed, saying, 'What's all lies?' Because surely—common sense, arriving late as usual, told me—Siobhan doesn't know who Emily is? How could she know? It's not as if she's been spying on me, is it? And then it hit me—the reason for this universe-crunching event: Emily works for a publisher; Siobhan is a writer. Emily's company must be publishing Siobhan's new book. It had to be a coincidence—nothing more.

But then I had another spasm of panic, another wave of paranoid thoughts making me reel: what if Siobhan finds out that Emily and I are together? Emily might mention that her boyfriend is a writer too; she might even say my name. I expect Emily talks about me at every possible opportunity. And if Siobhan discovers that this sweet, harmless girl is going out with a man she thinks of as a stalker, surely she'll tell her about my past, try to warn her off.

I was paralysed by all those ifs, not knowing what to do. And while I was paralysed, I realised that Siobhan was standing up and heading my way.

I rushed around the corner of the café and ducked down an alleyway. This was where the Aroma Therapy dustbins were kept. Hell, I was going to need therapy after this. I heard something move beside me and jumped, clutching my chest. A rotund moggy blinked at me then returned to the remnants of the tuna baguette it had dragged out of the dustbin.

I figured Siobhan must have gone by now, so I

239

poked my head out of the alleyway, startling an old woman. I considered going in to the cafe to see Emily, but I knew how I must look: wide eyed and flustered, smelling of sweat on a frigid London afternoon. I didn't want to arouse any suspicion in her. I really wanted to go home. I really, really wanted a cigarette. On the way back to my flat I stopped off and bought a packet of Marlboro's—full strength. I smoked three of them before I got home.

Simon was there—he'd taken the afternoon off work—and he was playing loud music that echoed the pounding inside my head. He gave me a quizzical look. 'Are you alright, mate?'

I nodded. 'Yeah, yeah. Fine.'

'You look like you've just witnessed a car crash or something.'

I took a deep breath. 'Could you turn the music down a bit? I've got a really bad headache.'

'Sure. No problem.'

'I'm going to go and lie down.'

I went into my room and lit up another cigarette. Now I would have to wait. It was all I could do.

Later . . .

By the time seven o'clock crawled around, I was working on my last remaining fingernail. Emily had told me she'd stop by on her way home. I was sitting here at the computer, playing Solitaire, when the doorbell rang. I heard Simon go to the door, and then there was a light knock on my bedroom door. As I opened it, I took a long, deep breath and muttered a two-word prayer.

She was smiling.

That meant Siobhan hadn't told her she was going out with a psycho. I'd been terrified that the only reason for this visit was so Emily could *a*) shout at me and tell me I was a bastard and a loser and that she never wanted to see me again, and *b*) collect the pair of knickers she left here this morning. She wouldn't want to leave them in the hands of a panty-sniffing freak like me, would she? (Actually, Siobhan knows I'm more likely to buy underwear than sniff it, but who knows how she might embellish the story?) But Emily was smiling, and that meant that Siobhan hadn't told her anything. Thank you, God.

Of course, that didn't mean I was in the clear completely. What if Siobhan and Emily had arranged to meet up again? What if they got really pally and Emily invited her to come out with us? Just thinking about it gave me goose bumps. So I knew that any reprieve might only be temporary.

'Hi, sweetheart,' Emily said, bestowing a firm kiss upon my lips. 'How was your day?'

'Oh . . . okay. Did some writing. Went for a walk. Nothing exciting.'

'Did you call me earlier?' She sat down on the bed and kicked off her shoes, wriggling her toes inside her tights.

'I . . . yes, I did. I wanted to see if you wanted to meet for lunch, but you'd already gone.'

'Oh.' She leaned over and kissed me again. 'I'm sorry. I didn't know.'

I shrugged. 'It's okay.' I gave her my most innocent smile. 'So, did you have a nice lunch?'

'Hmm. Actually, I was talking about you with someone.'

My blood went chilly. 'What? Who?'

She hesitated. 'I hope you don't mind me telling

people about you. I was just telling Sara from work about you and your mum.'

My sigh of relief must have been audible.

'You don't mind, do you? You had this really strange look on your face just then.'

'Did I? I was . . . trying not to fart.'

It was Emily's turn to pull a face.

'Of course I don't mind. As Oscar Wilde said, there's only one thing worse than being talked about, and that's not being talked about.'

'Ooh, I love it when you talk literary to me. Speaking of which, I took your stories in to show Pernilla.'

Shit—I'd forgotten all about that. But after meeting up with that moron Brian and finding he'd set Kathy's bloodhound of a friend on my trail and then seeing Emily with Siobhan, the worry about an editor seeing my stories before they're ready seemed pretty trivial. I said, 'I was going to talk to you about that.'

Emily nodded enthusiastically. 'She said she'd try to read them this weekend. I kept telling her how brilliant they are, and she said she'd read them if it was the only way to get me to shut up.'

So it sounded like it was too late to get them back. Oh well. Like I just said, it's the least of my worries. I'm just thankful that none of the stories are about people falling off fire escapes, or stalkers. All my stories are set further back in my past: my childhood and my schooldays. This journal is my only piece of contemporary autobiography, apart from a couple of stories about a guy who falls in love with the tutor at his writing class which I haven't let Emily see.

'Wouldn't it be great if she liked them?' Emily said. 'You might be a real, published writer. Imagine it!'

I did, and smiled.

'I bumped into a writer at lunchtime, actually.'

My blood temperature plummeted again. 'What was her name?'

She gave me a look. 'Her? Why did you say "her"?'

Well done, Alex. 'I don't know. I just assumed.' What a brilliant excuse. That'll really fool her. I wanted to punch myself.

But Emily didn't seem that bothered. 'It was weird, actually. She said she knew me from somewhere. Then we had this odd conversation which ended with her telling me I had something on my teeth. I didn't really like her, to be honest. I got this bad vibe off her, like there was something wrong with her. Attractive, well-dressed—but a bit strange.'

'Did she tell you her name?'

'Well, yes, she did. But when I got back to the office I looked her up on Amazon and couldn't find her. So I can't have remembered her name correctly.'

'What was it?'

'I told you, I didn't remember it properly. But I thought it was Jessica Thomas.'

Nothing like Siobhan McGowan, then. But why had Siobhan—and it had definitely been Siobhan; I'm sure I hadn't hallucinated the whole thing— given Emily a fake name?

There's something very odd going on. And whatever it is, it certainly isn't good news for me. I'm sighing as I type this: sighing long and hard. Fuck, if I could turn the clock back, I would never have signed up for that writing class.

Tuesday

I haven't had a chance to write here since Thursday because I've been with Emily most of the time; and when I haven't been with her all I've wanted to do is sleep. This whole thing is sucking away my energy, wearing me down and leeching me dry. Because things have got worse. I don't know how much more my overworked heart can take.

On Friday, a day I spent working on my new short story and sleeping, Emily called me at six and told me she wanted to go to the pub. 'I need a drink,' she said.

'Why? Have you had a bad day?'

She paused. 'Do you think I'm fat?'

'What?' I was taken aback.

'Do you think I'm fat?'

'Of course I don't.'

I haven't had much experience of this kind of thing, but I've read in numerous men's mags that you should never ever tell a woman she's fat. Even voluptuous is pushing it. Apparently, you can't even say things like, 'I like women to be a bit curvy', without triggering an outbreak of tears, gym membership and ultimately anorexia and death by starvation. So I said, 'You're not fat at all. Why on earth are you asking me that?'

She sniffed and said, 'I'll tell you later.'

I grabbed my coat and headed out the door, waving goodbye to Si and Nat. It was Arctic outside, a chill wind blowing nobody any good. The streets were quiet, sensible people huddled inside with the central heating turned up full. I thought about what Emily had said on the phone and hoped we weren't going to have a long conversation about her weight. I would rather be running my hands over her flesh than talking about it. The truth is, I guess Emily is a little bit overweight, certainly compared to the whippet-women who populate the magazines she reads. I know I've commented on it here before. And the truth is, I really do like her body. Her heavy breasts, her soft thighs. Yum. But I knew I wouldn't be able to use the words heavy or soft if she was having a body-image crisis.

I got to the pub and went inside, enjoying the smell of many kinds of beer and the warmth from the open fire as I searched for my girlfriend. There she was, sitting on her own in the corner. She had a half-full glass and a bottle of tonic in front of her. I gestured that I'd seen her and bought myself a pint of Guinness. As I waited at the bar, practically licking my lips in anticipation, I touched my own belly. The word 'six-pack' didn't spring to mind.

'Hi,' I said, kissing her as I sat down. I nodded at her glass. 'Tonic water? I thought you said you wanted a drink.'

'There's gin in it,' she said grimly. 'Though I shouldn't be drinking alcohol at all.'

I acted the innocent. 'Why not?'

'Alcohol is one of the most fattening things there is.'

'Yes, I know that. So why shouldn't you be drinking it?'

She didn't smile. Instead, she reached into her bag and pulled out a couple of magazines. One was called *Your Diet*, with a picture of a smiling housewife and a pineapple on the cover. The other was called *Flesh*, which, from the picture of a half-naked woman with the largest breasts and the biggest chins I'd ever seen and the tag-line ('For men who know that

245

big is beautiful!') was clearly a porn mag for those who appreciate the larger woman.

'Where did you get these?' I asked.

'They were sent to me.'

'What?'

'Somebody sent them to me at work. They were waiting in my in-tray, in a brown envelope with my name typed on the front. I thought it was just going to be an unsolicited submission from an author. Some of them have my name because sometimes Pernilla gets me to pp the rejection letters. So my in-tray is usually overflowing with thick A4 envelopes. I couldn't believe it when I opened it and found these inside.'

I picked up *Flesh* and leafed through it. The women inside were enormous, rolls of flab covering the part of the anatomy that most blokes buy porn mags to look at. It was mind-boggling really, thinking that some men must find this stuff a turn-on. Still, it's less harmful than a lot of the shit out there.

It wasn't harmless as far as Emily was concerned, though. I turned to her and saw that her eyes had filled with tears. 'Somebody's trying to send me a message—tell me I'm fat. That I need to go on a diet—or I'll end up like one of these disgusting pigs.'

I couldn't stop staring at the magazine. Eventually, Emily snatched it away and stuffed both the magazines back into her bag.

'Was there a note with it?' I asked.

'No, nothing. I guess the magazines delivered the message well enough on their own.'

Suddenly, I felt angry. I didn't know who had sent these stupid mags to my Emily, but I knew that I wanted to hurt them, to get back at them for the pain I could see on Emily's face.

'Who the hell would do this?' I said.

'I don't know.'

'Somebody in your office? Have you got any enemies there?'

She looked at me, mouth open. 'What do you mean, enemies? Why would I have enemies at work?'

I didn't reply, just thought about my own former workplace, and the porn sites to which I had subscribed my old boss. I felt sick.

'Pernilla said the magazines were probably sent in by an aggrieved author—someone we'd turned down. But maybe people do hate me at work,' Emily said, staring into the distance. 'Maybe they all got together and sent me these, hoping to drive me out. Get rid of the unsightly fat girl.' Her lower lip was starting to tremble.

I put my arm around her. 'Emily, you're not fat. And of course they don't hate you at work.'

'I am fat.'

'You're not.'

'I am.'

'No, you're not. You're beautiful.' I could feel tears welling up in my own eyes now, caused by the emotions that were building up in me. 'So beautiful. I love you.'

She looked at me. 'You're not just saying that?'

'No, of course not. I love you and I love your body. I really love your body.'

She smiled.

'Why don't we go back to your flat and I'll show you exactly how much I love it.'

This time she giggled, although the laugh and the subsequent joke did sound a little forced: 'You're just turned on from looking at the women in

247

that magazine.'

'Shit. You caught me out. Can we take it with us?'

We drank up and left the pub, splashing out on a taxi. Back at Emily's, we made love: intense, wordless sex that made us both sweat despite the chill in the room. We said goodnight and after a little while I turned over to sleep. A few minutes later, I realised that she was crying.

I turned around, pressing up against her back. 'Emily,' I whispered, 'what is it? What's wrong?'

She didn't reply. I held her until she fell asleep.

*   *   *

The weekend was fine—we didn't mention the magazines at all; Emily dumped them in the dustbin outside. Then, on Monday morning, someone banged on the front door. I had just woken up and was lying in bed with a book that I was only half reading, wondering if I might hear something from Pernilla about my stories. I sat up, images of a wild-eyed Siobhan or a troop of armed police at my door. I'm not sure which would be worse. There was another bang at the door and I forced myself to get up, commonsense telling me it was probably only the postman.

Commonsense was right. The postie handed me a plump brown Jiffy bag and a couple of pieces of junk mail. I closed the door and chucked the envelopes onto the side table, then inspected the Jiffy bag. It was addressed to Emily, c/o me. How odd. Why would somebody send something to Emily at this address? Then I realised—she had probably ordered something on the Internet and used this as her postal address, knowing that I'm usually here in

248

the mornings. Maybe, I speculated, she isn't allowed to receive personal mail at work.

It didn't even cross my mind that this could somehow be connected to the magazines she'd received at work. As Pernilla had said to Emily, that was probably just a malicious piece of revenge mail from an author who'd seen Emily's signature on a rejection letter. I took the package into my room, dropped it on the desk and went back to bed.

Emily came round that evening at seven. I greeted her at the door with a kiss which made her smile and press herself against me. A minute later, we were in bed, and a few minutes after that I was inside her, her teeth grazing my neck, her fingernails sharp against my arse, heating each other's winter-chilled flesh and making the headboard bang against the wall.

When I came I saw a flash of white light.

'Mmm,' she said, afterwards.

I kissed her, then remembered: 'Oh, a parcel came for you earlier.' I hopped out of bed, grabbed it and handed it to her.

She smiled. 'You bought me a present? Oh, Alex . . .'

'It's not from me,' I said, wishing I had bought her a present. 'Didn't you order something online?'

She shook her head. 'No. I haven't ordered anything.' She turned the parcel over in her hands. Then she said, 'Can you pass me my T-shirt?'

I did.

'I feel less vulnerable with some clothes on.' She pulled the T-shirt over her head, covering her breasts. She looked scared.

'What's the matter?' I asked.

She looked at me. 'I don't know who would send

me a present here. If it is a present.' She swallowed.

That's when I remembered the magazines. A small shudder ran through me. 'Do you want me to open it?' I asked. We were both staring at the package as if it might contain a bomb.

Emily said, 'No, I'll open it. It's addressed to me.' With trembling hands, she tore it open, then peered inside.

'What is it?'

'I can't see yet. It's in a black bag. Looks like—feels like—a bin-liner.'

She pulled the black bin-liner out of the Jiffy bag. There was, all of a sudden, a strange smell in the room. My heart was beating very fast. I put my hand on Emily's shoulder and she jumped.

'Alex! Jesus—don't do that!'

'Give it to me,' I said, holding out my hand, and Emily passed me the package. Slowly, I unwrapped it, and as the packaging fell away, the smell in the room became a stench and Emily screamed, leaping out of bed and running to the bathroom. I could hear her throwing up, but instead of going to comfort her, all I wanted to do was get it out of the room. I opened the window and threw it out. And then I ran to the bathroom myself. I watched Emily throw up the last contents of her stomach. All I could think was, who? Who would do this? And that's when it struck me, and I felt even sicker. Pernilla's words came back to me: that it was probably an aggrieved author.

I only know one person who meets *that* description.

27

Siobhan

It was a really horrible thing to do. I know. I know. But she deserves it. Why should everything be plain sailing for her, when she's fat and unattractive, when my own life is a total disaster? I'm aware that Alex, behaviourally, is borderline obsessive (and possibly even psychotic) but he's actually a very good-looking guy, and for some mysterious reason he absolutely adores her! I don't understand. He could have been mine. I keep hearing her whiny voice inside my head, saying 'my boyfriend', as if she's licking her forefinger and drawing the number one in the air in front of her, i.e. I've got one up on you, loser. Urghhhh, she's so SMUG.

I didn't plan it. It just happened, in a glorious collision of circumstance. I suppose after sending those magazines (if I was that overweight, I'd want a friendly hint from some kind well-wisher, of course I would. It's like having BO or bad breath—you need your friends to tell you otherwise you'd never know) the idea of posting things was still fresh in my mind. And it just so happened that I'd had this great big Jiffy bag lying around for ages waiting to be recycled. Can't even remember what came in it—oh, yes, those pink glass cabinet knobs I bought on eBay . . .

Anyway, I'd just peeled off the label, and was vaguely thinking, shame I don't have a manuscript to put in this and send off to Patricia, to be rapturously received and lauded to the heavens . . .

when I heard Biggles banging and crashing against the cat flap, like he'd suddenly gone blind and couldn't see where the door was.

I got up to look.

'What are you doing, you daft—' But the words stuck in my throat like a fishbone.

With one huge push, like childbirth, Biggles shoved his prize through the cat flap and jumped in after it, beaming proudly at me.

It was a massive dead rat. One that had been dead for quite some time, by the look of it. For God's sake, I thought cats wouldn't touch anything that wasn't fresh, what was the matter with him?

I had to press my lips together to \stop myself being sick. I couldn't even open the back door because the—thing—was blocking it, so I ran over and flung the kitchen window as wide as it would go, burying my nose in the pot of droopy basil on the windowsill.

'Oh Biggles, you idiot,' I moaned at him. 'Take it away, please take it away.'

But of course he didn't. In fact, by the way he was regarding it, I think even he was beginning to think he might have been a little hasty. I can cope with the odd dead sparrow, or even mouse—but this? It was like a horror movie on my very own kitchen floor.

'I'm sorry Biggles, but I am never going to allow you to lick me again,' I said out loud. 'Not now that I know where your mouth has been.' Funny, actually. That's something I was always quite tempted to say to Phil. But the thought of my sweet Biggles's jaws clamped around that stinky matted rat fur really did make bile rise in my throat, and I retched. What the hell was I going to do with it?

So I put on rubber gloves, ripped a bin-liner off the roll, and stuck one hand inside it. Then, with Biggles hovering anxiously around me, and holding my nose with my free hand, I edged gingerly towards the corpse, arm outstretched. The rat had thin hooked claws and its tail was fat, hairless, and much longer than I would have imagined rat's tails were. Its teeth were, of course, as yellow as my Marigolds. My stomach was roiling and jumping so badly that I had to shut my eyes.

When I felt my hand, through its black plastic and yellow rubber layers, close around the soft body, my teeth clenched, and the only thing stopping me vomiting was the knowledge that if I didn't do this now, I'd have to do it later. I picked up the rat, and turned the bin-liner inside out over it, letting go and feeling its weight thud heavily down to the bottom of the bag.

Then I threw up in the sink.

Now what, I wondered? There was no way I was going to go to the trouble of digging it a little ratty grave—some other predator would probably only excavate it for me later. I couldn't put it in the outside bin because the bin men had only just been. My kitchen was still smelling really bad, so I wrapped the bin-liner around the body as many times as possible, and then, for extra protection, slid the whole thing into the empty Jiffy bag.

I swear I only sealed it up to stop it smelling. I suppose it was lucky that I had a stapler in the kitchen drawer, and sellotape. But once the bag was closed, I could open the back door, put the thing outside, and air the place out. Because now there was the stench of sick to get rid of, as well as dead rat. My beautiful clean kitchen.

I chucked the rubber gloves into the bin, donned a fresh pair, upended the kitchen chairs onto the table, and mopped the entire floor with a solution of bleach, before throwing away the mop head. Next I poked all the regurgitated peas down the plughole— can't remember having eaten peas at all, but there you go—and bleached the sink. Finally I got down on hands and knees and washed the floor a second time with pine Flash and a J Cloth.

Then I made myself an industrial-strength gin and tonic, which I drank in the living room, my back aching from my exertions. The drink did relax me, but it also made me quite drunk and, if truth be told, somewhat maudlin. I shouldn't drink gin during the day. But honestly, I've had a terrible time of it lately. Nothing's gone right. I felt I deserved a little drink or two.

I'd just topped up the gin when the phone rang. Oh goody, I thought. Company. I hoped it might be Jess—she still hadn't returned my calls from a couple of weeks ago. But it was an unfamiliar woman's voice.

The exact details of our conversation elude me, but it turns out that the woman was a friend of Kathy's. She—the friend—had been away for a year somewhere, and had only just heard about Kathy's death, and couldn't believe she'd fallen off a fire escape. Apparently Kathy had never done it before— although, I mean, surely one can only fall from the top of a fire escape once? I didn't really understand what she was on about, if truth be told, but it was nice to talk to somebody sympathetic.

We chatted for some time—enough time for me to have another gin—and it got me thinking even more about how crap my life is. I mean, Kathy and

I were actually pretty good friends. We certainly could have been. I really liked her.

'I really liked her,' I found myself sobbing down the phone. 'She was a really, really good friend to me. I miss her so much.'

I'm not sure, but I think the woman on the end of the line was crying too. 'So do I,' she said. 'And I didn't even get the chance to say goodbye.'

'Nor did I,' I said, the tears coming thick and fast, dripping into the melting ice cubes in my glass. 'It's not fair, is it? Nothing's bloody fair.'

Nothing was fair. I mean, look at me. No boyfriend, no book, no job, no friends—and all the time Alex and Emily rubbing my nose in it with their smugness, and him about to get a publishing deal, knowing my wretched luck; and her laughing behind my back and wanting to give me a piece of her fat mind. The woman was saying something else.

'Wha'?' I think I might have been slurring my words slightly.

'I said, did you go to the funeral? I couldn't even get back for the funeral.'

'Yes, I went,' I said, fresh tears coming at the memory of that sad, sad day.

'Did you know any of Kathy's friends?'

'Nobody. I didn't know anybody there at all—oh, except Alex Parkinson. He was there.'

'Alex Parkinson from your writing class?'

That was odd. I didn't realise this woman knew about my class. And how did she know who Alex was? In fact, why was she ringing?

'Yes. Why did you ring me, again?' I was gradually becoming aware that I sounded a little odd.

'Like I said just now, I want to talk to everyone who knew Kathy. I can't believe that her death was

255

an accident. The police aren't doing anything.'

And there I was thinking she'd just rung to offer her condolences. Still, I was shocked to the core.

'You mean, you think Kathy was murdered?'

'I don't know. But I know she wouldn't have killed herself. So, were Alex and Kathy friends?'

I tried to remember, but all I could think about was Alex coming back home with me after the funeral, and us having a row about the clothes he'd bought on my credit card.

'No. Don't think so. He only came to the funeral because he was in love with me and guessed I'd be there.'

There was a sort of disgusted silence at the end of the line. It was only later I realised that that statement didn't put me in the best possible light. But it was true! That was the day Alex confessed his feelings for me, and, like an idiot, I kicked him out. Why am I such a moron? True love stared me in the face and I turned it away. And now he's all over Emily.

The woman hung up soon after that. Still don't really understand why she rang or what she wanted.

The rest of the day passed in something of a blur. I forgot about the rat for a while and had a little sleep on the sofa. It was only later when Biggles jumped up onto my chest and demanded to be fed that I remembered, and pushed him off, imagining him breathing dead rat in my face.

The sealed-up Jiffy bag was still outside the back door and, in my defence, I was still dizzy from the gin. I laughed at the thought that it looked like an exciting mail-order present, a nice, fat parcel waiting to be opened. I could just pop it in the post, I thought. It should just fit through the slot of that letterbox on the corner, if I flatten it a bit. But who could I send it to?

I didn't have to think about it for all that long, just long enough to look up Alex's address in my college records, write her name c/o him on a label, whack it on the Jiffy bag and walk to the post box.

I think I'm still a little bit drunk, even after that walk. Better just go to bed.

28

Alex

Thursday

Emily had to take the day off work yesterday, most of which she spent in my bed, eating sweets (her diet forgotten) and listening to an eighties compilation album over and over. She said she couldn't face seeing anyone after receiving 'the parcel', as it became known, euphemistically. A dead rat. Someone had sent her a dead rat. It was unbelievable. And the thing that made it worse was that Emily had a terrible fear of those long-toothed, long-tailed rodents. She had told me about it one night, lying in bed, when we were talking about things that scared us. Emily had said, 'When I read *1984* I didn't need to imagine what would be in my Room 101, because it was right there in the book. Rats.' She had shivered at the thought of it.

And I shivered at the thought of who might have sent it to her. The more I turned it over in my mind, trying to persuade myself that I must be mistaken, the more I was convinced. If I hadn't seen Siobhan talking to Emily, I would never have considered her as a suspect. But it was too much of a coincidence. I quizzed Emily, trying to find out if she'd made any enemies recently, but she was adamant that she's never had any enemies, apart from a couple of girls at school who used to pick on her for having puppy fat. Plus she couldn't believe that any 'aggrieved authors' could have discovered her home address, let alone her boyfriend's address. She was upset and bewildered, unable to figure out what she'd done and to whom.

But what the hell can I do about it? I can't tell Emily about Siobhan. I can't go to the police. Part of me thinks I should contact Siobhan, talk to her, ask her why she's doing this. I mean, I paid back the money I owed her. I'm out of her life now, moving on. I just don't get it. If she's trying to get revenge against me, why is she sending stuff to Emily? What is she trying to achieve?

And although I'd like to know the answers to my questions, I know that if I contact her it's bound to make things worse. I just have to hope that now she's carried out her little act of revenge, she'll be satisfied and stop. So, for now, I'm going to be an ostrich and bury my head. But if she does any more to hurt Emily, well . . .

I'll have to do something.

Just typing this is making me feel weak and sick. It's all I need at the moment, what with Kathy's friend and everything else. My life feels like that scene in *Star Wars* when Luke, Han and Leia are in the waste-disposal room, up to their waists in shit, when the walls start closing in.

Except I've got no R2-D2 to save me.

Friday

This morning, at 11 am, something wonderful happened.

I was sitting in my bedroom, brooding about the Emily/Siobhan problem, trying to decide if I'd be better off in Tibet, chilling out with a bunch of monks—women and sin forsaken forever—when the telephone rang.

Whenever the phone rings in this flat it might as well be a death knell, or the sound of a harpie calling me to the rocks. Sighing, I dragged myself to the living room and said a tentative, 'Hello?'

'May I speak to Alex Parkinson?' said a shockingly posh, strangely familiar voice.

'That's me.'

'Ah, Alex.' A kind of purr came into her voice, the sound a cat might make when it spies an exquisitely juicy mouse, and that's when I realised who it was. It was Pernilla. And as soon as it struck me, I had to sit down, my heartbeat almost drowning out her voice. 'I'm calling to tell you that I absolutely love your stories.'

I can't recall every word of the conversation: it seemed too unreal. But she went on to tell me that while she had been exceedingly sceptical about the literary credentials of her assistant's boyfriend, she had been bowled over by my astonishing stories. 'Your voice is so different yet authentic,' she said. 'I was thrilled—and also a little disturbed—by the way you got inside the mind of a chap who is so clearly on the edge of sanity in 'The Long Drop'. Wonderful.' I soaked up the praise like a desert welcoming rain. And after she'd buttered me up for a while, she told me that unfortunately they couldn't afford to offer me a ludicrous advance like those I might have read about in the Sunday papers, mainly because short-story collections are not huge money-spinners. But they could offer £5000 for a book of short stories and then we could talk about a novel. 'I think this could be the beginning of a long, successful career.'

I was reeling, hardly able to speak, and at the end of the call Pernilla said, 'Well, I'll let you absorb all this, then maybe you could call me after the weekend and we'll set up a meeting to talk about the book and your future.' She emitted an extra loud purr. 'I shall tell Emily to pick up a bottle of something fizzy on the way home.'

When I put the phone down I didn't know what to do. I felt as if someone had stuck a needleful of adrenaline into my heart. All my problems were forgotten and I was pumped full of energy, sparkle, joy. I wanted to call Emily but I knew she'd be sitting right next to Pernilla and would know about it already. I desperately wanted to spread the news—I needed a megaphone and a rooftop. I even had an urge to call Mum, but knew she'd merely greet the news with a 'So what?'

I decided to call Simon at work. He was thrilled. 'That's fantastic, mate. Wow. Hey, do you think one day they'll put one of those blue plaques outside our front door: Alex Parkinson, Novelist, lived here? We'll have to go out to celebrate later. Tell you what, I'll call the Indian and book a table and the four of us can go out. Or is the Indian not good enough for you writers? I guess you'd rather go to the Groucho or something.' He laughed and I laughed too, feeling even more giddy and ecstatic.

I kind of floated into my bedroom and sat down in front of the computer. I didn't have a megaphone and a rooftop, but I had email. I wanted to let everyone know so I composed a message, announcing my good news, and sent it to everyone in my address book, which isn't a huge number of people, to be honest. The people on the list included my old colleagues (who would no doubt be extremely pissed off to discover that they were soon going to be selling a book with my name on the cover) and even that idiot Brian, who once foisted his email address on me at the writing class, though I'd never had cause to contact him before. The only person I removed from the list before I sent the email was Siobhan.

Then I went out for a walk. The city looked so beautiful, so alive, and I could feel its history—its resonant literary past—seeping through the cracks in the pavement which actually seemed to contain a trace of gold. I stopped off at Waterstone's and found the space where my book would go, between Jefferson Parker and Adele Parks. I walked as far as the river and looked down at the grey water, the shadows of the buildings opposite reflected on its surface, and although I couldn't see my own reflection I felt like Narcissus, absorbed by myself, feeling the coat of self-doubt and loathing I've worn for so long dissolving, melting away.

Later . . .

Of course, that feeling didn't last for long.

Emily and I had celebratory sex as soon as she got here, then we got ready for our meal with Simon

261

and Natalie, both of whom were genuinely happy for me. We dressed in our best clothes and the flat smelled of the girls' perfume. It was dark outside, the air crisp, streetlights shining against a deep black sky, as black as the cab that would carry us to our destination.

We were waiting for the taxi when the phone rang again. I grabbed it, thinking it might be someone responding to my email, calling to congratulate me. But, for the second time that day, in a kind of sick, twisted symmetry, someone said, 'May I speak to Alex Parkinson?'

'Speaking,' I said.

She paused. 'My name is Elaine Meadows. I was a friend of Kathy Noonan's and I believe you went to the same writing class as her. I've been calling all . . .'

She might as well have walked into the room and delivered a karate chop to my windpipe. At the same time she was speaking I heard—as if from a great distance—Simon say, 'The taxi's here,' and I must have gestured that I would be one moment, because the three of them headed out to the cab.

'I heard that you went to Kathy's funeral. I wondered . . .'

'Sorry,' I said, 'who did you want to speak to?'

'Alex Parkinson. You said . . .'

I interrupted again. 'No, sorry—my name's Alex Parker. I must have misheard you. You must have got the wrong number.'

I dropped the receiver. I was sweating. Why the fuck did I lie to her like that? It looked so suspicious, so obvious. I hurried towards the front door, the taxi driver sounding his horn impatiently. As I shut the door behind me, the phone began to ring again.

*　　　*　　　*

The meal tasted of cardboard; the wine like dirty washing-up water. I felt sick, unable to concentrate on anything. Emily joked about it, saying I must be in some kind of shock, dreaming about success. Simon raised a toast—'To bestsellerdom'—and I held up my glass weakly. Maybe it wouldn't have been so bad if I hadn't felt so happy during the afternoon; it was like coming down from E, landing so hard that it knocked all the wind out of me. Kathy's friend had found me. It was all the fault of that arsehole Brian. If I saw him again, I'd throttle him; I'd stuff his socks full of rocks and chuck him in the Thames. It was so unfair. What the hell was I going to say if that woman called again—especially as I'd lied to her now? Goddamn it, Alex—it was such a stupid thing to do.

I needed time to think. Some space, away from here, away from the flat, from London and Elaine Meadows and Siobhan and dead rats and ghosts.

'Let's go away,' I said to Emily.

'What?'

'Let's go for a break somewhere, to celebrate.'

*　　　*　　　*

Later, Emily told me that she had also been thinking about how nice it would be to go away, to help her recover from the shock of receiving the magazines and the rat. 'Where shall we go?'

Across the other side of the restaurant was a man wearing an orange football shirt—the uniform of the Dutch football team.

263

'Let's go to Amsterdam,' I said.

*   *   *

When we got home, I went online to book our flights to the Netherlands, and also found a hotel for us. Emily was almost bouncing on the bed in anticipation. 'It's going to be great,' she said. I nodded.

While I was online I checked my emails. There was one from Brian:

Congratulations! That's really great news, Alex. I'd like to meet you for a drink so you can tell me all about it. How about tomorrow?
  Again, congrats
  Brian

Well, I thought, he might be an idiot, but he's the only person who's bothered replying to my email. I felt an unexpected warmth towards him. He wasn't to know that he was dropping me in the shit when he spoke to Elaine Meadows, was he? I quickly replied, saying we could meet up for a drink sometime, but not tomorrow as I was going to Amsterdam with my girlfriend to celebrate.

Then I joined Emily in bed. The drink had knocked her out and she was snoring. Without warning, I found myself wildly irritated, close to anger. Here she was, sleeping peacefully—well, it was peaceful for her; she couldn't hear her own room-rattling snores—whilst I was in the middle of a crisis. I took a few deep breaths until the irritation went away. I couldn't sleep though—there was far too much going on in my head, faces spinning like numbers on a roulette wheel. Women's faces. Siobhan, Kathy, Emily, an invented face for Elaine Meadows—she had carroty hair in my imagination and a witch's wart on her chin. And I thought about my mother, replaying many of the cruel things she said to me when I was a child. All that stuff about me being unwanted, ugly, stupid, evil. Maybe the follow-up to my book of short stories will be a misery memoir, dedicated to my mum.

Or a fucking prison memoir.

29

Siobhan

Haven't written for a few days. Been too busy. But thought could bring diary—something to do to wile . . . whyl . . . whil away the hours, sitting in coffee shops. Doing what you do in coffee shops in Amster . . . dam. Ha! Damn.

Bit out of it actaully. Keep making spelling mistakes and cant be assed to correct them. Tired. Head spinning. Pen too heavy think better go back to hotel to better thnik. Write more later

Later . . .

OK so now I know that pot makes me lose the use of my personal. pronouns (see above!), not to mention the ability to spell. I feel better now, but it took me a good few hours. Thank goodness I'm not meeting the people from the publishers' until tomorrow. I think I got a bit carried away, with my first solo foray into a coffee shop.

I managed to buy the gear, and even roll one for myself. Admittedly it looked like a rolled-up copy of the *Financial Times*, but then a nice Dutch bloke helped me tighten it up a bit. I didn't mind him butting in. I'd done the hard part—walking up to the counter and asking to see the menu, so they know you're after some gear, and not just a coffee. The Dutch guy was called Evan. I might go and meet him later—he said he'd be there after eight. I think he was hitting on me—stop press, MAN FANCIES SIOBHAN, shock horror; though he was stoned too so he was probably seeing me through dope goggles. I can't say that he really set my knickers alight but he seemed nice enough, if a little shifty. At least he spoke great English.

It was strong gear, too—Evan said it was called 'Afghan Gold'. He talked about it like it was some kind of fine wine. When I was writing that stuff above, after my new friend had gone, my pen felt so heavy that I could hardly lift it. It was like my brain had slowed down, and I didn't even really care that I was spelling things wrongly, or what I was writing. Very liberating, actually, to not care what you put down on the page.

And liberating to have a couple hours' respite from the pressure I've been going through at home, too. Finding out about Alex like that, and thinking that I was actually going to have a heart attack when I heard about his deal. Really, I literally couldn't breathe, and Barbara—those bloody writing students get everywhere—looked quite worried. I mean, things have got to a pretty bad state when an overweight septuagenarian with varicose veins worries about *my* health!

But the Alex thing is beginning to seem like some giant trick the universe is playing on me, for the sole purpose of tormenting me; I feel poisoned by it, like some bastard cherub dipped an arrow in a bucket of strychnine and fired it at me. There I was, minding my own business, trying lipstick shades on the back of my hand in Boots, wishing I had someone who would complain about the lipstick traces I'd left on his collar, or skin, when Barbara tapped me on the shoulder, looming up behind me like Fungus the Bogeyman with a shopping basket.

'Hello, Siobhan!' she says, friendly but somehow cautious, like a mental nurse talking to one of her patients. Like she's afraid I'm going to go off on one again (turns out that I was, kind of. But there was still no need for her to act like that). 'Are you feeling better? We were all ever so sorry when you left, you know. The class isn't the same without you.'

I smiled weakly. 'Thanks Barbara.' I wondered if I should apologise—hadn't I said something quite nasty to her? I couldn't remember if it was her or Mary, so I decided against apologising unnecessarily.

'We've got a very nice young man teaching us now. He's quite hot on homework though—works us much harder than you used to! He's had a book published, you know.'

'So have I,' I said, pretending to be offended that she hadn't remembered, when actually I was very offended. My hand now had six different pastel lines drawn on it in lipstick. I decided on a raspberry-coloured one, and scrubbed off the others with a tissue.

'Oh yes, dear, well, you writers are such a talented bunch, aren't you? And have you heard the wonderful

267

news about Alex?'

I nearly dropped the raspberry lipstick. 'Alex?'

'Yes, remember him? I always thought his work showed such promise.'

'Alex,' I repeated, somehow knowing what was coming.

'Got a publishing contract, he has, for his stories. And they want him to write a novel too. Brian told us last night in class. Alex wasn't there because he's gone to celebrate in Amsterdam with his girlfriend. Isn't that lovely for them? He got an awful lot of money, too, I understand. Fifty thousand pounds, at least.'

Fifty grand? Fucking Alex got fifty grand? Well, at least it wasn't half a million, but still—50K for a few minging short stories and a not-even-written-yet novel? My advance was long ago swallowed up by the bricks and mortar of my house. The house where Phil and I were supposed to live happily ever after.

And he's taken that piglet on holiday to Amsterdam . . . I felt faint.

'Are you all right, dear?' said Barbara, looking panic-stricken. 'You've gone a funny colour. Are you going to have another of your turns?'

I could have punched her. I clenched my fist around the lipstick. I don't have 'turns', for God's sake! She made me sound like some ancient grandmother.

'I've got to go. Nice to see you, Barbara. Do send my love to the rest of the class.'

I pocketed the lipstick and marched out, panting with shock.

*　　　*　　　*

So that's how come I'm sitting in a hotel in Amsterdam, wearing a stolen raspberry lipstick (it's a bit too pink for my liking, actually. Wish I'd taken the Ginger Spice one) and coming down off an extremely strong joint. I wonder how I go about finding out where Alex and the Piglet are staying? I feel empowered, as it happens, exhilarated by the chase and the challenge and the change of scenery. If I want things to happen in my life, I have to make them happen. If I want to get back at Alex and the slag of a girlfriend who slagged me off, I have to do it myself. Instead of sitting on my ass grumbling about him like some sad, weak loser.

*   *   *

It was easy to get out here. I rang Patricia and reminded her of that offer by the Dutch company to do a reading, so she rang my Dutch editor, Mareliese. Mareliese said there wasn't enough time to organise a reading, but if I was coming over anyway, she'd love to take me to lunch, and into a few bookshops to sign some stock. They couldn't pay for my flight, though. But it wasn't expensive on EasyJet, and by that time I'd made up my mind. And it was nice to have an official reason to be here.

I also rang Alex's flat and spoke to his flatmate, pretending to be someone from an agency wanting to represent him (a great excuse to ring, I thought). His flatmate confirmed that he was away in Amsterdam until next Thursday. I invented a name and phone number, and told him to get Alex to call me.

Mareliese recommended a lovely hotel. It's where all the authors stay when they come to Amsterdam to do promotion, and there are signed copies of all their books in a little library next to reception. I wondered if Alex might have plumped for this one too, but there was nobody by the name of Parkinson when I checked. And anyway, he probably doesn't know about it. Yet.

The room's a bit expensive, but I thought, sod it. I need a break. So I went for a canal-view one, with huge black-framed windows running down the length of it, and the dark water sliding past outside. The building opposite has twenty-eight windows, all with shutters. It must have been some kind of warehouse originally. The windows are all different sizes—big down the middle, flanked by smaller ones, and then with these two tiny round windows right at the top; bits of wood jutting out above them which must have been where the pulleys were attached. It looks like a pair of eyes with eyebrows. Freaked me out a bit when I was high, actually.

If I try hard enough, I can pretend that I'm here because I've won some prestigious Dutch award for Best First Novel, or something. Or I'm about to be picked up and taken to a radio station for a national radio interview.

*　　　*　　　*

I've just rung thirty hotels in my *Rough Guide to Amsterdam*, starting with the most expensive ones, assuming that Alex will want to splash out, now he's rich and everything. No Alex Parkinsons. Maybe they only stayed two nights and then went to Rotterdam or somewhere. I'll try a few more then I'm giving up . . .

. . . Ha! Well, I was wrong about Alex wanting to

splash out. I've finally found him, on my thirty-fifth call, to a hotel listed under the 'budget' heading in the guide book. I double-checked it was him, by asking if he was with his girlfriend Emily, and he was. Bingo. Unfortunately their hotel seems to be quite a way away from here. And I haven't decided what exactly I'm going to do anyway.

Think I'll go out for some dinner and a wander, get some air. And maybe back to the coffee shop to see if Evan's around.

Monday

What an excellent night! Evan is such a laugh. I can't remember when I last laughed so much. His friends were an interesting bunch, too. A bit lacking in the tooth department, some of them, and there was a little too much talk of breaking people's limbs for my liking; but I'm sure all that was just macho bollocks. Big lads, they were. I've never seen quite so many tattoos. The air was as heavy with testosterone as with pot—but I loved it. I loved the uncomplicated masculinity of their company. They really made me feel welcome, like a little sister.

Evan's friend owns that coffee shop, which is why he's always in there. I had all sorts of different flavoured beers, including a raspberry one, to match my lipstick, and God knows how many hits off how many different joints.

I was really out it. Evan walked me back here and we had a bit of a snog on the bridge, but— thankfully—I declined to let him come back to my room. He's not my type. Too . . . I dunno . . . meathead-ish, I suppose. But not stupid—we had

271

some long, long talks. Or rather, I talked, and he listened. I couldn't seem to stop, actually. It was so great to have a sympathetic ear, and I really felt he understood my plight.

I told him all about Alex, and what he'd done to me: breaking into my house, using my credit card, following me home. And about how the Piglet bad-mouthed me to her friends for no reason. I think I told him about Phil two-timing me too, and about not having a job. I think—oh blimey—I might even have cried at one point. But Evan was lovely. He held me close and stroked my face and handed me joints to puff on and said, 'I'd sort Alex out for you, if I could get my hands on him.'

Evan had very large hands.

I remember sort of sitting up and saying, 'He's in Amsterdam at the moment, as it happens.' Then I remember taking the scrap of paper with the name of Alex's hotel on it out of my bag and showing it to him. Him nodding, and stretching out one of those big hands for the scrap. Asking me to write down Alex's surname too. I wrote it down.

Evan looked at the piece of paper and slipped it into his top pocket. The moon shimmered on the black surface of the canal and, all of a sudden, I felt cold and exhausted. I asked Evan to walk me to the door of my hotel. Then he turned away and walked back across the bridge, and I remember marvelling at how someone who'd smoked so much dope could have so much purpose in their stride.

30

Alex

Amsterdam

Emily threw the rucksack on one bed and herself on the other, sprawling on her back, breasts bouncing beneath her shirt, arms and legs spread, star-shaped.

She let out a long, relieved sigh. 'This is exactly what we need—a few days of peace. Away from horrible magazines and horrible dead rats—and I was going to say away from Pernilla, but I suppose I've got to be nice about her now.'

I smiled at her, then looked around the room. Not bad for the price. The view was of a brick wall, but it wasn't an English brick wall, and that's what mattered. No mini-bar, but there was a TV and— praise be—a trouser press. Just what every weary traveller needs.

'Shame about the twin beds. This is supposed to be the sex capital of Europe, isn't it? And they give you twin beds.' Emily had wanted to go to this hotel that she'd heard about at work—some place where authors always stay. But I decided it wouldn't feel right, not yet—not until I've actually got that book with my name on the cover in my hands. And I haven't got any of the money yet, so, having a rare attack of level-headedness, I booked us into this cheapish hotel. Now, looking at the separate beds, I wished I'd splashed out a bit—not that £5000 is going to last very long.

Emily rolled over on her side and hitched an eyebrow. 'We'll just have to snuggle up in one bed, won't we?'

I came over to give her a kiss; Emily tried to catch my arm, to pull me onto the bed, but I resisted. Despite my complaint about the twin beds, I wasn't really in the mood. My thoughts kept strobing, flicking from one thing to another:

Kathy falling from the fire escape . . . literary glory . . . Siobhan telling me I was a stalker . . . the dead rat in the Jiffy bag . . . Elaine's telephone call . . . Emily and Siobhan in the café . . . the things I can spend my advance on . . . my mother telling me I'd never amount to anything . . . that time I hid in Siobhan's wardrobe . . .

Round and round and round they go. And although my main worry involves Kathy and her fucking friend, and my main source of happiness is my literary success (oh, and Emily, of course—how could I forget?), it's odd how many of the scenarios that whizz through my head involve Siobhan. It's as if she's still at the centre of my life, my nemesis. When I think about her sending the rat to Emily, and the magazines, and seeing them together, I feel so confused: angry and stupefied. I don't know what to do about her. Should I confront her? Warn her to stop? I really don't know. And I promised myself that while I was in Amsterdam I wouldn't think about it. I wouldn't think about her.

I looked at my girlfriend. 'Let's go and explore,' I said.

*   *   *

We spent the afternoon doing touristy stuff: the

Van Gogh museum, the Anne Frank house, which made Emily cry. We dodged bicycles and took a ride on a canal boat which was full of Japanese women clutching Louis Vuitton handbags. We walked through the red-light district, and I remarked on how healthy the prostitutes in the windows looked, so unlike the stereotypical smack-addled whores who frequent films and TV shows. Emily asked me if I'd ever been with a prostitute and I lied. I didn't tell her about the girl in Bangkok, five or six years ago, about the five minutes I spent in her company and the feeling of self-loathing that lasted a hell of a lot longer. Amsterdam was dirty and beautiful, and I fantasised about living in a canal-side apartment, writing novels about the strange and fascinating characters who paused on the bridges beneath.

I asked Emily if she fancied going to a coffee shop and having a smoke but she shook her head.

'Dope makes me really sick,' she said. 'You can get some if you want but you'll have to smoke it alone.'

I tutted, but tried not to let my irritation show. 'Oh. It doesn't matter. I'm not really into it. Let's just go for a drink, yeah?'

We were near an Irish pub so we went inside and ordered Guinness and a couple of portions of chips, which we ate with mayonnaise. Fantastic. Kings of Leon were playing in the background. Even better.

I drank my pint fast and it made my head spin a bit. From where we sat I had a pretty good view of the street. It was growing dark outside, the character of the city changing as the streetlights came on: the locals headed to their houses while the sex-and-drug tourists hurried out into the town, looking for the thrills they had to work harder to find at home.

Emily was talking about how she'd felt in the Anne Frank museum, about how sickening it was that someone betrayed her and her family—when I suddenly felt as if I'd been punched in the stomach.

Because Siobhan walked past the window.

I stopped listening to what Emily was saying. I looked at my pint of Guinness like a drunk in a movie who's just seen an alien or a talking pig. I must have hallucinated her. I must have. What the fuck would she be doing in Amsterdam? There was no way she could have followed us . . . was there? No, it must have just been someone who looked like her. I wanted to get up, go out into the street and check, just to be safe, but how could I? Emily was still talking about Anne Frank and I was still nodding along, even though in my head I was hundreds of miles away.

But I had to know.

'. . . and there was only a week to go before the end of the . . .'

'I have to go to the loo,' I said abruptly, standing up.

She blinked up at me, the sentence frozen in her mouth. 'What?'

'The loo. Sorry. Urgent.'

Luckily, the toilets were around the corner from where we were sitting, quite near the exit. I rushed off and, looking over my shoulder to make sure Emily couldn't see me, I left the pub. Standing on the pavement outside I looked in the direction I'd seen 'Siobhan' go—up towards the Van Gogh museum. But the light was dim and I couldn't see anyone who looked like her. I jogged forward a few paces, straining to see, but it was hopeless. I turned and went back into the pub, genuinely needing to

276

pee now. Standing at the urinal, I muttered reassuring words to myself. The guy beside me zipped up quickly and scarpered. Then a memory came back to me—something that had been niggling me since we'd decided to come here. I remembered the email I'd deleted off Siobhan's computer, in which her editor had mentioned an invite to Amsterdam. Maybe Siobhan came here sometimes, if her book was popular here. But it would still be a huge coincidence.

When I got back to our table, Emily said, 'You were ages.'

'Sorry. The guy standing next to me kept talking to himself and my bladder got shy.'

'You poor thing. But you're not shy of barmen, are you?'

I ordered another Guinness for Emily and a Diet Coke for myself. I figured it was better if I didn't have anything else to drink. One more pint and I might see Kathy drag herself past the front door.

We stayed in the pub for a while (I didn't stay teetotal for long; my next drink was black and thick and had a shamrock crafted into the head) and Emily and I reminisced about our relationship; how we'd met, etc, etc. I'm not sure if most couples do this: talk about their relationship after being together such a short time. Still, Emily is my longest-standing girlfriend by quite some way. She's the record holder. I think I'm a lowly fourth in Emily's longevity chart: some guy called Craig holds pole position with a chart-topping stay of three-and-a-half years, a length of time I can hardly imagine.

Would Emily and I still be an item forty-two months down the line? We could be married, have a kid and a shared gym membership. Right now, I would kill for some stability and peace of mind. I looked at Emily again, a Guinness-foam moustache lining her upper lip, and tried to picture myself spending the rest of my life with her.

'Shall we go to a club?' I said, needing to get out of the pub.

'A nightclub? That's a good idea. There's a really cool place just round the corner.'

'How do you know it's really cool?'

'It said so in the guide book.'

The club was pretty empty at first, but filled up rapidly until it was a melee of bumping and grinding bodies, made up of some of the coolest and sleaziest people I'd ever seen. While Emily was in the toilet I was chatted up by a beautiful 'woman' with the biggest Adam's apple I've ever seen. I joined Emily on the dance floor and tried to move in time with the music, which I think I just about managed. Emily surprised me by being a fantastic dancer, all raised arms and swooshing hair and energy; guys were forming a disorderly queue to dance next to her. She was drenched with sweat by the time I managed to drag her away from a guy with a gold front tooth.

'Hey,' Emily laughed, 'I was enjoying myself.'

'So was that guy you were dancing with. Look.' I pointed at the bulge in his trousers and Emily shrieked with wide-eyed laughter.

'This is such a cool place,' she said. 'Why don't we move to Amsterdam?'

'Well . . . we could.'

She kissed me, open-mouthed and sweaty. 'We could come to this club every week.'

God, it was tempting. Get out of England. Escape and never go back. What a wonderful idea. As a writer, I could live anywhere. But then Emily

278

reverted to boring reality and said, 'If it wasn't for my job', and the idea fizzled out as quickly as it had been born.

Something about this exchange really annoyed me. It seemed so typical of that small-minded attitude to life that I was always so determined not to have. Dashing your dreams before they have a chance to live, just because trying to make them real would take effort and might be scary. I've always tried to be different: leaving my hometown the second I could, going travelling, pursuing my literary ambitions . . . okay, so I've also got myself into a lot of trouble, especially recently, but no one could ever say my life has been boring. But when I looked at Emily, I saw—and I really do hate to say this—a glimpse of the future I never wanted. I had seen it sitting in the pub. Emily had narrow horizons; and, worse, she was weak. Her reaction to the magazines and the rats had started a train of thought that had been running through the back of mind for a while, coming to the forefront now. I have always admired women who fight; strong women. And although part of me wanted to protect Emily and hated to see her suffering, there was another part of me that wanted to tell her to, well, be a man.

I hated myself for having these thoughts, and as soon as they surfaced I told myself not to be stupid. Emily was the best thing in my life, I reminded myself. The only woman who ever loved me.

*   *   *

It was just after midnight when we got back to the hotel. As we approached, walking up the narrow street that led alongside the canal, past a dodgy-in-

279

extremis-looking basement coffee shop and various homes and offices, I became vaguely aware of a couple of guys standing outside the entrance of our hotel. There was another tourist couple ahead of us, and I saw these men say something to them before they went into the hotel. My first thought was that they might be more drug dealers.

As we neared the hotel entrance, I realised that the two guys were eyeing us—or rather, eyeing me. They were both tall, blond and muscular and pretty imposing. A couple of brick shithouses. I felt a premonitory stab of fear.

Emily let go of my hand and started to look in her bag for our room key, head down, ignoring the men. Then, as we stepped past them, one of them said, in a light Dutch accent, 'Alex?'

I automatically turned, just as anyone would if they heard their name, immediately affirming that I was indeed called Alex, and the taller and least ugly of the two took a step towards me and punched me in the stomach.

I doubled up, gasping for air, feeling like I was drowning. I was aware of Emily a few paces ahead of me, and the two men forming a wall between us. One of the men leaned towards me and said very quietly, in his best Hollywood English, 'We don't want shits like you in our city.' I had a horrible sense of déjà vu, and then he shoved me and I toppled over, landing on my side, my cheek scraping the asphalt. I could hear Emily, saying, 'What are you doing?', a hysterical lilt in her voice, and the second brick shithouse—the one who hadn't hit me yet— saying to her, 'What are *you* doing—with a creep like this?'

I tried to get up, but a kick in the chest returned

me to the pavement. I closed my eyes and the world swam. I could taste blood and hear a high-pitched whine. When I opened my eyes I didn't see stars— just the gutter, a crumpled cigarette packet inches from my face. I was still gasping for breath, curling up to protect myself, all instinct now, my body taking over from my confused and shocked brain.

Brick Shithouse One bent down and said, 'This is only a taster.' He put his hand on the side of my head and pressed it hard against the ground. I opened my eyes and looked at him, maybe hoping that eye contact would make him realise that I was more than a punchbag. His eyes were cold; actually, he looked sleepy, his pupils dilated. I knew I would never forget his face.

Emily was still making noise but I couldn't see her from where I was. I didn't know if the guy was holding her back or if she was holding herself back through fear. I tried to turn my head to see but the first shithouse still had his hand on my head, his thumb digging into my scalp. I swivelled my eyes towards him again and croaked a single word: 'Please.'

He seemed to contemplate something for a moment, then he nodded, apparently satisfied, and stood up.

After that, the two of them jogged away, calmly.

31

Siobhan

I slept like a baby—pot does that to me—but woke up groggy and muzzy-headed, and with a nagging unidentifiable feeling of unease. It stayed with me during my solo breakfast in the small but bright dining room, nobody else around except a silent waiter clearing up the croissant crumbs of the earlier breakfasters. What couldn't I remember?

Snogging Evan—well, that was a mistake. But at least I had the good sense not to let him come back with me. Telling him my problems—nothing wrong with that either. It was very cathartic.

I don't think I'll go out of my way to see him again, though. In fact, I'm going to steer clear of that coffee shop. And something is definitely niggling me about what happened last night.

*   *   *

It wasn't until I was in a cab on the way to lunch with my Dutch editor that I remembered:

I gave Evan Alex's name and his hotel. After he said he'd 'sort Alex out' for me if I wanted. Oh God.

I'm sure Evan wouldn't really have done anything, though. I'm sure he was only trying to act all macho to impress me. Once he realised there wasn't a shag in it for him, I'm sure he wouldn't have bothered hauling ass all the way over to Alex's hotel . . .

Would he?

Now that I think about it, there was an awful lot

of talk last night of heads being kicked in and retribution being exacted. Not by Evan, though. I wouldn't have stayed up late flirting with a thug; I mean, I do have some standards. But what if his mates egged him on? And I suppose there is the remotest possibility that I very slightly exaggerated the wrongs Alex and his girlfriend had perpetrated on me. Well . . . if I'm honest, I made them sound like Ian Brady and Myra Hindley.

Even if Evan did do something to Alex, I don't have anything to feel guilty about. He asked for it.

It's just, I suppose, I feel a little bit—what? It's hard to pin down but weirdly enough, I think I feel a little bit worried about Alex.

I was thinking about all this so hard that I didn't even notice that my cab had pulled up outside what looked like a sandwich shop.

'Here you are, miss,' said the cabbie, a tired-looking middle-aged man with a droopy moustache.

'Are you sure?' Mareliese had said she was taking me to lunch, and so I was expecting at least a place with white linen on the tables and a maitred'. Not formica and a queue at the till.

It seems that my capacity for optimism is stuck on 'high', in the face of repeated disappointment. This was indeed our venue for lunch. Mareliese was a dumpy lady in her mid-forties with an unfashionable mass of out-of-control corkscrew curls which kept shedding into her egg salad sandwich. She seemed to begrudge me even a paltry three-quarters of an hour of her time, and banged on continuously about how busy she was with her surprise 'hit' of the year, a novel written by a man who'd had a sex change called *Kicking the Balls Into Touch*. Yawn. I ordered the most expensive thing on the menu—a seafood

283

salad (which turned out to be a couple of crabsticks and some barely defrosted prawns, hidden in a huge bowlful of lettuce) and kept trying to turn the conversation back to *TLA* but she didn't seem that interested, beyond saying that the bookstore round the corner had four copies which I could sign—if I liked. And that it had done 'OK' in Holland, but it would have been much better if I could have come over and done one of the literary festivals or a reading some months ago when she first suggested it. Now people had forgotten about me and moved on to the next big thing . . .

Oh please, I felt like saying. Contain your enthusiasm for me and my book, all this fawning is quite embarrassing. My thoughts kept drifting back to Alex, with a sort of appalled anticipatory thrill. I even had an image of me at his hospital bedside, his face pale and bruised on the pillow, a sickly puppy, wan with gratitude and overcome with emotion at my presence. (Emily of course was out of the picture, as Alex had seen the error of his ways and ditched the bitch long ago.)

Mareliese made her excuses and escaped, after pointing me in the direction of the bookstore, without even offering to accompany me to the signing. I did walk over there, and searched long and hard along the shelves for both the English version of *TLA* and the Dutch translation, but failed to find either. I asked a lanky male assistant, who brightened.

'Yes,' he said, in heavily accented English, after consulting his computer. 'We have it. Please follow me.' He strode purposefully across to the back of the store, to a crate on the floor full of dog-eared books with torn or stained covers. Kneeling down with an expression of intense concentration, he plunged his hand into the crate, right down to the bottom, rummaged around and triumphantly pulled out one rather battered copy of *TLA*.

'Here!' he beamed, thrusting it at me.

'I've changed my mind,' I said abruptly, turning around and walking out of the shop. Bloody great. What a waste of time.

*   *   *

It was a beautiful sunny day, and the water in the canals sparkled, superficially disguising their murky depths. I strolled alongside one for a while, past a small, fragrant flower market, where I bought two packets of tulip bulbs, and several gift shops. I stopped in one and bought Paula a money-box Dutch clog, as a thank you for agreeing to feed Biggles while I was away (I hope he's OK. I hope she hasn't forgotten), and then walked on further.

I'm now in a coffee shop—having actual coffee this time—writing this diary and wondering if Alex's bloated body is being dragged out of a canal somewhere. I can't stop thinking about it, although whether out of mere curiosity or concern I still haven't quite decided . . .

No. It's no use, I've got to know.

Later . . .

I remembered the name of Alex's hotel and got a cab over there, wishing that I'd thought to bring my disguise. My heart was pounding as I walked into the dingy little lobby with its smeary faux-marble counter, and my head was practically swivelling 360 degrees in my attempts to keep an eye out for Alex or whatsherface—Emily.

'I'm here to meet a friend of mine,' I whispered to the receptionist. 'Alex Parkinson. Is he—um—alright, do you happen to know?'

Her face instantly settled into creases of sympathy. 'Jah, it was very bad,' she said, tutting. 'They took him off in an ambulance last night.'

'An ambulance?' Oh God, it wasn't just my imagination working overtime. Evan really had done something to him. 'Is he in hospital?'

The receptionist looked at me with dual suspicion and guilt, realising that she had been less than discreet. 'I am sorry, I thought you knew what had happened.'

'Well, um, yes and no. Not exactly. I just got a message that he was hurt.' I felt sick with nerves now. What if Emily walked in? Or Alex—unless he was in traction somewhere. How could I explain my presence, or worse, what if the receptionist let on that I knew Alex had been hurt? Or—horrors—what if Evan had said in Emily's earshot, right before plunging a six-inch knife into Alex's heart: 'This is from Siobhan'. . .

'So—could you tell me if he's here or in hospital?' Or dead, I thought in a panic. Sweat was actually running down the side of my face, even though it wasn't at all hot. That bloody Evan. What had he been thinking? I could go to jail!

'He's not in hospital. He stayed here last night. After he'd talked to the police.'

Not dead. But talking to police. Oh God.

'He and his friend have checked out. They are

going home this afternoon. I think they went to have some lunch first. Would you like to leave a message for them?'

'Don't worry,' I said. 'I think I know where they went for lunch. I'll catch up with them there. Thanks for your help. By the way, is there a Ladies' I could use first?'

I did actually really need the toilet. It must have been nerves. The receptionist pointed me in the right direction, and I shot off, on legs of jelly. Locking myself in a cubicle, I tried to shepherd my straying, panicked thoughts into some sense of cohesion.

Right. Alex wasn't dead, but bad enough to have needed an ambulance. He couldn't be in too bad a state though, because he'd gone out to lunch with Emily. So his injuries were clearly more superficial than had at first been believed. Probably just a black eye, maybe a couple of stitches. I heaved a sigh of relief, then instantly began to panic again. He'd been talking to the police. I just had to pray that Evan had the sense not to mention my name, otherwise I really was in trouble.

Still on the loo, I delved in my handbag for my compact, to powder my terror-shined face. My fingers closed around an unfamiliar plastic bag, which I pulled out, puzzled. I was holding a small Ziploc bag containing a rather large amount of cannabis, a mess of leaves and stalks compacted into a clump the size of a squashed tennis ball. How the hell had that got there?

Then I remembered. Evan, mid-snog last night, had murmured, 'Here's a little present for you.' I'd thought he was referring to his large and frankly intrusive tongue, but he must have slipped the pot

287

into my handbag then. I was momentarily touched—how sweet of him! Giving me drugs and beating up Alex for me. Bless. I considered writing him a little thank you note, and then decided against it. Better for me to disassociate myself, and deny any knowledge of him. I'd have to dump the pot, too. Thank goodness I'd found it before I went through customs!

I was about to tip it down the loo when I thought, no, while I'm still in Amsterdam I don't need to worry. I pocketed the bag and decided that I might as well indulge myself a little before going home. I could just leave it in the hotel room for the cleaners to enjoy—if I hadn't finished it all by then.

I flushed the toilet and emerged, repairing my make-up at the mirror before cautiously opening the door back into the lobby. It was still deserted, but I slunk out with great trepidation and hid behind a large luggage rack with two rucksacks on it. I still had to make extra sure I didn't bump into Alex and Emily coming back in.

A label on one of the rucksacks caught my eye: Emily Norris-Bottom, it said. I sniggered out loud, stifling it quickly. Could that really be Emily's surname? Oh, how I'd have enjoyed writing that on the Jiffy bag with the magazines/rat, if only I'd known it before. To double-check, I looked for identification on the other rucksack and, sure enough, there it was: Alex Parkinson.

Well, I could deal with coming face-to-face with their luggage, just as long as I didn't have to see them in person. A door across the lobby opened and a very elderly looking porter emerged, meandering slowly towards me. I was surprised—I didn't think a hotel this grotty would run to a receptionist and a porter—but still, never mind.

Checking that the coast was clear, I was about to make a dash for it when I had a sudden flash of inspiration.

Before I could think it through, I'd pulled out the bag of pot and stuffed it into the side pocket of Emily's rucksack. Then I scurried out of the hotel, thankfully unobserved.

If she got home without being stopped, she could call it a little gift from me. If she got caught by customs—well, then she could call it revenge.

I got a cab back to my hotel, determined to relax and enjoy the rest of my holiday on my own. No Alex, or Emily, or Evan. Just the pleasure of my own company, a couple of art museums, a nice restaurant or two, and some good books.

But I was still on tenterhooks, waiting for the knock at the door saying that the police wanted to speak to me on a matter of intent to cause GBH, or worse, attempted murder. How did my life suddenly get to be this dramatic?

32

Alex

Amsterdam (continued)

Right on cue, as soon as the brick shithouses had vanished into the Amsterdam night, a member of the hotel staff came running out to find me lying on the ground, Emily kneeling beside me. I looked up and saw the young woman who had checked us into the hotel; she was followed by a couple of other members of staff; and—predictably—a number of guests who had made their way from the hotel bar to gawp at me. Something for them to mention on their postcards home. I closed my eyes again. I didn't want to get up. I was starting to feel quite comfortable lying in the gutter.

'Is he okay?' asked the hotel receptionist.

Emily said, 'Call an ambulance.'

I opened my eyes and started to push myself onto all fours. 'No, I don't need an ambulance.'

'Call the police,' said Emily.

I shook my head, pushing myself to my feet. Emily held me by the elbow. She felt even shakier than I was. I said, 'Don't worry. I don't need the police.'

'Alex, don't be an idiot. What do you mean, you don't need the police?'

I tried to think of a reason that would make sense. 'It's too much hassle. I just want to go to bed.'

Another member of the hotel staff, a guy my age, came over. He told us he was the assistant manager. 'I think we need to call the police. We have to think about the safety of our guests.' A murmured chorus of approval came from the crowd.

Emily was looking at me very strangely.

I said, 'Okay. Whatever. But I didn't see much. I won't be able to tell them anything.'

The assistant manager went inside to call the police and we followed. The warm air in the lobby made my head spin. I sat in a big armchair with saggy upholstery. Emily sat beside me and said, 'Well, I saw everything. I got a really good look at them. They were big and muscular and looked . . . Dutch.' She trailed off, biting her lip.

The onlookers shuffled away, bored. Nobody had died or been consigned to a wheelchair. The assistant manager came back and said, 'The police will talk to you at the hospital. I called an ambulance as well.'

'But I told you I don't need one,' I moaned.

He looked at me like I was a stubborn and stupid child. 'We don't want people saying we don't look after our guests, do we?'

The ambulance didn't take long. The paramedics put me into a fold-up wheelchair and pushed me out to the ambulance. The pain in my chest was getting worse and I wondered aloud if something had been fractured or broken. Emily sat in the back of the ambulance, still chewing her lip and looking worried.

'Alex . . .' she started, but I groaned and said, 'Please, not now . . . it hurts to talk.' The paramedic guy beside me nodded and Emily fell quiet. I felt guilty, knowing how anxious she must be, remembering all the secrets I had, but right then it honestly did hurt to talk. In several ways.

We reached the hospital and they wheeled me off to a room where a doctor checked me over, then they took a couple of X-rays and told me I was going to be fine. 'Nothing serious—no need for worries,' said the doctor, patting my arm firmly. 'Looks like you got on the wrong side of someone?'

I closed my eyes and looked at the pretty patterns.

'Anyway, the police will be here soon, then you can go back to your hotel room.' He winked at Emily. 'He's okay, but you'd better leave him alone tonight. No, how do you say, bone-jumping for a day or two.'

A pair of policemen turned up shortly afterwards. I had expected a couple of uniformed hippies with big moustaches, but they looked like policemen the world over. Bored and superior. They asked me my name, address, the purpose of my visit to Amsterdam, etc. Their English, like everyone in this city, was excellent.

'Do you have any idea why these men attacked you?' the older policeman asked after Emily and I had described the brick shithouses. (I think I actually used those words.)

'No,' I replied.

Emily was looking at me from over the policeman's shoulder, her eyes narrowed.

'I guess it was just a random mugging.'

'But they didn't steal anything,' said the other cop.

'No. Maybe they heard someone coming out of the hotel and got scared. We were lucky.'

'Hmm. And they didn't say anything to you?'

'No. Nothing.'

Emily's eyes became slits.

'And they didn't try to hurt you, miss?'

Emily shook her head. 'They didn't touch me.'

The policemen looked at each other. The older one sighed. 'Random violence. It is a growing problem everywhere, I think. Even in your country.'

'Especially in my country,' I said.

He nodded sadly. Then they said they would be in touch if they needed to ask me any more questions, and left. Emily walked out of the room and returned a few minutes later. 'There's a taxi on the way. And when we get back to the hotel, we need to talk.'

Great, I thought. Just great.

* * *

I lay down on one bed and Emily sat on the other. She leaned forward and said very quietly, 'Why did you lie to the police?'

'What? I didn't.'

'You did, Alex. You told them those men didn't say anything, but they did. I'm sure they did.'

'Well . . .', I said, dragging out the first word to give myself another nanosecond to think. 'They said something in Dutch but I didn't understand it.'

'Alex, they said your name!'

'No they didn't.'

That made her pause, her brow furrowing with self-doubt. 'I'm sure . . . I'm sure I heard them say your name just as we were going into the hotel. I had my back to you—but I heard someone say Alex.'

I opened my mouth to lie, then paused, hating myself. But what else could I do? One of the men had said my name—that's why I turned around—and there was only one explanation: Siobhan must be in Amsterdam; I really had seen her through the pub window. And somehow she had found out where we were staying and had sent some thugs after me. I wondered if she had been watching while they beat me up, smiling to herself, discovering that revenge is indeed sweet. Not that I ever hurt Siobhan. Scared her, maybe. Inconvenienced her. But surely I hadn't done anything to merit this—to merit her following us to another country, for God's sake, and setting a pair of gorillas on me. What was wrong with her? While I was lying in the hospital bed I had realised how stupid it had been to run here. I should have gone to see Siobhan as soon as I'd suspected that she was responsible for the magazines and dead rat. And I should also have found a way of dealing with Kathy's friend. I had made another mistake.

It was time I stopped running away from my problems.

Except I still didn't want Emily to know about Siobhan. It would ruin everything; I would lose the only woman who didn't hate me; the only woman in this fucked-up scenario who wasn't capable of sending me to prison or hospital. Emily was the only one who cared for me. And another thing—hiding the truth from her had almost become a reflex. So I opened my mouth and told another big fat porky.

'I honestly didn't hear anyone say my name, Emily. And I would have heard it—you always hear when people say your name, don't you? I think you must be mistaken.'

She was quiet for a moment. 'But I'm sure one of them said something to you just before they ran off.'

'He said something in Dutch.'

She looked at me for a long moment. And then she started to cry, not making any noise, just sitting there, still staring at me, fat tears rolling down her cheeks. Then her lower lip started to wobble and she covered her face with her hands.

I sat up, feeling sick with guilt, hating myself more than ever. 'Emily . . .'

She lay down and turned away from me, facing the wall. She said, 'I need to sleep.' I crossed over to her bed and put my hand on her shoulder but she was as still as a rock, her muscles tense. It was hard to believe that only a few hours ago she had been the dancing queen of Amsterdam, surrounded by men, her face alight with happiness. I said her name again and she said, 'Let me sleep.'

I was relieved. I wasn't going to have to talk about it any more.

*　　　*　　　*

The next morning, as soon as I woke up, I took a bath. My chest and stomach muscles felt like I'd lost a fight with a gorilla—rather, two huge Dutch gorillas, doing their best to send Amsterdam's peace-and-love image up in a cloud of smoke. My cheekbone was badly grazed where it had scraped the pavement, and I held a flannel against it. My head pulsated and hummed; it hurt inside and out.

After a few minutes, I heard Emily get out of bed. She came into the room and said, 'I want to go home.'

'Okay.' I wasn't going to argue, knowing what the guy had really said to me as I lay in the road: *This is only a taster*. It sounded like a 'this town ain't big enough for the both of us'-style threat. Stay one more night and I might end up saying hello to whatever lived at the bottom of this city's canals.

Emily left the room and I slid deeper into the water. I felt a surge of anger towards Siobhan. The stupid bitch; she was a maniac; what the hell did I ever see in her? And, in answer to my question, I remembered her face, and her body, that body that was so much slimmer and more toned than Emily's. I remembered her smell, and the sound she made as she splashed about in the bath.

I rubbed the towel against my bruises, reminding myself what Siobhan had done, sparking anger. I held on to it. Siobhan equals pain—my pain and Emily's. I had to stop being stupid; I had to stop thinking about Siobhan and comparing her to Emily. Siobhan was slim—so what? I like Emily's curves. Siobhan is strong and determined and creative and Emily is . . .

Shut it, Alex, I shouted inside my head, pressing the towel against my bruises again. I loved Emily, not Siobhan. Siobhan was a menace. A threat. And if she did one more thing—then I'd give her a real reason to be scared of me.

After dressing, I went downstairs with Emily and told the receptionist that we wanted to check out, and asked if they could call the airport to get us a flight that afternoon or evening. They were really helpful. It was almost as if they wanted to get rid of us. After that, we went upstairs and packed, emptying our room and taking our rucksacks downstairs. The receptionist had told us that if we were going to leave that day we needed to vacate our room, which wasn't a problem. Downstairs, we were told that they'd got us on a flight at three that afternoon, and that we could pay at the airline desk.

I looked at my watch. 'We've got a couple of hours to kill.'

'I'm hungry,' said Emily.

*   *   *

We went for lunch at a nearby Italian restaurant. My treat, as I announced once we'd sat down. Three times during the meal I almost confessed everything, mainly because I couldn't bear the dreadful silence that hung between us like a shroud. Of course, I didn't confess—just made several valiant attempts at small talk, trying to get Emily to laugh by cracking jokes about the waiter's moustache and the restaurant's décor. My attempts were doomed. I wasn't in top form anyway—I kept looking over my shoulder to see if my friends from last night had decided to make good on their threat and offer me a full course of Dutch violence.

After lunch, we went back to the hotel to check

out and pick up our luggage. We took a taxi to Schiphol airport and I watched the city centre recede, vowing silently that one day we would return, when all the mess in my life had been cleaned up. I reached over and squeezed Emily's hand. To my great relief, she squeezed back and gave me a small smile. Then she shuffled closer and leaned her head on my shoulder.

'You do love me, don't you?' she whispered.

'Of course I do.'

That was all she said.

The taxi got stuck in traffic and I started to look at my watch agitatedly, worried that we were going to miss our flight.

The driver heard me tutting and said, 'No worries. I will get you there.' But the traffic wasn't moving, and neither were we. Emily stared out of the window, a deeply melancholic expression on her face.

'I've got a headache,' she said, after we'd been sitting in traffic for about twenty minutes.

I kissed her temple. And we waited some more.

Finally, we arrived at the airport, paid the driver and lugged our rucksacks out of the boot, loading them onto a trolley and rushing into the building. We spotted the EasyJet desk and raced towards it. We had two minutes left to check in, but just before we reached the airport desk, Emily said, 'Hang on. I need the headache tablets.' We stopped and she opened the side pocket of her case. 'I'm sure they're in here.'

As she groped around inside the case, a puzzled look appeared on her face. She withdrew her hand from the pocket and we both looked at the small plastic bag she was holding.

'What the fuck?' Emily said.

The bag contained enough dope to keep Cheech and Chong happy for a fortnight. Emily held it like it was a bomb, and looked at me accusingly. I hoped that she could see I was as shocked as her. But then I looked up and saw that a member of the airline staff was coming towards us, pointing at her watch.

'Put it in your pocket,' I hissed.

'What?'

'Put it . . . oh shit.' I grabbed it from her and stuck it in my front pocket, turning away from the woman in the EasyJet uniform who was almost upon us. 'Flight 342 to London?' she asked. 'You need to check in now.'

'Yes, sorry,' Emily said. 'I was just looking for my headache tablets.' She stuck her hand back in the rucksack pocket and pulled out a box of Anadin, brandishing them triumphantly, as relieved as I was that she hadn't just produced a bag full of heroin and syringes.

The woman hurried us over to the desk and we plonked our rucksacks on the conveyor belt.

'Did you pack your bags yourself?' the woman asked robotically.

'Yes, yes,' we nodded in unison.

'Has anyone had the opportunity to interfere with your luggage?'

'No, no.'

She handed us our boarding passes and told us which gate to go to. We walked off as quickly as we could. I was sweating; I couldn't have looked more suspicious if I was wearing a T-shirt with a marijuana leaf on it and a shit-eating grin. I expected some cop to appear at any moment and say, 'Alright Cheech and Chong, hand it over.'

Emily muttered, 'You moron.'

'What? I didn't know it was there.'

'You've got to dump it. What if we get stopped and searched?'

'Jesus.' There were no bins in sight and we were surrounded by people. How the hell was I supposed to discreetly get rid of a huge baggie of dope, especially when we were moving rapidly towards the departure gate, about to miss our flight? I tried to work out the chances that we would get stopped before we boarded the plane. And then, as we neared the departure gate, I saw a uniformed customs officer. With a dog. A dope-sniffing dog.

'Oh. My. God.' Emily grabbed my arm.

'Act cool,' I said.

'Dump the fucking dope,' she said.

To my left, appearing in my field of vision like an oasis in the desert, was a Gents' toilet. I left Emily with the trolley and ran inside, trying to look as if I really needed a pee. The cubicle was occupied. I wondered if I was too young to have a heart attack. But then the cubicle opened. I could have kissed the hugely fat man who exited it, until I got a whiff of what he'd left behind. I pushed past him and slammed the cubicle door behind me, immediately taking out the bag of Mary Jane and emptying it into the stinking bog. I stuffed the bag behind the loo and flushed, rushing back out to find Emily at the desk with lots of grumpy, impatient-looking airline staff. We were just in time. I looked back at the man with the dog. The dog looked at me. I swear the fucking thing winked.

*   *   *

Emily didn't talk to me much on the plane. She

was convinced I had hidden the bag of dope in her rucksack. And it was difficult to protest my innocence with the other passengers listening in. Luckily, it was a short flight, and on the tube from Heathrow I pleaded my innocence until she told me to shut up.

'I'm going back to my place,' she said. 'I'll call you tomorrow.'

As she got off the train, I said, 'I'm sorry, Emily.'

I expected her to say something like, 'So am I'. But she didn't say a word. Just slung her rucksack onto her back and headed off. And to be honest, I was pleased to see her go. I'd had enough emotional shit for one day.

*   *   *

When I got back to my flat, Simon and Nat were sitting in the front room, smoking a joint. 'Want some?' said Simon.

I pictured the police dog winking at me. 'I don't think so.'

'Why are you back? And what happened to your cheek?'

'It's a long story.'

I turned to leave the room, but Simon said, 'Some woman called for you while you were away. Five times. She refused to believe you weren't here.'

'Silly beetch,' said Nat, giggling.

'Anyway, she finally got the message, but not before leaving a message of her own. There's a bit of paper stuck to your door with the details on it.'

My trainers felt like they were made of lead as I walked to my room and tore the note down from my door. It said: 'Please call Elaine Meadows on

8 823 6544. Or she's going to the police.' Underneath, in brackets, Simon had added, 'What have you been up to?' Then he'd drawn a smiley face.

33

Siobhan

Saturday. Late.

My birthday's nearly over; I'm drunk and weary and my tongue, lips and teeth are stained dark with red wine, but I think I feel better, about everything. I'm home again, and it's suddenly got so cold outside that I've lit the fire. Now I'm sitting here writing, enjoying the warmth and flickering light and—yes—enjoying the solitude of my home. All the windows and doors are locked up securely, of course, but I don't feel scared any more.

I didn't invite any of them back after the meal; Mum and Dad like to get to bed early, Jess had a babysitter, and Paula and her new boyfriend Gary were clearly off to do what couples do . . . Besides, after the dramas in Amsterdam, I feel a bit like retreating into my nest and letting things calm down a bit.

It would be nice to have Biggles to stroke, but he's in self-exile in my bedroom; I don't think he likes the smell of the fresh paint. Probably just as well—there are enough bristles from the paintbrush stuck along my skirting board without needing a load of cat hair rubbed in it too. I'm into this painting lark, it's very therapeutic. Think I'll do the banisters next.

I've been painting like a maniac for two days, since I got back, and it's helped a lot. Phil always promised to do it for me when he moved in but—predictably—couldn't tear himself away from whatever sporting event was on television on any given weekend. So I did it myself. I haven't ever decorated anything before, but I knew what you had to do: sandpaper it, put masking tape along the edges, and paint it—I mean, how hard is that? I'm feeling well pleased with myself.

This room is a mess, though. I seem to be less obsessively tidy than I used to be. Maybe it's because I don't have to clear up after Phil any more. I don't know, but I quite like being bohemian and spontaneous. It's more fun than running around with a can of Pledge every five minutes.

* * *

It's been ages since I saw Mum and Dad, and Dad was looking much better now his slipped disc is on the mend. Paula and Gary were all over each other, and I didn't even feel a twinge of envy (though I suspect this might have been more to do with the fact that Gary is 5'4" and paunchy), and it was fantastic to see Jess. We've made a pact to meet up once a month minimum, from now on, and really get our friendship back on track. She apologised for 'neglecting' me but of course I understood—I mean, children are so time-consuming, so everyone says. She also told me how worried about me they'd all been, which gave me a warm glow. I do have friends and family who love me. That's important.

They toasted my birthday, and I made a little speech. Told them all I was going to give up writing and get a proper job. Admittedly I was a little bit upset that nobody leaped up and shouted, 'No, please don't do it, Siobhan, the world would be such a dark place without your talent!' but I guess I can live with that. They were all encouraging and said how brave I was, and how it was the right thing to do. 'After all,' said Mum, 'there's nothing stopping you writing another novel in the future if you get inspired again, is there?'

Must go to bed. I've drunk my Resolve and my litre of water, so I'll be up in the night to pee, but at least I shouldn't have a hangover in the morning.

Oh—there was one conversation I want to write down, between me and Paula, when Gary went to the loo, and she asked me what I thought of him.

'He's lovely,' I lied, suddenly pretending to be very engrossed in scratching small splashes of white gloss off my forearms. 'And he seems to really adore you.'

'Do you think he's fanciable?'

I picked harder at the dried-on paint. I didn't want to upset her. 'Well, yes, although he's just not my type.'

Paula refilled our glasses, I remember, drunkenly spilling a swill of it onto Mum's napkin. The red soaked through the white cotton like a bloodstain and Mum tutted. Paula scrunched up the stained napkin and handed it to a passing waiter, asking him to bring Mum a clean one, and then she said to me—just curiously, not in a nasty way—'What exactly is your type, Siobhan? All your boyfriends have been so different that I have no idea.'

For some reason, it wasn't at all difficult to answer. Without hesitating, I replied: 'Impulsive; creative—definitely; and talented. Not hairy. Tallish. Slim. Passionate. And someone who knows how to buy clothes for a woman. That would be my ideal man.'

It's only now I'm home that I realise I was describing Alex. How weird is that?

*　　　*　　　*

But so what? That's all behind me now, and I just have to accept that I blew it. I should've gone out with him when he first asked, back when he really liked me, before it all got so weird. And it definitely got way too weird in Amsterdam. I ought to consider myself very, very lucky Alex doesn't have a clue that what happened with Evan was anything to do with me—and the rat and the magazines before that . . . I wonder if they got caught at the airport with the pot? I must say, I do feel guilty about that. I wouldn't want Alex to go to jail. Emily I'm not so sure about . . . But no, I suppose even she doesn't deserve that. I'm looking back now and wondering what on earth I was thinking . . . It's just not me, all that revenge stuff.

All of a sudden I feel quite mature and wise. I will start looking to the future, to my new life as a . . . whatever it is I'm going to do instead of being a novelist. But I'm too tired to think about it now, what with all the painting, and then all the drinking. I'm going to bed.

Good grief, that was the doorbell. I'll ignore it—must be a cabbie with the wrong address, or a late night pizza or something.

*　　　*　　　*

There it is again. Better go and check, I suppose.

304

34

Alex

Ever since I started writing my journal I've become addicted to recording my life. Which is why, even now, I'm typing—even though I'll probably have to trash all the files as soon as I've finished. Still, I'm used to living on the edge. Accustomed, in fact, to going right over it.

After getting back from Amsterdam and reading the message from Elaine Meadows, I knew what I had to do.

I walked down the road to the only public phone box in the area, pleased that this anachronism still existed in our mobile-choked country even if it is mainly used these days as a display cabinet for prostitutes' leaflets. I felt good, strong. It was as if making the decision had cleaned away the cobwebs of fear that had blighted my life for so long. I was sick of being scared. Tired of jumping when I heard a siren, of waking up in a puddle of cold sweat in the middle of the night. Sick and tired of the mental exhaustion that inaction brings. Now I was going to stop being a coward. I was going to do something, and as I picked up the phone and dialled the number that Simon had jotted down, I ignored my trembling fingers and told myself again that this was the only way to solve my problems.

'Elaine Meadows.'

'Hello, Elaine, this is Alex Parkinson.'

'Oh. Alex. I've been . . .'

'I know, I know. I'm sorry about what happened

before. And I'm sorry I haven't called you back. I've just returned from a trip abroad and my housemate just gave me your message.'

'Okay. I want to . . .'

Again, I didn't let her finish. 'Have you given the police my name yet?'

'I only made that threat about the police to scare you, to get you to contact me. All I want to do is talk to you. I just want to know the truth about what happened.'

'Good.' I paused. 'I was with Kathy the night she died.'

She inhaled sharply.

'I want to explain it to you. I want to show you. Can we meet tomorrow evening?'

She sounded like a strong woman: her voice didn't shake or betray the way she was feeling. She simply said, 'Okay. Where and what time?'

'Where do you live?'

She coughed. 'Well, actually, I live in Kathy's flat.'

That shook me.

'When I got back from my travels, I needed a place to stay and Kathy's parents said I could stay here for a while if I wanted.'

'Right. Well, okay, let's meet at your place at seven.'

'Can't we meet earlier?' she said.

'No. I've got some other stuff to do.' This was a lie, but I could hardly tell her I wanted to wait until it was dark before I met her. Before hanging up, I said, 'Elaine, I don't want anyone else there tomorrow. No friends. Certainly not the police, because my story is pretty unlikely. If there's anyone else there I won't tell you a thing. You'll never get to hear the truth. Okay?'

She agreed straight away.

I put the receiver down and stood in the phone box for a while. She lived in her dead friend's flat. How weird. How ghoulish. In one way, this character defect made what I was going to do seem easier. So why did I feel like I was going to puke? It was the weakness coming back, and I forced myself to push it away. I closed my eyes, clenched my fists, gritted my teeth. Be strong, Alex. A man's gotta do what a man's gotta do. I was powerful, a master of my own fate, in control of my own destiny. Everything was going to turn around, because I wanted it to. Everything was going to be alright, because I wasn't scared any more and I wasn't going to take any more crap!

I left the phone box and stepped in a pile of dogshit.

*   *   *

The next morning, I typed up an account of what had happened in Amsterdam in my journal, Brick Shithouses and all. Then Emily turned up.

She was acting a little strangely, a false smile on her face. She asked for a cup of tea (weak, no sugar, like always) then said, 'So what have you been up to this morning?' She didn't mention Amsterdam at all. I had expected her to start quizzing me about the dope and the thugs as soon as she got through the door. I was relieved—I really didn't want any more grief from her—if a little puzzled.

'I've been writing,' I replied.

'Oh. A short story? Pernilla will be happy.'

'Er . . . yes.'

'Can I read it?'

'No. I scrapped it. It wasn't very good.'
She nodded.

Taking a deep breath, I said, 'I'm going out tonight. I got a call from an old friend. This guy that I used to know. I promised I'd meet him for a drink. Is that okay?'

'Sure.'

'Really? Are you certain?'

'Of course. I'll stay here, though, if that's alright. I haven't seen Nat for a while.'

'Okay.'

We sat in silence, Emily with a smile curled at the corners of her mouth, me feeling totally baffled. She was up to something. But I didn't have the time or energy to work out what it was. I was mostly just pleased that I was going to be able to get out of the flat and keep my date. I almost laughed. My date with destiny.

* * *

It was raining when I left the house. Simon and Natalie were out, but Emily had decided to stay at mine anyway. She was still acting mysteriously (very uncharacteristic of her), but I had more important things on my mind than her odd behaviour.

I didn't take an umbrella; I enjoyed feeling the rain on my face and in my hair. Earlier that day I had washed my hair and been alarmed by the number of hairs that fell away from my head, clinging to my soapy fingers, reminding me that I wasn't going to be young forever. I wondered if my dad was bald and, if so, at what age he started to lose his hair. Mum hardly ever spoke about him except to slag him off and tell me I took after him; she

308

certainly never gave me any biological details. I wondered what he would say if I tracked him down, called him up and told him everything I'd been through recently.

He'd probably just hang up.

But I wasn't going to feel sorry for myself. Not any more. I strode through the rain, my head held high, past the bookshops where my short stories would soon be on sale, past the college where I met Siobhan, towards the place where I watched a woman die. And then I was there, pressing the buzzer that now bore the name Elaine Meadows.

She buzzed me in. Climbing the stairs, I felt the now-familiar ache of my bruises, saw the faces of the men who had beaten me up. And then I was looking into the face of the woman who could have caused me a lot more pain.

I recognised Elaine from her photo in the paper, but I was shocked by how diminutive she was. Since I'd read that newspaper article I'd begun to see her as this behemoth, casting a huge shadow over my life. But she looked like Kylie Minogue's smaller sister. She had long auburn hair and a face that had been in the sun too long, with deep crow's feet spreading from the corners of her eyes.

She let me in and I noticed that she was breathing heavily. So was I.

'So, you've been here before,' was the first thing she said.

I nodded. 'Just the once.'

'The night Kathy died.'

'That's right.' A moment of silence. 'Have you got anything to drink?'

She beckoned for me to follow her through to the kitchen. 'I've got beer, or do you want something strong? Whisky? Vodka?'

'Beer's fine.'

We went back into the living room and she gestured for me to sit down. I looked out the window, thinking for the second time what a wonderful view it was. Perhaps that was why Elaine couldn't resist this flat.

'There's nobody here, is there? Nobody hiding in the bedroom?'

She shook her head. 'You can go and check if you like.'

'You're very calm,' I said. 'For all you know, I could be a vicious murderer who killed your friend and is about to do the same to you.'

She blinked. 'Then I guess I'm taking a risk.' She smiled. 'And I suppose I should warn you, I studied judo in Japan. So if you try anything . . .'

'You were in Japan? Me too. I lived in Tokyo.'

'I was in Tokyo and Osaka,' she said.

'Oh, yeah, I visited . . .' I stopped myself. What the hell was I doing? Chit-chatting? I reminded myself why I was here. I couldn't afford to build any kind of attachment to this woman. She was the enemy, the woman who could take away my freedom. She had vowed to find the person who was responsible for Kathy's death, and I was the only suspect.

I could tell her the truth about what happened but I knew she wouldn't believe me. Who would? It was such an unlikely story. Which was why I had to do this.

'Isn't it strange, living here?' I said, unable to resist the chit-chat after all. Knowing that by asking her questions I was delaying what I was going to do. But I also knew that I was going to need at least one bottle of beer inside me before I did it.

'I like it,' she said. 'Did you hear about *obon* when

310

you lived in Japan?'

'You'll have to remind me.'

'The Japanese believe that every summer their dead relatives come back to visit them. That's why so many people leave Tokyo in August and go back to their hometowns. I always liked the idea of that— of the dead visiting their old homes. Which is why I like the idea of hanging around and meeting up with Kathy's spirit when she comes calling.'

'Were you . . .?'

'An item? Lovers? Yes, we were. She was the love of my life.'

'So why did you go away?'

She shrugged. 'Things go wrong, don't they?'

I could relate to that. Even if I couldn't relate to the idea of waiting for your ex's ghost to come creeping up on you. I took another big swig of beer, closed my eyes, focussed.

'I want to show you what happened,' I said, standing up.

'Show me?'

'Yes, out on the fire escape.'

She looked doubtful. But I said, 'Look, Elaine, you need to trust me. I have to show you; it's too complicated just to tell you. Otherwise I'm going to leave now and then you'll have to wait for Kathy's spirit to come and explain it instead.'

I saw her weigh up her options. She didn't know anything about me. But there was something about her that made me confident that she would accept my invitation. I couldn't put my finger on it at the time—this vibe she was giving off—though I understand it now.

She put her drink on the carpet and stood up. 'Alright. Let's go.'

She opened the window that led to the fire escape and I said, 'After you.'

She stepped out onto the metal structure and I followed her. It was still raining and the wind had really picked up, howling around the building, forcing me to raise my voice so Elaine could hear me.

'We were both drunk,' I said, 'and Kathy said we should go up onto the roof where the view was better. I didn't really want to go, but she was insistent. We came out here and then—well, let's go a little higher and I'll show you.'

She looked doubtful now, but I also knew she was so desperate to know the truth. She had clearly been obsessing over it ever since she'd got back from her travels. That was the power I had over her: only I could set her mind at rest. If only the truth was more plausible. Because I was convinced that, if I didn't do something drastic, the following was going to happen:

After I told Elaine what had happened she would call the police and tell them what I'd said. Of course, the police would want to talk to me because I was a witness who hadn't stepped forward before, which was suspicious in itself. Then they would start digging in my past and find out about Siobhan. Next, they would talk to Siobhan and decide that I was jealous of Kathy because I thought Kathy and Siobhan were about to embark on a lesbian affair. That gave me the motivation to murder Kathy.

Standing on the fire escape, the rain making the metal slippery, I knew that if I walked out of that flat with Elaine still alive, the police would have me in an interview room by the next morning.

'This is where she fell from,' I said. We were

standing near the top of the fire escape, a few steps from the roof. I pointed towards the adjacent block of flats and said, 'Look,' so that Elaine turned away from me.

I began to reach out. All I had to do was push her and she would go over the edge, down to the same spot where Kathy had landed. *Grief-stricken woman commits suicide.* It would have perfect symmetry. Nobody knew I was here. There was nothing to connect me to this. Push her, and it would all be over.

I reached out further.

*   *   *

On my way home, I stopped at Camden Lock and sat down on a bench overlooking the water. Traffic rushed down Camden High Street. Teenagers queued outside a nearby music venue, their whole lives ahead of them. I lit a cigarette and enjoyed each drag. I could hear a couple screaming at each other in a nearby flat and I wondered if they thought they loved each other. Did they fight and scream and then collapse into bed, professing eternal love while the next row brewed inside them? Did they have a child who was listening now, cowering in the next room, desperate to grow up and get out? A child who heard his parents alternately fighting and fucking in the name of love.

Love.

It's a bitch.

Elaine Meadows loved Kathy but something went wrong and she left the country. But she never stopped loving her. When she turned back to me on that fire escape, after I had realised that I couldn't

313

do it, that I could never kill anyone, that I would rather die in prison for a crime I didn't commit, she had tears rolling down her face.

'She was drunk,' I told her, 'and she came up the steps too fast. And she slipped—it was simple as that. I reached out to try to grab her but she was beyond my reach.' I was crying myself now. 'And I ran, all the way home, and I didn't tell anyone that I'd been here, because I was convinced that everyone would think I pushed her. I was so scared and so fucking stupid. And I'm so sorry.'

'Let's go inside,' she said. She sounded . . . resigned.

We went back into the living room and Elaine fetched a couple of towels so we could dry off.

'Are you going to call the police now?' I said.

'No.'

I looked at her.

'I believe you, Alex.' She touched my shoulder. 'All I wanted was to know the truth—that's what I told you, wasn't it? I'm not going to talk to the police.' She lowered her voice. 'Between you and me, I think they're a bunch of arseholes and they think I'm a stupid, obsessive woman who can't accept the simple fact that her dyke friend got drunk and fell off the fire escape.' She paused. 'To tell the truth, I was going to tell them about you acting strangely when I phoned you, but every time I'd tried to make them listen to me before, they never took me seriously.'

'I wouldn't blame you if you called them now. I . . . I feel responsible. And, the thing is, I did think about hurting her. I thought she was going to come between me and the woman I was in love with. I had a motive—that's why I thought everyone would

314

think I killed her.'

Elaine let my confession sink in, and for a moment I was convinced she was going to change her mind, walk over to the phone and dial 999. But she said, 'Who was this woman?'

'This woman?'

'The one you said you loved. The one you thought about killing for. Are you with her now?'

I shook my head. 'No I'm not. I blew it with her. She hates me.'

Elaine frowned. 'So it was all a waste. You thought about killing for this woman—loved her that much— and then it ended. Just like that? Did you fight to keep her?'

'Yes, I . . .' I trailed off. Had I fought? Did I do everything I could to make Siobhan love me? Jesus, I did a lot of things I shouldn't have done, but when it came right down to it, I gave up, didn't I? I moped around, felt sorry for myself, and then Emily came along to take my mind off it. And I'd convinced myself I loved Emily, that she was my saviour. But what if she was just a plaster on my wound—the wound on my heart that never actually healed?

*   *   *

I sat on the bench listening to the rowing couple for a little while longer, then headed home, thinking about Elaine Meadows and her desire to know the truth. The last thing I had seen her do was shake her head at me then turn back towards the window. I saw her move her finger towards the condensation on the window, drawing something there.

I had closed the door, leaving her in peace. There was something I had to tell Emily.

315

But when I got back to the flat she had already found out.

*   *   *

I opened the door to the flat and headed towards my bedroom, realising as I passed the living room that Emily was sitting in there, on the floor, her back against the sofa. I stood in the doorway.

'What are you doing?'

She looked up at me, her face pale, her eyes pink. She had a big pile of A4 pages on her lap and my first thought was that it must be a manuscript that she'd brought with her from the office. Then Emily started reading from it:

'"Siobhan was very lucky to have this place. Now all she needed was someone to share it with. Somebody like me . . . I love you so much, she'd say. And then she'd get that naughty glint in her eye and say, Why don't you fuck me?"'

'That was just before you hid in her wardrobe, and just after you'd sat on her toilet seat like some kind of perverted freak.'

'Emily.'

'And how about this bit?' She flicked back through my journal, which she had printed out in its entirety. 'This is the bit where you push the woman off the fire escape.'

'Emily, I didn't. Give me that.' I tried to grab the journal but she screamed.

'Get away from me, you fucking pervert. You . . . murderer.'

'Emily,' I said again, trying to remain calm. 'Did you read all of it?'

'I read enough. Not all of it, but enough.' Her

voice was twice as loud as I'd ever heard it before. Her nose was running where she had been crying. 'I flicked through to the end, to the bit in Amsterdam. All those lies, Alex. All those fucking lies. And that bit where you wrote about how weak I am and how you'd hate to be fucking saddled with me for the rest your life. Weak, am I? You'll see. You'll fucking see.'

'Sshh . . .'

'Don't fucking shush me, you bastard! You knew that this woman—this oh-so-perfect woman—set those blokes on you. God, I wish they'd broken your neck. And it was her, wasn't it—it was her who sent me the rat and those magazines? And you knew all along but didn't do anything? Why? Why?'

'Please . . .'

'No! I want to see this Siobhan. I want to see who my competition was; who I was trying to live up to—without even knowing it. I'm going round there now.'

'Emily, don't be stupid.'

'Don't call me stupid! And you can't stop me—I know her address. It's in here.' She waved the journal at me. 'I'm going to go round there and tell that bitch she can have you.' She stood up. That's when I smelled the alcohol on her breath and saw the empty wine bottle beside her.

'I'll come with you,' I said. Maybe I could stop her en route, or at least slow her down. 'Let me just get a jumper. It's cold out.'

'I need a piss,' she said, marching unsteadily into the toilet, cradling the pages of the journal tightly against her big soft breasts; the breasts that I'd liked so much but which now made me feel stifled just looking at them. I didn't know what to do. Should

317

I phone Siobhan? No, I didn't have time. I rushed into the bedroom and saw the journal on screen. There was so much stuff in it—so much shameful stuff. I quit the program and immediately dragged it into the trashcan. I emptied the trash, without a flicker of regret. Now I just had to get the hard copy off Emily and destroy it.

Emily came out of the toilet and went straight down the stairs towards the front door. I forgot about the jumper and followed her. She had the journal tucked in tight under her arm.

I tried to be belligerent. 'I can't believe you read my private journal.'

'Fuck off,' she said. Then, after a few moments, she said, 'I needed to find out what had been going on in Amsterdam, and I knew you kept a journal. It wasn't hard to work out the password. At first I hoped it might be my name, but no. So I tried the name of the person you love most: Alex. Your own name. Although you don't only love yourself, do you? You love her too. Siobhan.'

'I used to,' I said weakly, wishing I'd kept my password as *Tara Lies Awake*. Emily would never have guessed that one.

She glared at me. 'No. I think you still do. Otherwise you would have told me about her. You wouldn't have tried to protect her.'

We were walking so fast that it only took fifteen minutes to reach Siobhan's house. There was a light on downstairs. I had been hoping that Siobhan might be out. I was so nervous about seeing her—and not just because of Emily and my fear that she might try to knock Siobhan out.

It was because Emily was right—I still loved Siobhan. I had been denying it for months, since I had thrown myself into my relationship with Emily, who had been so good to me, so good for me. My first chance to have a proper, healthy relationship. But that's all it had been—me trying to be normal; like everyone else. I was so shocked that somebody without any bizarre abnormalities or mental illnesses liked me, and so grateful, that I had convinced myself that I was happy. I mean, I don't want to rewrite history—I did like Emily, and I enjoyed playing the boyfriend role. But that's all it was: acting; making myself into one of those people who was in love with the idea of being in love. I think that, maybe, if I'd met Emily at a different time, it might have been okay, even though she was boring and didn't make my pulse race and my pupils dilate and my heart ache (I couldn't even get it up the first time we went to bed; what kind of sign was that?). Maybe we could have had a lasting relationship. Because the main thing wrong with Emily was that she wasn't Siobhan.

When Elaine said that Kathy was the love of her life, my first thought hadn't been, 'That's how I feel about Emily'. It had been, 'That's how I felt about Siobhan'. Except it wasn't just past tense.

It *isn't* past tense at all.

Emily rang the doorbell and, after a few moments in which my heart performed several somersaults that would have taken gold at the last Olympics, Siobhan opened the door.

She looked like she'd been out on the town, her lips stained with red wine. She was wearing the Prada clothes I'd bought her—but they had paint all over them. Seeing her made me catch my breath. She looked incredibly sexy—and also shocked. And very pissed off.

Just as Emily did.

'It's you!' Emily said. 'From the coffee shop. I don't believe it.'

Siobhan looked from Emily to me. 'What is going on, Alex?'

She said my name. Said it so naturally, like it was a name she used every day. I gulped.

'What's going on,' said Emily, waving the journal, 'is that I've just discovered all about you and Alex and other rats—ones that come in a sealed envelope. And I want . . . I want . . .' Emily trailed off. I guess she hadn't thought that far ahead.

'You'd better come in,' Siobhan said quietly, looking over our shoulders where her neighbours' curtains twitched. And we went with her into her living room. I noticed immediately that there were birthday cards on the mantelpiece.

'Is it your birthday today?' I asked.

She nodded.

'Happy birthday.'

Siobhan laughed. Not just a chuckle but a big, loud belly laugh.

Emily stood there with her mouth open. 'What's so funny?'

'This is just so bizarre.' She was a bit drunk as well, I realised now. 'Here you both are, wishing me a happy birthday. And, Emily—Emily Norris-Bottom,' she giggled, 'it looks like you brought me a present.'

Siobhan reached out for the journal and Emily raised it to give it to her. But before Siobhan could take it, I grabbed it and took a couple of steps backward.

'What is it?' Siobhan asked, squinting at it. 'Is it your book?'

I said, 'Do you remember at the writing class you told us to keep a journal? This is it. I've kept it completely up to date.'

'And you're the star,' Emily said to Siobhan.

I sighed. 'That isn't true. But what this journal represents,' I said, holding it up, 'is the past. And earlier tonight, I made a decision. A big decision. I decided that it's time for a new beginning. I've done some idiotic things over the last few months. But now I'm going to move on. Alone.' I gave Emily a meaningful look. Her mouth fell open again.

I took my cigarette lighter out of my pocket and sparked a flame, setting the edge of the journal alight. I threw the whole thing into the fireplace, where the remains of a fire still glowed red. A cloud of malevolent-looking ashes rose, then settled slowly back down again. Emily gasped and tried to get past me to retrieve the pages but I held her back, and, anyway, it was too late. The fire had taken hold, and the pages started to float up the chimney, the smell of them filling the room. All those words; my life since the middle of last September. Up in smoke.

Emily was trembling, staring into the flames. 'That's right,' she said. 'Burn the evidence. There's still a copy on your computer, though.'

'I deleted it. While you were in the toilet.'

'It doesn't matter,' she said, tapping the side of her head. 'It's all in here.' She turned to Siobhan. 'Enjoy him while you can.'

She walked out of the room and out of the house, slamming the door behind her.

'This is too much,' said Siobhan. 'I need to sit down.'

I could see her looking at the ash on the carpet, a frown line creasing her brow. She looked so adorable.

She sat on the sofa and I stood in front of her, not knowing what to do.

'What did she mean, "Enjoy him while you can"?'

'She meant . . .' But instead of explaining, I said, 'I'm still in love with you.'

Siobhan looked into my eyes. I held her gaze. There were butterflies the size of crows going mental in my stomach. Behind me, I sensed the fire going out. But in front of me, Siobhan touched the sofa beside her and said in a soft voice, 'Sit down.'

I did what she said. The room was silent except for the hum of electricity and the rustle of fabric as Siobhan reached out for me.

'This whole situation,' Siobhan whispered, 'is completely fucked up. Isn't it?'

'More than you know,' I said.

'What's Emily going to do?'

'I don't care.'

She took hold of my hand. Her skin was warm. Then she smiled and said, 'I don't think we've been introduced.'

'I . . .?' Then I looked into her eyes, at the way she was looking at me, and I got it. The way people who are meant to be together understand each other. This was going to be our fresh start. Just for this moment, we had no history. I said, 'My name's Alex. Nice to meet you.'

'Nice to meet you too, Alex. I'm Siobhan.'

She kissed me. She tasted of ash and wine.

'Siobhan. That's a beautiful name.'

I kissed her.

'Thank you.'

She unfastened the top button of my shirt and slid her hand across my collarbone.

'Let's go upstairs.'

*   *   *

She was even more beautiful than I imagined. I breathed her in, put my head against her silk skin and listened to the blood inside her body. I kissed her hair and felt the flutter of her eyelashes against my cheek. I kissed her mouth and smelled the wine that stained her lips. I put my mouth between her legs and she tasted even better than I'd dreamed. I slid inside her and she whispered, 'Slowly.'

After we'd made love, we lay pressed together with a purring cat lying on top of the quilt by our feet. And we talked—for hours. I don't have time to record everything we said. I don't want to. But we both spoke without inhibition about the way we felt, about the future and what we wanted. Siobhan commented again upon the amazing fucked-upness of our situation, although we both avoided mentioning the less impressive parts of our unconventional courtship. This was our new beginning, after all.

I told her I loved her. I told her about Kathy and Elaine, terrified as I was telling it that she would pull away from me. But she just listened quietly, then said, 'From now on, you have to make me a promise. No more lies. No more running away from the truth. No more keeping journals that need to be burned because they're full of so many secrets.'

She was quiet for a moment. 'Did you read my diary when you hid in here before?'

'A bit of it.'

'What did you read?'

I smiled in the candlelight. 'Oh, something about wanting a man with a dick like a truncheon who'll

323

make you come three times in one night.'

She laughed. 'So, are you going to give me what I want?'

'Um—well, I don't know about the truncheon bit—it's more of a . . .'

'Alex?'

'Hmm?'

'Shut up.'

*　　　*　　　*

At six o'clock the next morning the doorbell rang. I got up and looked out the front window. There was a police car parked by Siobhan's front gate. Emily, I found out a little later, had called the police and told them that I had confessed to her that I'd murdered Kathy.

'Oh shit.' I beckoned Siobhan over to the window. 'How far do you think I'll get if I slip out the back door?'

She shook her head. 'No more lies, remember, Alex. No more hiding. Just go and tell them the truth. I'm sure they'll believe you.'

*　　　*　　　*

They believed me alright—like I believe in the tooth fairy. They questioned me for hours, and by the end of the day they'd found several people who'd seen me with Kathy that evening in the pub. I told them to go and talk to Elaine Meadows. And they did. But when they got there she wasn't in the flat.

She was dead.

Her body was lying in exactly the same spot where Kathy's body had been found.

'She must have jumped,' I told the police. 'She must have decided that she wanted to be with Kathy. Two spirits together, living in that flat, so she could be with her all the time, not just at *obon*.' The police loved that.

'So you saw Elaine Meadows last night?' said the detective in charge of the case.

'Yes. I went to see her to . . .' At which point I stopped talking and asked for a solicitor.

*   *   *

So here I am, in a cell, awaiting trial for the murders of Kathy Noonan and Elaine Meadows. Apparently, the case relies almost entirely on the testimony of Emily, whose anger with me seems to be all-consuming: this is her way of punishing me and keeping Siobhan and me apart. And I guess she really believes that I did it. Thinking back over what I wrote in the journal, I suppose it was pretty ambiguous.

The police also have forensic evidence that I was in the flat the night Elaine jumped, not that I've denied it. I feel slightly responsible for Elaine's death—if I hadn't gone round there and stirred up all those old feelings . . . although she might just have been waiting to find out the truth about what happened before she joined the love of her life in death. I wrote earlier that I'd sensed something strange—some weird vibe—and now I understand it: she had a death wish. She was just waiting to join Kathy—she'd *wanted* me to push her. I understand that now; that desperate desire to be with the one you love. Still, I would have appreciated it if she'd left a suicide note absolving me of all responsibility.

325

How thoughtless of her.

There are only two positive things left in my life. One is that my publisher is even more excited than ever about my literary career. 'Think of the publicity,' said Pernilla, who also told me that she had let Emily go because 'the poor girl is a wreck, and her efficiency has nose-dived drastically.'

The other, of course, is Siobhan.

Siobhan, my angel, as I lie here at night, listening to my cellmate grunting as he jerks off in the other bunk, I think of you and that beautiful night we spent together. Even though my body is in a cage . . . Oh shit, here comes the warden. And I don't think he's big on romance. But listen, Siobhan, if this was a letter, I'd sign off with four kisses, and a heart with an arrow right through it—like the heart I watched Elaine etch into the condensation, just before I left her flat.

Epilogue

22nd April.
My darling Alex,

Reading between the lines, you sounded miserable in your last letter. How are you holding up? I want to hold you up, and never let you go. I promise I will do that for you, in whatever way I can, whatever happens.

I know I keep saying this, but you never seem convinced so I will say it again: the truth will out, darling. I'm sure that you won't end up in prison. Emily couldn't possibly lie under oath. She'll realise that she can't punish you in that way: that she's playing with your life. I'm sure she'll come around. She's just relishing her impression of a roaring mouse for now, that's all. She'll calm down.

I'm sorry that you ever met her. It's my fault. If I hadn't been so blind, and so weird with you when you first said you loved me, none of this would have happened. I drove you into her arms, and I feel terrible about that.

Like I said the night before they took you away, I've always been slow on the uptake. I don't know why. I either choose the wrong man (Phil being a prime example), or, in your case, can't recognise a good thing when I see it. I mean, you bought me designer clothes, and I still turned you down! How mad is that? I can't believe I fixated on the money part of it—I'm

*not tight, darling, I promise—from now on,
what's mine is yours (not that you'll be rich, I
warn you!), but I was just afraid. I was afraid of
your intensity, and the effect it had on me when
you looked at me that way.*

*It's so funny—at dinner that night, my
birthday, someone asked me what my ideal man
would be like. It was only later that I realised I
had given an accurate description of you, my
love, both physically and mentally. You were
what I wanted all along. I was just too
overwhelmed by your devotion, and the way that
it came like a bolt from the blue. Or maybe I felt
that I didn't deserve it—that's always been a
problem of mine; and, now that I think about it,
probably the reason I've ended up with so many
losers before. I've never allowed myself to truly
love anybody, in case they left me.*

*And now here we are, apart! For who knows
how long . . . No, sorry, Alex, ignore that. I'm
trying so hard to think positive, but every now
and then I think 'what if . . . ', and panic. I
can't bear the thought of you going to prison for
years.*

*But you won't. Like I said, Emily's not evil.
She knows you didn't really do it, and she
wouldn't let that happen. Even though I know
how true it is that hell hath no fury, etc, etc. And
I wish she wouldn't have said whatever it was
that's she's clearly said to Natalie and Simon—
they still put the phone down when I try to ring
them. Natalie was quite nasty to me last time I
tried, actually. I'm glad they wrote you a note;*

but it's really not fair that they're blaming me for all this! I'd do anything to get you out of there.

And no, in answer to your question, your mum didn't ring me back either. I'm sorry. I think under the circumstances it was good of you to let her know what's going on.

I'm going to change the subject now before I drag us both down. Guess what—I got a new job! Reading manuscripts for a hot new literary agent; an ex-editor called Mark Molesey. It's very part-time, which is perfect. I want flexible hours so that I will always be able to visit you, angel. And I've already sent him your stories and told him about your deal, obviously, and he's keen to represent you for the novel that I know you're going to write.

I'm so proud of your writing success. I was jealous at first, but that was before you were part of my life, and also when I thought that I still had ambitions to be a 'faymuss awfor'. Reading all these manuscripts for Mark has made me realise that, actually, I am a good writer. And so are you. I've decided that I'm not going to do any more writing for a while though—just give myself a break from the pressure of it. I don't want to write another novel until—or even unless—I get that deep, mad yearning for it. I've learned that you have to really want things in order to deserve them: want them and fight for them, like you did for me. I'm so incredibly touched that you did that for me, after I'd very nearly wrecked everything.

I'll sign off now. There's a man coming to

clean the carpets, and I have to go and buy
Biggles some flea powder—oh the excitement!
Anyway, I'll be visiting tomorrow, so this
afternoon I'll be baking my Victoria sponge with
a file in. Maybe next time will be the time the
guards let me through with it. I can't wait to see
you, angel. Every part of me is waiting for you,
however long it takes, body and soul.
   All my love,
   Siobhan xxx